THE REALMS
—— OF THE ——
GODS

ALSO BY TAMORA PIERCE

SONG OF THE LIONESS QUARTET

Alanna: The First Adventure (Book I)

In the Hand of the Goddess (Book II)

The Woman Who Rides Like a Man (Book III)

Lioness Rampant (Book IV)

THE IMMORTALS QUARTET

Wild Magic (Book I)

Wolf-Speaker (Book II)

Emperor Mage (Book III)

The Realms of the Gods (Book IV)

THE REALMS
— OF THE —
GODS

TAMORA PIERCE
THE IMMORTALS

Atheneum Books for Young Readers
NEW YORK LONDON TORONTO SYDNEY NEW DELHI

ATHENEUM BOOKS FOR YOUNG READERS
An imprint of Simon & Schuster Children's Publishing Division
1230 Avenue of the Americas, New York, New York 10020
This book is a work of fiction. Any references to historical events, real people,
or real places are used fictitiously. Other names, characters, places, and events
are products of the author's imagination, and any resemblance to actual events
or places or persons, living or dead, is entirely coincidental.
Text copyright © 1996 by Tamora Pierce
Afterword copyright © 2015 by Tamora Pierce
Cover illustration copyright © 2015 by Mélanie Delon
All rights reserved, including the right of reproduction in whole or in part in any form.
ATHENEUM BOOKS FOR YOUNG READERS is a
registered trademark of Simon & Schuster, Inc.
Atheneum logo is a trademark of Simon & Schuster, Inc.
For information about special discounts for bulk purchases, please contact Simon &
Schuster Special Sales at 1-866-506-1949 or business@simonandschuster.com.
The Simon & Schuster Speakers Bureau can bring authors to your live event. For
more information or to book an event, contact the Simon & Schuster Speakers
Bureau at 1-866-248-3049 or visit our website at www.simonspeakers.com.
Also available in an Atheneum Books for Young Readers hardcover edition
The text for this book is set in Stempel Garamond.
Manufactured in the United States of America
This Atheneum Books for Young Readers paperback edition September 2015
2 4 6 8 10 9 7 5 3 1
The Library of Congress has cataloged the hardcover edition as follows:
Pierce, Tamora.
The realms of the gods / Tamora Pierce. — Atheneum Books for Young Readers
hardcover edition.
pages cm. — (The Immortals ; 4)
Originally published by Atheneum in 1996.
Summary: While in the mystical realms of the gods along with Numair, Daine learns
the secrets of her past and the implications for her future as she and Numair are
compelled to return to the mortal world of Tortall to help fight against the immortals.
ISBN 978-1-4814-4029-5 (hc)
ISBN 978-1-4814-4028-8 (pbk)
ISBN 978-1-4391-3209-8 (eBook)
[1. Fantasy. 2. Human-animal communication—Fiction. 3. Supernatural—Fiction.]
I. Title.
PZ7.P61464Re 2015
[Fic]—dc23   2014043355

*To Claire Smith and Margaret Turner,
who teach me that heroism includes facing
sorrows each and every day with courage,
humor, and practicality*

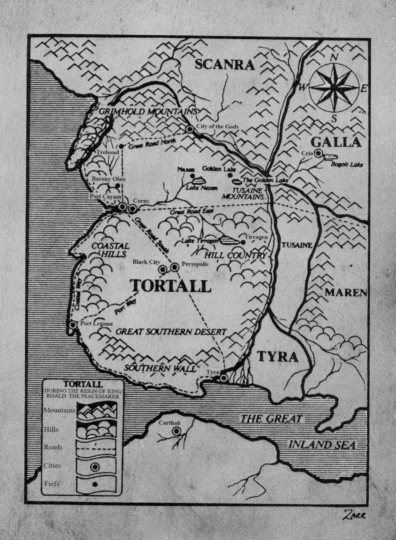

Acknowledgments

When I complete a series, I like to thank all those who assisted me in some fashion. With The Immortals, I had a great deal of help from general reference and wildlife sources. While I have thanked some persons or groups in the book for which I most needed their help, I would like to thank them again, so they know the debt I owe them, but also so that anyone who also has an interest in these areas can find them. My heartfelt thanks to:

Subscribers to *two* computer networks, including but not limited to CompuServe's Pacific Forum, members of the Australia Section, particularly Douglas

Dow, who gave me invaluable tips on duckmole (platypus) lore; Barbara Delaplace, CompuServe's Science Fiction Literature forum, who has given me sound advice on professional matters.

America Online: the KMart Shoppers, particularly MaxEntropy for her extra assistance with duckmole information; Steven and Lisa Dawson for the loan of their imperious orange-marmalade cat; Virginia Caputo, who helped me to find a different name for platypi and named Broad Foot; also, KO Gen and the KO staff, Guides and kids of America Online's Kids Only, where I have found such friendship, warmth, community, advice, enthusiasm, and input as I never would have expected to come from a computer. {{{{{Gen & Co.}}}}}

Richard McCaffery Robinson, for his valued critical comments, his eleventh-hour naval and plot pointers, and his way of cheering up woebegone persons under deadline: Our friendship alone is worth every penny I pay to CompuServe!

Ellen Harris, who would be very happy to do a Daine doll.

Cat Yampell, for her enthusiasm, moral support, and her own wonderfully wacky writing—I hope she gets the recognition that she deserves.

Ms. Vivian Ellner and the kids of U.N.I.S., who have invited me to read for their book fair three years in a row.

Tas Schlabach, who helped set Daine's feet on the path of the horse-hearted.

My foreign editors, agents, and publishers, who have kept me afloat: in the United Kingdom, Jacqueline Korn and the staff of David Higham Associates, and Julia Moffatt and David Fickling at Scholastic Children's Books (and David Wyatt, who does most cool covers!); in Europe, Ruth Weibel and Liepman AG, which has been tireless on my behalf, and Barbara Kiiper, my editor at Arena Verlag, her staff, and Arena's dedicated translators.

Robert E. J. Cripps, Celtic Wolf Medieval and Renaissance Style Crossbows, for making me look at crossbows in an entirely new light.

The wildlife researchers and experts whose work I relied on for insights, ideas, and research, and whose efforts to preserve wildlife deserve aid and applause across the world: L. David Mech, researcher and writer on wolves; Farley Mowat, the author of Never Cry Wolf; Marty Stouffer and his Wild America television series; The Nature Conservancy; the National Wildlife Federation; NYZS The Wildlife Conservation Society;

Sir David Attenborough, whose many programs and books on nature changed the way I looked at it; and the International Wolf Center of Ely, Minnesota, which tries to make it possible for future generations to hear pack-song.

Friends whose contributions are intangible but vital all the same, including Amelia and Molly Bonnett, whom I got to meet at last; Nikki Johnson, who went from fan to friend; Kelly Riggio, whom I think of far more than my rare letters would lead her to believe; Iris Mori, because *Benkyo ni narimashita* (It's been educational, literally!); Heather Mars, who's earned a much-deserved degree after wading through quanta, vectors, and m-m-m-math; Stacy Norris, who is never afraid to speak her mind; and my inspirational helper, Andy Foley, who has made me laugh (on purpose) at times when I could use a laugh.

Peter, James, Rich, Tim, and all the other wonderful people at Books of Woinder, still my favorite bookstore.

Jean Karl of Atheneum, who has borne with me during crazy times, and Howard Kaplan of Atheneum, for the work he's put in.

And, as always, my own personal family constellation: my husband Tim, who nurses me through my deadlines as I nurse him through his; Raquel, who at last sighting had submerged in nineteenth-century New York for *her* current book; Thomas, whose approach to artistic growth and experience always gives me guidance on staying young from the neck up; my sister Kim, who rescues people and keeps them alive for a living; Pa and Ma, who teach me to age with Attitude; Melanie, Fred, and C.J., who share my love of animals; and the agents, accounting department, assistants, and receptionist of Harold Ober Associates, who do so much for this grateful ex-employee and client.

CONTENTS

PROLOGUE

A MAGICAL BARRIER HAD SEPARATED THE REALMS of the gods from the mortal realms for over four hundred years. While it stood, mortals were safe from the legendary creatures known as immortals, so named because, unless they were slain, they lived forever. Giants, Stormwings, griffins, basilisks, tauroses, Coldfangs, ogres, centaurs, winged horses, unicorns: In time all became the stuff of children's tales, or the concern of scholars who explored the records of times long gone.

In the eighth year of the reign of Jonathan and

Thayet of Tortall, mages in Carthak found the long-lost spells that were the keys to gates into the Divine Realms. Ozorne, the Carthaki emperor, turned those spells to his own use. His agents opened gates into other kingdoms, freeing immortals to weaken Carthak's enemies for later conquest. Even those immortals who were peaceful, or indifferent to human affairs, created panic and confusion wherever they went. Gate after gate was opened. No thought was spared concerning the long-term effects on the barrier.

In the autumn of the thirteenth year of Their Majesties' rule, Ozorne's great plan came to a halt. In the middle of peace talks with Tortall—whose agents had revealed his involvement in the current troubles of his neighbors—Emperor Ozorne made a final attempt to regain his advantage. He ignored omens that proclaimed the gods were most displeased with his stewardship of his kingdom. For his pains, he was turned into a Stormwing and barred from human rule. His nephew took the throne; the gate spells were destroyed. By that time, however, the barrier had been stretched in a thousand places to cover the holes made by the magical gates. Its power flickered like a guttering candle.

* * *

At the dawn of the Winter Solstice, the shortest day of the year, all those with any magic—Gift, immortal, and wild—woke suddenly, laboring to hear something that was not a sound. In Tortall, Numair Salmalín, one of the world's great mages, sat up in bed, pouring sweat. Though he could not see them, he *knew* what all the other mages in the palace and city were doing. The king, awake and at work in his study, knocked his chair over when he jumped to his feet. Harailt of Aili, dean of the royal university, flailed in bed and fell out with a thud. Gareth the Elder of Naxen pressed a hand to his laboring heart; Kuri Taylor swayed on her feet, half fainting. Even those with wild magic registered on Numair's senses. Onua of the Queen's Riders jumped out of her dawn bath, shrieking a K'miri war cry. Stefan Groomsman dropped out of his loft, landing safely on bales of hay while the horses who loved him whickered in concern.

And Daine, Numair's teenage friend and ally of the last three years, sat up in her bed-nest of cats, dragon, marmosets, martens, and dogs, eyes wide in the gloom, soft lips parted. The young dragon Skysong trilled without stopping, her voice spreading in a series of rippling pools, soon to reach and fill the palace itself.

"Kit, hush," Numair heard Daine say, though the

girl didn't try to enforce the order. "Numair, what is it?"

He didn't question her knowing that he could hear what she'd said, in spite of hundreds of yards and a number of buildings between them, any more than she questioned it. In that moment, as the sun climbed over the horizon, any wall seemed vague and ghostly. "It's the barrier," he replied softly, but she heard every word. "The barrier between the realms. It's—gone. Evaporated."

He could feel her blink, as if those long, dark lashes of hers touched his cheek. Suddenly he learned something that he'd never considered before. For a brief moment, that fresh knowledge erased even his sense of magical cataclysm.

"The immortals—they'll be on us like a ton of bricks," she said, her voice matter-of-fact. "I'd best get up."

1
SKINNERS

THE STORMWING SAT ON A LOW WOODEN PERCH like a king on his throne. All around him torches flickered; men spoke quietly as they prepared the evening meal. He was a creature of bad dreams, a giant bird with the head and chest of a man. As he moved, his steel feathers and claws clicked softly. For one of his kind, he was unusually clean. His reddish brown hair had once been dressed in thin braids, but many had unraveled. His face, with its firm mouth and large amber eyes, had once been attractive, but hate deepened the lines at mouth and eyes. Dangling around his neck was a twisted, glassy lump of rock that shimmered in the torchlight.

Now he stared intently at a puddle of darkness on the ground before him. An image grew in the inky depths. In it, a tall, swarthy man turned the reins of his black-and-white spotted gelding over to a young hostler. Beside him, a girl—a young woman, really—lifted saddlebags from the back of a sturdy gray pony. When the hostler reached for *her* reins, the mare's ears went flat; lips curled away from teeth.

"Cloud, leave be," ordered the girl. She spoke Common, the main language of the Eastern and Southern Lands, with only a faint accent, the last trace of her origins in the mountains of Galla. "It's too late for you to be at your tricks."

The mare sighed audibly, as if she agreed. The hostler took her reins carefully, and led mare and gelding away. Grinning, the girl slung the bags over her shoulder.

She is lovely, thought the Stormwing who had once been Emperor Ozorne of Carthak. The boys must swarm around her now, seeing the promise of that soft mouth, and ignoring the stubborn chin. Or at least, he amended his own thought, the ones with the courage to approach a girl so different from others.

Boys who don't mind that she converses with passing animals, not caring that only half the conversation can be heard by two-leggers. Such a brave boy—or man— would try to drown himself in those blue-gray eyes, with their extravagant eyelashes.

Ozorne the Stormwing smiled. It was a pity that, unlike most girls of sixteen, she would not make a charm this Midsummer's Day to attract her true love. On the holiday, two days hence, she—and her lanky companion—would be dead. There would be no lovers, no future husband, for Veralidaine Sarrasri, just as there would be no more arcane discoveries for Numair Salmalin, Ozorne's one-time friend.

"I want the box," he said, never looking away from the dark pool.

Two new arrivals entered the image in the pool. One was an immortal, a basilisk. Over seven feet tall, thin and fragile-looking, he resembled a giant lizard who had decided to walk on his hind legs. His eyes were calm and gray, set in a beaded skin the color of a thundercloud. In one paw he bore his long tail as a lady might carry the train to her gown.

The other newcomer rode in a pouch made of a fold of skin on the basilisk's stomach. Alert, she surveyed everything around her, fascination in her large eyes with their slit pupils. A young dragon, she was small—only two feet long, with an extra twelve inches of tail—and bore little resemblance to the adults of her kind. They reached twenty feet in length by mid-adolescence, after their tenth century of life.

"Numair! Daine! Tkaa and Kitten—welcome!" A tall, black-haired man with a close-cropped beard, wearing blue linen and white silk, approached the new arrivals, holding out a hand. The swarthy man gripped it in his own with a smile. As the young dragon chirped a greeting, the basilisk and the girl bowed. Jonathan of Conté, king of Tortall, put an arm around mage and girl and led them away, saying, "Can you help us with these wyverns?" Basilisk and dragon brought up the rear.

Something tapped the Stormwing's side. A ball of shadow was there, invisible in the half-light except where it had wrapped smoky tendrils around a small iron box. The Stormwing brushed the latch with a steel claw; the top flipped back. Inside lay five small, lumpy, flesh-colored balls. They wriggled slightly as he watched.

"Patience," he said. "It is nearly time. You must try to make your mistress proud."

Mortals approached the camp. They stopped on the far edge of the Stormwing's dark pool; the image in it vanished. Two were Copper Islanders. They were dressed in soft boots, flowing breeches, and long over-tunics worn by their navy, the elder with a copper breastplate showing a jaguar leaping free of a wave, the younger with a plain breastplate. The third man, a Scanran shaman-mage, was as much their opposite as anyone could be. His shaggy blond mane and beard were a rough contrast to the greased, complex loops of the Islanders' black hair. Hot though it was, he wore a bearskin cape over his stained tunic and leggings, but never sweated. Few people ever looked at his dress: All eyes were drawn to a large ruby set in the empty socket of one eye. The other eye glittered with cold amusement at his companions.

"Still watching Salmalin and the girl?" asked the senior Islander. "My king did not send us for your private revenge. We are here to loot. The central cities of Tortall are far richer prizes than this one."

"You will have your richer prizes," Ozorne said coldly, *"after* Legann falls."

"It will take all summer to break Legann," argued the Islander. "I want to reunite my fleet and strike Port Caynn now! Unless your spies have lied—"

"My agents can no more lie than they can unmake themselves," replied the Stormwing coldly.

"Then an attack from my fleet at full strength will take port and capital! I want to do it now, before help comes from the Yamani Islands!"

Ozorne's amber eyes glittered coldly. "Your king told you to heed my instructions."

"My king is not here. He cannot see that you forced us into a fruitless siege only to lure a common-born man and maid into a trap! I—"

The Stormwing reached out a wing to point at the angry Islander. The black pool on the ground hurled itself into the air. Settling over the man's head and shoulders, it plugged his eyes, ears, nose, and mouth. He thrashed, ripping at the pool. It reshaped itself away from his clawing hands, flowing until it pinned his arms against his sides. The onlookers could hear his muffled screams.

When the man's thrashing ended, Ozorne looked at the remaining Islander. "Have *you* questions for me?"

The younger man shook his head. Droplets of sweat flew from him.

"Consider yourself promoted. Bury that," the Stormwing ordered, meaning the dead man. He looked at the Scanran shaman-mage. "What do you say, Inar Hadensra?"

The man grinned. Crimson sparks flashed in his

ruby eye. "My masters sent me to see that Tortall is stretched thin," he said in a cracked voice. "Where our forces go is no matter, so long as this bountiful realm is weak as a kitten in the spring."

"Wise," Ozorne remarked with a shrug of contempt.

Fire blazed out of the ruby, searing Ozorne's eyes. He covered his face with his wings, sweat pouring from his living flesh, but the agony went on, and on. A harsh voice whispered, "Remember that *you* are no longer emperor of Carthak. Take care how you address me." The pain twisted and went icy, chilling Ozorne from top to toe. Each place where his flesh mixed with steel burned white-hot with cold. "The power for which I plucked one eye out of my own head is enough to defeat the magic of a Stormwing, even one so tricky as you."

When Ozorne's vision cleared, he was alone with the dark pool on the ground, and the shadow next to him. "I'll gut you for that, Inar," he whispered, looking at the box. "But not before I settle my score with Veralidaine and the one-time Arram Draper." Grabbing his iron box in one claw, he took off, flapping clumsily into the night sky.

* * *

11

Two days later, the girl and the man who had drawn Ozorne's attention hovered over a cot in a guard tower at Port Legann. Their eyes were locked on the small blue-white form curled up in a tight ball at the cot's center. The dragon's immature wings were clenched tight on either side of her backbone. The tall gray basilisk Tkaa was there as well, gazing through a window at the courtyard below.

"I don't like her color," Daine said. "She's never been that shade before. Pale blue, yes, but—going white along with the blue? It's as if she's turning into a ghost."

"She is weary," replied the basilisk, turning away from his view. "For a dragon as young as Skysong, the effort of will required to send a wyvern about his business is tiring. She will be fine when she awakes."

"What if the wyverns return before then?" Numair Salmalin showed the effects of the spring's fighting more than Daine or Tkaa. Too many nights with little or no sleep had etched creases around his full, sensitive mouth and at the corners of his dark eyes. For all that he was only thirty, there were one or two white hairs in his crisp black mane of hair. "The king was— unpleased—when *I* attempted to fight them last time."

Daine smiled. *Unpleased* described Jonathan's

reaction to Numair's use of his magical Gift on wyverns as well as *breeze* described a hurricane. "You were ordered to keep your strength in reserve," she reminded him. "Archers can do for wyverns as well as you, and there might come something archers *can't* fight. *Then* he'll need you."

"The wyverns should not return for at least a day," the basilisk added. "They too used up their strength, to defy a dragon's command for as long as they did."

"I can't believe they ran." Daine pushed her tumble of smoky brown curls away from her face. "She's not even three years old." She and Kitten had risen at sunrise to handle the attacking wyverns; there had been no time to pin up her hair, or even to comb it well. With a sigh, she picked up her brush and began to drag it through her curls.

Numair watched her from his position next to the sleeping dragon. He could see weariness in Daine's blue-gray eyes. The two of them had been in motion since the spring thaws, when Tortall's foreign enemies—an alliance of Copper Islanders, Carthaki rebels, Scanran raiders, and untold immortals—had struck the northern border, western coast, and a hundred points within the realm. With the wild magic that enabled Daine to ask the animals and birds of Tortall to fight the invaders, Kitten's dragon power, Tkaa's ability to turn any who vexed him to stone, and Numair's own great magical Gift, they had managed time after time in the last twelve weeks to stave off disaster.

Port Legann was their most recent stop; the four had ridden all night to reach the king. Remembering that ride, just two days ago, Numair wondered how much more of this pace they would be able to stand.

The rest of the country was in little better shape. "Our true allies are pressed to the wall," King Jonathan had told them over supper on the night of their arrival. "Maren, Galla, Tyra—immortals hit them at the same time they hit us. Emperor Kaddar does his best to guard our southern coast, but he's got a rebellion on his hands. The emperor of the Yamani Islands has promised to send a fleet, but even when it comes, it will be needed to relieve the siege on Port Caynn and on Corus."

Kitten stirred in her sleep, interrupting Numair's thoughts. "Shh," he murmured, stroking her. The dragon twisted so that her belly was half exposed, and quieted again.

A boy stuck his head in the open door. "'Scuze me, m'lord Numair, Lady, um—um—sir." His confusion over the proper title for a basilisk was brief.

"His Majesty needs you now, up on the coast wall, the northwest drum tower. If you'll follow me?"

Now what? was in the looks Daine and Numair exchanged, before the girl remembered the dragon.

"Kitten—"

"I will remain with Skysong," Tkaa assured her.

Daine stood on tiptoe to pat the immortal's cheek. "You're fair wonderful, Tkaa." She and Numair followed the runner at a brisk walk.

A man, a commoner by his sweat-soaked clothes, knelt at the king's feet, drinking greedily from a tankard. Beside him was a tray with a pitcher and a plate of sliced bread, meat, and cheese. The king, in tunic and breeches of his favorite blue and a plain white shirt, leaned against the tower wall, reading a grimy sheet of parchment. In direct sunlight, Daine could see that Jonathan had also acquired some white threads in his black hair since the arrival of spring.

"This is Ulmer of Greenhall, a village southeast of here," the king said when he saw them. "He has ridden hard to reach us, and his news is—unsettling."

Watching the man eat, Daine realized he didn't kneel just from reverence to his monarch—gray with exhaustion, he was too weak to stand. It seemed that all he could manage was to chew his food.

"'Unsettling'? I don't like the sound of that," Numair remarked.

"The village headman writes that five *things* came out of the Coastal Hills near Greenhall the day before yesterday. They kill what they touch—"

"Skin 'em, with magic," Ulmer interrupted. "Can't shoot 'em." He refilled his tankard with trembling hands. "I mean, *y' can*, but it does them no hurt. Swords, axes—" He shook his head. Realizing that he'd interrupted the king, he ducked his head. "Beggin' your pardon, sire."

"It's all right, Ulmer." To Numair and Daine, Jonathan added, "Sir Hallec of Fief Nenan went to fight them at sunset yesterday. They killed him." He grimly rolled up the parchment. "Fortunately, the Skinners don't move after dark, and are slow to start in the morning—they seem to need to warm up. The people of Greenhall have fled, but . . . there are rich fields in this part of the realm, as you know. We will need those crops this winter." He looked at Numair, then at Daine. "I'm sorry. I know you're exhausted, but—"

"You need your other mages to deal with the enemy fleet, and the siege," Numair said. "This *is* why you've kept me in reserve, Your Majesty."

"The wyverns—" the runner who had brought them said. He blushed when the others looked at him.

Daine understood his worry. The giant, winged, legless dragons breathed a yellow fog that gave humans a dry, long-lasting cough and made the eyes burn and blur. The crew of one of the great catapults, breathless and half blind, had dumped a boulder among their own soldiers. Legann's only insurance against another wyvern attack was Kitten. Wyverns might resist, but they *had* to obey an order from one of their dragon cousins.

"Kit stays," the girl said firmly, looking at the king. "Tkaa knows more about helping her than I do, anyway."

"She won't protest?" Jonathan asked. He knew the young dragon well.

Daine shook her head. "She doesn't like us being apart for long, but she's gotten used to it since the war began. Sometimes we're more useful when we're apart."

"I'll guide you to—home." Ulmer tried to get up, and failed.

"There's no need," said Numair gently. "If you do not object, I'll take the knowledge of the route to your village from your mind. You're in no condition to ride."

"I'll pack for us both, and give the word to Tkaa," Daine said. "Meet you at the stables soonest." She turned to go. A hand grabbed her sleeve. Puzzled, she looked at the king. "Be careful," he said, giving her the parchment letter. "These Skinners sound like nothing that anyone has encountered before."

Daine smiled at this man whom she had served with love and respect for the last three years. "Numair will set them to rights, Majesty," she said. "Just make sure you're still here when we come back."

"I think I can manage that much," the king replied, and released Daine's sleeve. "Unless they get reinforcements, we can hold them all summer if we must." He and Daine tapped their own skulls with closed fists, their version of knocking on wood. "Look at the bright side. It's Midsummer's Day—maybe the gods will throw some luck at us!"

"Midsummer—do you know, I'd fair forgotten?" Daine smiled wryly. "Maybe I'll look in a pond along the way and find out who my true love will be."

Jonathan laughed. Daine grinned, bowed, and trotted off, waiting until she knew he could no longer see her before she let her smile fade. With Numair's magical Gift to hide their presence, there would be no problem in leaving the city—it was how they'd entered it in the first place. Her concern was for the king—and for the queen, commanding at the embattled capital; for Alanna the Lioness, the King's Champion, in the far north since the spring; for the many friends she had made all over Tortall.

We need Midsummer luck for the fair, she thought, returning to their rooms. All along, the enemy's known what we're about before we do it. We need luck to counter him, and luck to find his spies. I don't know where it's to come from, but we need it *soon.*

They left Port Legann separately. Numair rode his patient gelding, Spots, carrying his pack and Daine's. While two of the three roads that led into the city were still open, they were unsafe; he cloaked himself and Spots magically, as he'd done on the way into Legann. Daine herself flew out in the shape of a golden eagle to see if she could find the Skinners and get an idea of what she and Numair were up against.

She soared on columns of warm air that rose from the land. From the upper reaches, the walled city and its surroundings looked much like a wonderfully detailed map. The enemy's main camp lay a few miles off the north road. On the road itself, a mixed band of enemy soldiers and immortals was camped. On the eastern and southern roads, soldiers in Tortallan colors had dug in to keep the way open for help and supplies. From aloft, she also saw the motley fleet that waited outside Legann, thwarted from entering the harbor by the great chains stretched across its mouth.

In her years in Tortall she had lived among warriors and mages, and could read a battle situation like a book. What she read now gave Daine hope. The enemy army was about equal to Legann's; if they had any magical surprises, they would have used them before. With armies that were matched, and neither side having the advantage in magic or weapons, the battle on land and at sea was a stalemate. The king was right: Legann might hold all summer, particularly if they could keep at least one road open.

She wheeled, turning her eyes east. Twenty miles from the city, a wide swath of pale brown, black, and gray, naked of greenery, straddled the east road. Trees stripped of leaf and bark thrust into the air like toothpicks. As she approached, she saw, and smelled, corpses—most of them animals—bloated and stinking in the heat. They came in all sizes, from the smallest mice to cows and sheep. The closer Daine came to that dead zone, the fewer animal voices she heard. Most of the Beast-People who could do so had fled.

Gliding over the last bank of living trees, she found the Skinners. There were five in all: wet, flesh-colored, two-legger things. They had no eyes, ears, noses, or mouths, but they didn't seem to require such niceties. They forged ahead blindly, touching anything that lived. When they did, plants became dull instead of glossy. Tree bark vanished. Within seconds, vegetation went dark, brittle, dead. As the creatures touched things, parts of their own flesh changed color—brown, green, reddish, like bark or leaves in texture. Those patches would grow, shrink, and vanish rapidly.

She had come upon the Skinners as they worked their way through a village. They ignored small obstacles, like tossed-aside buckets or sacks of food that had been left in the street. If the object was big—a well, or an abandoned wagon—they split up, walked around, and rejoined to walk abreast once more.

High overhead, Daine reached into the copper fire of her wild magic. Gripping it, she cast it out like a net, letting her power fall gently onto the Skinners. She didn't expect it to stop them. Wild magic only helped her shape-shift and talk to the People. Still, if wild magic was something she had in common with these things, perhaps they could talk. Perhaps she could get them to break off their mindless, deadly ramble.

Her net touched something—and suddenly a hole yawned in the center of her magic. She felt the closeness of things she couldn't name; they shifted and rolled just at the corner of her mind's eye. Creatures that should not exist wailed in voices that made her ears bleed; dreadful scents reached her nose and tore at the delicate tissues inside. She lost control over her eagle body and dropped.

In losing her form, she broke the magic's grip. Frantically Daine shifted into the first shape that came to mind. Just before she hit the ground, crow wings grabbed the air and dragged her aloft. When she was safe in the new form and out of reach, she looked down.

The Skinners had formed a circle. Their eyeless heads were turned up, as if they could see her. She scolded with the excitement of fear, cursing them in a crow's beautifully nasty vocabulary.

Her foes were not impressed. Spreading out in a line, they began to march forward. Daine shuddered. What had she sensed? What were those things made of? She would have to ask Numair. For now, she slowly made herself an eagle again. A bird of prey was a better glider than a crow, and she needed the eagle's sharp eyes.

Below, the monsters lumbered on. The leftmost Skinner was about to step over a small hutch when it stopped. Bending down, it grabbed at the small door, yanking it off its hinges. A rabbit streaked by on its way to freedom. Before Daine could even guess what was happening, the Skinner seized its prey and held its prize up by the ears.

The hare convulsed. Its fur and hide vanished, ripped off in an eye-blink. Patches of fur appeared all over the Skinner, dull against the gleaming stickiness that was its own flesh. The hare now dangled, motionless. The thing dropped it, and touched a patch of fur that had appeared on its belly. The patch grew, then shrank, and was gone.

Horrified, Daine called up her magic again while the Skinners walked on. She searched the village for more abandoned animals. There was a chicken coop on the edge of town. Its occupants could sense nearby monsters; they shrieked their alarm. She didn't stop to remember that she despised chickens for their stupidity and their smell. Once more she dropped, taking on her true shape as soon as she touched the ground.

Fumbling at the rope latch on the coop, she glanced around. More than anything, she wanted to see the Skinners before they saw her. The rope gave. Chickens erupted from the coop, showering Daine with feathers, scratching her and squawking in her ears. "Stop it, you idiotic birds!" she whispered. "Shut up, clear out, and get away from here!"

She used her magic to give them brief wisdom. The chickens raced into the forest, away from the approaching monsters. Daine took eagle shape for the third time, watching the Skinners from high above as she waited for Numair to arrive.

He threw off his cloaking spell when he and Spots reached the dead zone, and Daine glided down to meet him. Taking her pack, she dressed behind a tree as she reported what she had seen. When he dismounted, she unsaddled Spots and sent the gelding into the still-living woods, out of the Skinners' path.

Numair passed her crossbow and quiver to her. "Can we beat them?" he asked.

Daine's blue-gray eyes met his dark ones. "I don't know," she said truthfully. "I've never seen the like of these things." Putting a foot in the crossbow's stirrup, she drew the bowstring until it hooked over the release.

The man sighed and dropped his cloak over their packs. Black fire that sparkled with bits of white appeared around his body. "Give me that quarrel," he

said, holding out a hand. She obeyed, passing over the
bolt that she'd been about to load. He closed long
fingers over it, lips moving, then handed it over.

Daine placed the quarrel in the clip, then led him
to their quarry. The Skinners had finished with the
village of Greenhall and had entered a nearby peach
orchard. Half of the trees were stripped of their bark.
Even the green fruit had lost its skin.

Numair looked ill. "Is it all like this?" he asked.

"Worse. There's acres of it, clean back to the hills."
She raised the bow to her shoulder, taking deliberate
aim. The Skinners, in the middle of the orchard, turned
to stare at them—if they could stare.

Daine shot. The quarrel flew straight, and buried
itself in one Skinner's head. Numair gestured; an explosion tore the air. The Skinner blew apart, showering its
companions with pieces of itself. The others looked
around in apparent confusion.

Daine started to grin, but stopped. Swiftly each of
the Skinner chunks doubled, redoubled, and spread.
Each sprouted a pair of stumps to stand on, and
stretched. Now there were ten Skinners, five large
and five smaller ones. Their attention fixed on her and
Numair, they came at a run. Daine slipped another
bolt into the clip of the bow.

The mage raised a hand. Black fire jumped away from him and swept over the monsters, pulling them into the air. The Skinners thrashed and broke through his control, hurtling to the ground. Slowly, they got up.

"I hope the owner of this orchard forgives me," muttered Numair. Stretching out his hands, he shouted a phrase that Daine couldn't understand. The ground before the advancing Skinners ripped open. They dropped into the crevasse.

Numair trotted toward it, Daine right behind him. "If I can seal them into the earth, that may be the end of it. I certainly hope so." Halting at the edge of the crack, they peered in. "I *hate* simply blasting them with raw power like this. There is always a spell to uncreate anything, though the consequences may be— oh, dear."

The Skinners were climbing the sides. Numair jerked Daine back, shouting a word that made her ears pound. The earth rumbled, knocking them down; the crack sealed.

"Please Goddess, please Mithros, let that stop them," whispered Numair. Sweat dripped from his face as Daine helped him to stand. "Grant a boon on Midsummer's Day—"

Daine heard something behind them and whirled.

Ten feet away, crude hands erupted through dirt. "Numair!" she cried, and shot the emerging Skinner. Unmagicked, her bolt had no effect. The creature rose from the ground as if it climbed a stair.

Numair cried out in Old Thak. The creature that Daine had shot turned to water. The man whirled to do the same to another Skinner. Half out of the earth, it dissolved.

Five spots near them exploded as Skinners leaped free of the ground. Daine screamed. Numair reached to pull her closer, and discovered that someone else had the same idea. Two pairs of hands clutched the girl by the arms, dragging her into a patch of air that burned silvery white.

"No!" shouted the mage, wrapping both arms around Daine. The phantom hands continued to pull.

Sinking into white pain, Daine heard a man shriek, "Curse you, follow them! Follow, *follow, FOLLOW!*"

Unseen by her or Numair, an inky shadow leaped free of the grass to wrap itself around her feet. Girl, man, and shadow vanished into bright air.

Every inch of her throbbed. Hands gripped her; she fought. "The Skinners! They'll kill Numair, they'll kill the People, they'll kill the crops! Let me *go!*"

A female voice, one that she knew, said, "If she doesn't rest, she won't heal. He's just as bad. Both keep fretting about those monsters."

"I'd best take care of it, then." The second, gravelly voice was even more familiar.

"Why?" The speaker was an unknown male. "Leave mortal affairs to mortals."

"Nonsense," barked the gravel voice. Whiskers tickled her face; a musky scent that she knew well filled her nose. "Listen, Daine. Numair is here, with you. He's safe. I'll fix those Skinners. I can handle them. Now rest, and stop fussing!"

She sneezed. "All right, Badger." If her old friend the badger god said that things would be taken care of, she could believe him, even if all this was only a dream.

The woman's voice was fading. "I'll tell Numair."

The next time Daine woke, the pain gnawing at her had turned to a dull, steady ache. Cloth rustled nearby; the faint odor of sweet pea and woods lily filled her nose. Like the female voice she'd heard, she knew that scent well. She opened her eyes.

A blurred face hung over her. Daine squinted, trying to see. The face became clearer: blue eyes, a dimple at the corner of that smiling mouth, creamy skin, straight nose, high cheekbones. The whole was topped with a braided crown of heavy golden hair.

In a second the girl forgot the last four years. She was twelve again, and in her bed in Galla. "Ma?" she croaked. "I dreamed you was dead." With a frown, she corrected herself—she knew how to speak like cultured folk nowadays! "I dreamed you *were* dead."

Sarra Beneksri—Daine's mother—laughed. "Sweetling, it was no dream, I *am* dead."

Some of Daine's confusion faded. "Well, that's all right, then." She tried to sit up. "Where am I?"

Sarra moved pillows to help her. "You're in the realms of the gods."

Moving dizzied the girl. "How'd I get *here*? And why do I hurt so?"

"We brought you. Sadly, passage between realms was fair hard for you. Here's something to drink against the pain."

"Talk about familiar," Daine grumbled, taking the offered cup. With each swallow, she felt an improvement; by the time she'd swallowed all of the liquid, her pain was nearly gone. "Your messes have gotten better," she remarked with a grin.

"It's the herbs here." Sarra pinched Daine's nose gently. "They're stronger. Open your eyes wide." She used her fingers to pull back Daine's eyelids. "Where were you born?"

"Snowsdale, in Galla. Why are you asking?"

"To see if your mind's unhurt—though it being you, I wonder if I'll be able to tell."

"Ma!" squeaked Daine with a laughing outrage.

"How old are you?"

"Sixteen." Memory returned in a rush. "Where's Numair? The Skinners—"

Her mother stopped her from getting up. "Easy. Master Numair is here, and safe. The badger took care of those skinning monsters. He turned them to ice, and they melted. They won't trouble anyone now."

"So I didn't dream that." Daine sank back against her pillows gratefully, fingering the heavy silver badger's claw that hung on a chain around her neck. "Where did they come from, do you suppose?"

"You know as much as me," was the reply. "I've never seen the like of them."

"Sarra?" The voice coming from the next room was deep, male, and unfamiliar.

The woman's face lit up. "In here, my love. She's awake."

The door opened, and a man dressed in a loincloth entered. Although the doorway was unusually large, the crown of antlers firmly rooted in his brown, curly hair forced him to duck to pass through. He was tan and heavily muscled, with emerald eyes. Daine was unsettled to notice that there also were olive streaks in his reddish brown skin.

"So." He touched his antlers uneasily as she stared at them. "We meet at last."

"This is your father," Sarra told Daine. "This is the god Weiryn."

2
MEETINGS
WITH GODS

HE LOOKED SO—ODD. NO ONE ELSE'S FATHER HAD antlers, or went half naked. What was she supposed to say? "Hullo, Da." She hid trembling hands under her blankets.

"Daine!" Sarra cried. "Is that the best you can do? He's your da!"

The girl couldn't begin to describe her feelings. Only months ago, she had learned that the horned man she saw in visions was her father, and that he was a god. She had tried not to think about it ever since. "It's not like you ever told me who he was, or what he was," she reminded her mother. "Not even a *hint*."

"I thought we'd have time later," replied Sarra. "I never meant to be killed by bandits!"

"Daine?" Numair came to the door, looking pale and tired. "You know that the badger destroyed the Skinners, yes?"

"Ma told me. You don't look so good."

He smiled. "I'll survive. Are *you* all right?"

"I hurt a little." She couldn't help but note, with some amusement, that except for the tips of his horns, Weiryn was shorter than her friend.

Numair smiled twistedly. "I am informed that passage between the realms has an adverse effect on mortals." He clung to the doorframe.

Silver fire glimmered on the floor, and a large badger appeared. Daine smiled as her mentor waddled over. He looked up at her with black eyes that were bright in his vividly marked face. "Hullo," she told him. "So we've you to thank for handling those Skinners?"

"You wouldn't rest until you knew they were dealt with." Balancing on his hindquarters, the god rose to plant his forepaws on her covers. Her nose filled with his musky, heavy scent.

Gently she scratched him behind the ears. Since she had left her Gallan home, the badger had visited her, teaching her the use of her wild magic, and warning of danger to come. The claw she wore around her neck was his; he could always trace it to find her.

Sarra frowned at Numair. "You are supposed to sit, and stay sat." She made a tugging gesture at the wall beside the mage. That part of the room began to move; the floor buckled and rose. The wall stretched to meet it, then sagged to create a chair. "Down, Master Salmalín!" ordered Sarra. Meekly, he did as ordered.

Daine's jaw dropped. "But—Ma, you can't—You never—"

"Things are different here," the badger said. "In the Divine Realms, we gods can shape our surroundings to suit ourselves."

"Sometimes," added Weiryn.

"Wonderful," the girl said weakly. She was not sure that she liked to see unliving things move about under their own power. "Tell me—how did we come here? The last thing I remember is the Skinners."

Weiryn and Sarra traded glances. "You were in danger of your life, against a foe you could not fight," the god said. "We had meant to bring you only, but this—man"—he glared at the mage—"refused to let go of you. We were forced to bring him as well."

"I just thank the Goddess that you met the Skinners

on one of the great holidays, when we *could* pull you through to us," added Daine's mother. "Otherwise you would have been killed. It fair troubles me that no one we've asked has ever heard of those creatures."

Light bloomed through the curtains on a window that filled one of the walls, growing steadily brighter, then fading. Just as it was nearly gone, another slow flash came. "Oh, dear," remarked Sarra as Weiryn opened the drapes. "They're still at it."

"What's going on?" Numair asked, lurching to his feet.

"Will you *sit*?" cried Daine's mother. "Men! You're so stubborn!" Numair quickly sat, this time on the bed. Sulkily, the chair that Sarra had made for him sank into the wall.

Daine stared at the view. The ground here dropped away to meet a busy stream. There were no trees between stream and house, although the forest grew thickly on the far side of the water. In the oval of open sky overhead, waves of rippling pea green, orange, yellow, and gray fire shimmered and coursed.

"What is it?" she whispered. Numair took her hand and squeezed it gently. "I feel that it means something bad, but it's so beautiful . . ."

"It means that Uusoae, the Queen of Chaos, is

fighting the Great Gods," said the badger. "That light is her magic and her soldiers, as they attack the barriers between our realm and hers."

"She has been at it since Midwinter." Weiryn put an arm around Sarra. "Normally the lights that burn in our sky reflect your mortal wars, but this is far more important."

"Thanks ever so," muttered Numair. Daine grinned at him.

Sarra looked at her daughter and said reproachfully, "Speaking of war, I never raised *you* to be always fighting and killing. That's not woman's work."

"It's needful, Ma. *You* taught me a woman has to know how to defend herself."

"I never!" gasped Sarra, indignant.

"You taught me when you were murdered in your own house," Daine said quietly.

Sarra turned back into Weiryn's hold, leaning on his chest, but not before the girl saw tears in her mother's eyes. A hand patted her ankle; a broad head thrust itself under her elbow. Against her mother's hurt, she set Numair's smile and the badger's approval.

"Sarra, our war in Tortall may seem unimportant to the gods, but not to us," Numair said. "Daine and I must return to it. They need every fighter, and every mage."

Daine nodded, and closed her eyes. She felt dizzy. Her bones were aching again.

Sarra glanced over and saw what was wrong. "We'll talk of that later," she said crisply. "You both need to drink a posset, then sleep again. It will be a few days before the effects of your passage are over." She went to the hearth and ladled something from a pot into a pair of cups. One she gave to Numair, the other to Daine. "Drink."

The liquid in the cup smelled vile, but Daine knew better than to argue. She gulped it down when Numair did, praying that her stomach wouldn't reject it.

"Back to bed, sir mage," ordered Sarra.

"Good night, Daine," Numair said. The badger echoed him.

"G'night," she murmured, eyes closing already. She sank back among pillows that smelled of sun-dried cotton. "Oh—I forgot. G'night—Da."

She heard a deep chuckle; a hand smoothed her curls. "I am glad that you are here and safe, little one."

Daine smiled, and slept.

Waking slowly, she heard familiar voices, and thought she dreamed them.

The speaker was a mage, Harailt of Aili. "—from

Fiefs Seabeth and Seajen." He panted, as if he'd been running. "A Yamani fleet's been sighted to the west. The bad news is, somehow the Scanrans knew they were coming. They fled overnight."

"Father Storm's curses!" That voice was Queen Thayet's. "How does the enemy get his information? I'd swear on my children's lives that there's no way for a spy to report our plans—and yet the enemy continues to stay one step ahead!"

"I'll ask the mages to start using truthspells and the Sight, and see if we can identify an enemy agent." Harailt sounded worn out.

"Please do," replied the queen. "And when we find him—or her—I hope that person is good with his gods."

Daine opened her eyes. The little room was silent, and bathed in sunlight.

What a strange dream, she thought, and sat up.

There was an even stranger animal on her bed.

At first she thought that someone had played a very bad joke on a young beaver; her visitor had that same dense brown fur. No beaver, though, had ever sported a duck's bill. The tail was wrong, too. It was the proper shape, but it was covered with hair. As the creature, a little over two feet in length, toddled up the length of her bed, she saw that it had webbed feet. Reaching her belly, it cocked its head first one way, then the other, examining her with eyes deeply set into the skull, near that preposterous bill.

"G'day, Weiryn's daughter," the animal greeted her. "Glad to see you awake."

Daine had stopped breathing—she made herself inhale. "Are you a—a god?"

"We're all gods here, except for the immortals," replied her visitor.

She sat up carefully. "Excuse me for asking, but what *are* you, exactly?"

"I am Broad Foot, the male god of the duckmoles."

"Duckmoles? I never heard of them." His fleshy bill *was* the same shape as a duck's, but with comblike ridges inside the bottom half. "May I pick you up?"

He nodded. "Mind the spurs on my hind feet, though. I've poison in them."

She lifted him gently. The fur under her fingers was springy and thick. Examining broad, webbed feet armed with heavy claws, she handled the rear ones— and their venomous spurs—with care. "What on *earth* do you eat?" she asked, putting him down.

"My people eat shrimp, insects, snails—frogs and small fish if we can get any. I usually eat the same

things as my people, though gods are more venture-
some. Sarra cooks the best fish stew in the Divine
Realms. I spend warm seasons here, just for that."

"You come here for Ma's *cooking*?"

His eyes twinkled. "That's right. She sent me to
tell you that she has food ready for *you*, if you care to
dress and come out."

Daine eased out from under the blankets, careful not
to dislodge her guest, and saw that she wore a cotton
nightgown. "How long have we been here?" she asked
Broad Foot.

"Four days. See you in the garden." Silver fire
bloomed; the duckmole vanished.

Four days was too long. What were Kitten, Tkaa,
and King Jonathan doing now? Did they know that
Numair and Daine weren't dead? Frowning, she washed
her face and cleaned her teeth; all that she needed to do
those chores lay on a table.

Looking about, she saw a simple red cotton dress
at the foot of the bed. Under it lay a pink shift, under-
clothes, and red slippers. She wished they were a shirt
and breeches, but knew she might as well put them on.
There was no sign of her old clothes, but even if she
could find them, she doubted that they would be in
very good condition.

Once dressed, she had to sit briefly to catch her breath. The weakness and ache weren't as bad as they had been, but she was still shaky. Tidying her bed required another rest before she could leave the room. She did not see the pocket of shadow that separated from the gloom under her bed and followed her.

The main room of the cottage was empty of people. Looking around, she saw the things that she would expect in her mother's house, as well as three heavy perches—as if very large birds often visited. She guessed that other bedrooms lay behind closed doors. Two doors, however, stood open. Outside one, a path led downhill into a forest. Going to the other, she looked into a walled kitchen garden. A small well, a table, benches, and an outdoor hearth were placed on the open grass. Her mother sat at the table, peeling apples. The duckmole sat on the table beside her, pushing a bit of peel with his bill.

Sarra beamed as Daine sat opposite her. "It's long past breakfast, but I thought you might still want porridge." She filled a bowl from a pot on the hearth. Pitchers of honey and cream were on the table; Daine used both. The porridge was rich, with a deep, nutty taste that shocked her. It was stuffed with bits of dried fruit, each tasting fresh-picked. The cream and honey also were intensely flavorful. She ate only half of the bowl, and put it aside. Her mother drew a mug of water from the well. That was easier to swallow, although it was as powerful as if it came from an icy mountain stream.

Sarra frowned. "You should be hungrier, after all that sleep and the pain from crossing over."

"You forget how things tasted when *you* first came here." A fluffy orange-and-white-marbled cat leaped onto the table to sit in front of Daine. She stared at the girl with large amber eyes, pink nose twitching. "In the Divine Realms, you eat the essence of things, not the shadow. I am Queenclaw, goddess of house cats."

Respectfully, the girl bowed. Queenclaw was an impressive creature. "It's a very great honor, meeting you."

"Of course it is." The cat began to wash.

"How'd you come to be here, Ma?" Daine asked. "I thought the mortal dead go to the Black God's realm."

Sarra cut her apples. "So I did," she replied. "Your father came for me there. He petitioned the Great Gods to allow me to live with him. They decided it was well enough." She eyed Daine warily. "You blame me for not telling you about him?"

Daine looked at the cat, who was still washing, and

at the duckmole, who was grinding apple bits in his bill. She'd forgotten her ma's way of discussing private things before others. "It might've helped later, is all. Ma, we can't stay, you know. We're—"

Queenclaw hissed, and leaped off the table. Briefly Daine suspected her of creating a diversion, until she saw that a black shape, almost like a living ink blot, was tangled in the cat's teeth and claws. It wriggled and shifted like water, trying to escape. Only when the duckmole jumped down to stand on one of the thing's tendrils did it quiet.

"What is that?" the girl wanted to know.

"I've no notion," replied Sarra, frowning. "I've never seen anything like it. Unless it's one of Gainel's—the Dream King's. It *could* be one of his nightmares."

"No," Queenclaw said, looking up. "He's strict with his creatures. They lose their power over mortals if they're allowed to wander, so he keeps them close."

"We'll hold it for Weiryn to look at when he returns." Sarra reached down, white light spilling from her fingers. When it touched the shadowy thing, Queenclaw and Broad Foot moved away from it. Kneeling, Sarra picked the creature up, using the white fire as a kind of scoop. "What manner of beastie are you?" she asked, frowning.

The creature rolled itself into a small, tight ball.

"I command you, give me your name!" ordered Sarra. There was a crack, and a smell of blood. *"Darking?"* She looked at the animal gods. "Have you heard of it?"

"Never," Queenclaw said, washing a forepaw.

Broad Foot shook his head. Vanishing in a wave of silver fire, he reappeared on the table next to the girl. "Easier than climbing for a little fellow like me," he explained.

Daine's mother shrugged, dropping the creature into her apron pocket. "That will hold you for now." She drew a line of white fire across the pocket's opening. Seeing it, Daine was uneasy: Sarra's magical Gift had always shown as rose-pink fire, not white.

"Don't fuss," the woman told her pocket as the darking began to thrash inside. "You'll just—" She fell silent abruptly and cocked her head as if she listened to someone.

When Daine opened her mouth, the cat placed a paw over it, silencing her. "Hush," Queenclaw whispered. "Someone needs her." Fur tickled Daine's nose; she sneezed.

"You are known to the Green Lady, Isa," Sarra remarked, oddly formal. "You seek aid for a breech birth? Who is the mother?" She listened, then sighed. "Nonia. I see."

Daine frowned. They had known an Isa and a Nonia in Snowsdale. Her mother had always claimed that Isa would be a good midwife, if she could ever stop having children of her own. Nonia was barely a year older than Daine herself.

"Harken, Isa. You must turn the babe before it comes. No—listen to me, and I will help." Absently, Sarra walked into the cottage, looking at something very far away.

Daine was the only one who saw the darking— whatever it was—drop to the ground through a hole in its pocket prison. She thought, just like Ma to fix the opening with magic and forget there's a hole in the bottom. She said nothing as the darking vanished into the shadows by the cottage wall. If Queenclaw and Broad Foot hadn't seen its escape, she wasn't going to tell them. After all, the darking hadn't done any harm.

"She's not the same as she was back home," she whispered, more to herself than to the cat or the duck-mole.

"Of course not." Queenclaw stretched. "Only gods or immortals may dwell here."

"You're telling me that Ma—*my* ma—is a god."

"There was a need," Broad Foot explained. "The northern forests had no one to watch over village gardens and childbearing—the Great Mother Goddess can't be *everywhere*. It wouldn't have worked if your mother hadn't liked such things already. Since she does, she became the Green Lady."

"Is she my ma, then?" demanded the girl. "Is she who she was, Sarra Beneksri?"

"Are you who *you* were?" asked the cat.

About to say that of course she was, Daine stopped herself. Daine of Snowsdale could no more heal animals—or turn into one—than the sun could rise in the west. She got up, ignoring a slight dizziness that overtook her. "Please excuse me. I need a walk."

"Be careful," both gods chorused.

"Do you wish a guide?" added Broad Foot, concern in his voice. "Some mortals find the Divine Realms overwhelming—"

"No company, thank you," Daine said, heading toward the gate.

Outside the wall lay a well-marked path. To her right it curved around the house. To her left it crossed a log bridge over a stream and led into the forest. Near the trees a rocky bluff rose in tumbles of earth and stone until it breached the leafy canopy. Anyone who climbed it should have a view that would stretch for miles.

Crossing the bridge, she found that her head had cleared; strength was returning to her legs and arms. She left the path at the foot of the bluff, taking a track that wound through piles of stone, leading her gently upward. When she stopped for a breath after steady climbing, a nearby chuckling sound drew her to a spring hidden in the rocks. A couple of sips of water were all that she needed: Her veins seemed to fill with a green and sparkling energy that carried her on upward.

There was plenty to think about as she climbed. Her ma, a god? She loved her mother, but there was no denying that Sarra needed looking after. Without it, she would seek plants on a cloudy day without taking a hat. Gods were dignified, all-knowing, all-powerful creatures, weren't they?

She knew that lesser gods entered the mortal realms only on the equinoxes and solstices, and her mother had said it was good they met the Skinners on Midsummer Day. There were degrees of strength among gods, then. If this was so, then perhaps lesser gods weren't all-anything, and Sarra could now be a divine being.

"There would be *worse* goddesses than Ma, I guess," she remarked, then sighed.

She left her thin, pretty slippers under a bush when they began to pinch. Thickening the soles of her feet by changing them to elephant hide, she climbed on in comfort. The way was rocky and steep. By the time she reached the rocky summit, she was gasping.

Below was the forest roof, an expanse of countless shades of green, pierced by clearings, streams, and ponds. Turning, she found mountains that stabbed into the sky, their heads wrapped in cloud, their shoulders white with snow.

"Oh, glory," she whispered, and went to see what lay below on that side. Passing a dip in the rock, she halted. A pool of some eerie substance was cupped there. It shimmered with green, yellow, gray, and blue lights, much like the colors that she'd seen in the sky the night before. They moved over its surface in globes, waves, or strips. Watching the pool made her giddy. She swayed, and put out a hand.

"Don't touch it!" a voice behind her warned.

She fought to yank her eyes away in vain. There was something terrible in those moving colors, something that she rebelled against as it drew her in. Pain flared on her ankle; it broke the pool's grip. She stumbled back a few steps.

"Careful!" Clinging to her foot was a lizard, a striped skink. "I'm sorry I hurt you, but I thought you needed help." Green with white and black stripes and a yellow muzzle, she was large for her kind, a foot in length. Her black eyes glinted with intelligence.

Daine bent to pick up the lizard. "So I did." She crossed to the far side of the bluff, putting yards of stone between her and the shifting pool. There she sat, placing the skink beside her. An inspection of her ankle showed that it bled a little. "Thank you."

"You're welcome." The skink jumped on top of a nearby rock to put herself at eye level with the girl. "The next time you find a Chaos vent, don't look into it," the lizard advised. "It'll pull first your mind, and then the rest of you, into the realms of Chaos."

"Chaos vents?" She licked her finger and dabbed at the bite, cleaning it off.

"You'll find them all over the Divine Realms," replied the skink. "They serve as gods' windows into the home of Uusoae, the Queen of Chaos."

"You'd think they'd put warning markers on such things," grumbled Daine. "And why are the gods keeping these windows open if they're fighting this Uusoae?"

"The vents have always been in both the Divine and Chaos realms, whether they're at war or not," explained the skink. "Father Universe and Mother Flame ordered things that way. Are you over your scare?"

"I think so." Daine leaned back, bracing herself with her arms as she looked at the view. "Why didn't I sense you?" she asked. "I should've known you were here the moment I got in range." In the distance, a hawk wheeled over an opening in the trees. Her finely tuned ears picked out the distant call of crows, jays, and starlings. "I never *felt* any of the People. I can't hear you in my mind."

"Nor will you," the skink replied calmly. "We are not mortal animals, Veralidaine Sarrasri—we are gods. If we are killed, we are instantly reborn in new bodies. We have our own magic, powerful magic. Mortals cannot hear us, or know us."

Daine rubbed her ears. "I feel deaf. I feel—separate from everything."

"It's all right," said her companion. "Bask awhile. The sun will do you good."

Daine smiled to think that sunning would help, but she obeyed. The rock warmed her and banished the fear caused by the Chaos vent. Below, woodpeckers tapped trees; squirrels called alarms. Nearby a pika chirped. From the mountains behind them, first one, then another, then more wolf voices rose in pack-song. She grinned, hearing the feeble, shaky notes of wolf pups joining their elders, perhaps for the first time.

The wind shifted, and brought with it a hint of wood smoke. Looking for the source, she found her parents' house and garden, cradled in the bend of the stream that ran past her window. A white plume of smoke trailed from the chimney.

"Look," said the skink. "To the west."

A large, dark bird of some kind flew up from the tree canopy in a twisting pattern. Daine couldn't see it clearly; one moment it was shadowy, the next almost transparent. It was larger than any bird of prey, though not as big as a griffin. She would guess that it was four or five feet long, with a seven-foot wingspan. Up it flew, its spiral tightening. When it seemed as though it spun like a top in midair, the bird opened its wings to their widest, spread its tail, and faced the sun.

Daine gasped as spears of orange, yellow, red, white, and even scraps of blue light flared from the creature's feathers, turning it into airborne flame. It flashed its blazing wings three times, then folded, shedding its fire, or covering it. Once more it was simply a nondescript bird, now flying downward in a spiral.

The skink sighed with pleasure. "Sunbirds," she said. "They do this from noon until sunset. I never get tired of watching it."

For a while they sat in quiet comfort, enjoying this vast scene before them. In the distance an eagle screamed. The breeze changed, to come out of the south, carrying with it the scent of water from still pools and busy streams.

The skink's head shifted. Daine looked and saw three bird forms rise from the trees in that distinctive corkscrew flight pattern. Eagerly she watched the sunbirds climb far above the leafy canopy. At last the three faced the sun, spreading wings and tails in an explosion of color. Daine gasped at the brilliance of the hues: There were more dabs of blue and green light among these birds, even a strong hint of purple under the flame.

There was also something like a picture. Startled, she closed her eyes; the image was clear on the insides of her lids. Queen Thayet and Onua, Horsemistress of the Queen's Riders, stood back to back on the wall before the royal palace in Tortall. Stormwings fell on them, filthy and open-clawed, mouths wide in silent shrieks. Grimly the two women, armed with small, recurved bows, shot arrow after arrow into the flock overhead, hitting Stormwings almost every time. A mage raced along the wall to join them, raising both hands. Something glittered like crystal in his palms.

The image faded. Opening her eyes, Daine got up. "I have to go," she told the reptile, who watched her curiously. "It was very nice meeting you."

"Come back when you can visit longer," the god replied.

Daine frowned at the skink. "Why are you being so nice?" she asked. "I'd have thought a god would be more, well, aloof."

The skink couldn't smile, but Daine heard amusement in her voice. "When you were a little girl, you once saved a nest of young skinks from two-leggers who wished to torture them. For my children, I thank you—and I hope to see you again."

Daine bowed to her, then began her descent. She had to stop more often to rest this time. A drink from the spring helped, but her legs were trembling by the time she reached the bottom.

Weiryn was there, waiting, strung bow in one hand, a dead hare in the other, quiver of arrows on his back. "Your mother is worried about you." His leaf-colored eyes were unreadable. "It's not always a good idea to wander here, these days."

Daine wiped her sweaty face on her sleeve. "I know what I'm doing," she said shortly. "And what is *that*?" She pointed to his kill. "Surely a god doesn't need to hunt."

"Don't vex that tender heart of yours," he replied. "As gods themselves, my prey are reborn into new bodies instantly, or there would be no game anywhere in these realms. And a hunt god *must* hunt." He turned and walked toward the cottage. Daine fell in beside him. "Didn't those mortals teach you anything? The tasks of gods bind us to our mortal followers."

"But you don't need to eat. You're gods."

"We don't need to, but it's fun. Which reminds me—I don't like how *you've* been eating lately. What kind of hunter's daughter won't touch game?"

Daine sighed. "One that's *been* hunted, in deer shape and in goose shape." She tried to smile. "I'm down to mutton, chicken, and fish, Da. I'm just too close to the rest of the People to be eating them."

Weiryn shook his antlered head. "To think that—" He whirled, dropping the hare. "I *thought* so."

"What?" she asked.

In a single, fluid movement, he put an arrow to his string and shot. His arrow struck, quivering, in a patch of shadow under a bush.

Daine frowned. *Something* keened there, in a tiny voice she heard as much in her mind as in her ears. Trotting over, she saw that the shaft pinned an ink blot. What had Ma called it? A darking? "What did you do that for?" she demanded, cross. Gripping the arrow, she yanked it out of the creature. It continued to flutter, crying, a hole in its center. "You don't even know what it is!" She tried to push the blot in on the hole in its middle.

"I don't have to," was the retort. "It came into *my* territory without leave, sneaking about, following us. Now, don't go coddling it—"

Sitting, she picked up the darking and carefully pinched the hole in its body, holding the edges together. "It's fair foolish to shoot something when you don't even know what it is." The darking ceased its cries; when she let it go, the hole was sealed.

The god picked up the hare. "When you are my age, you may question what I do. Now, come along. Leave that thing." He set off down the trail.

Daine looked at the darking. "Do you want to come with me?" she asked, wondering if it could understand. "I won't let him hurt—"

The darking fell through her hands to the ground and raced under the bush. That's a clear enough answer, thought Daine. "Don't let him see you again," she called. "For all I know, he'll keep shooting you." She trotted to catch up to her sire.

"I never thought a daughter of mine would have these sentimental attachments," he remarked. "Pain and suffering trouble gods, but they don't burden us as they do mortals."

Daine thought of the two-legger goddess that she had met the previous fall, the Graveyard Hag. Certainly *she* hadn't been troubled by the ruction that she had caused. "Maybe that explains more than it doesn't," she replied grimly. "Though I believe gods would be kinder if things hurt them more."

Her father turned to look at her. "What makes you think our first duty is to be kind?" he wanted to know. "Too much tenderness is bad for mortals. They improve themselves only by struggling. Everyone knows that."

She blinked. He sounded like those humans who claimed that poverty made the poor into nobler souls. "Of course, Da. Whatever you say."

Sarra met them on the other side of the log bridge. She kissed her mate, then ordered, "Go skin and dress that hare, and not in the house." He left, and she looked at Daine. "You shouldn't wander off like that, sweet. You're not well yet—"

"Ma, if I'm well enough to climb that" — she pointed to the bluff that thrust out of the forest — "then I'm well enough to go home. Me 'n' Numair can't be lingering here."

Sarra blinked, her mouth trembling. "Are you so eager to get away from me? After not even a full day awake in my house?"

Daine's throat tightened. "I don't want to leave *you*. Don't think it!" She hugged her mother. "I missed you," she whispered. "Four years — I never stopped missing you."

Sarra's arms were tight around her. "I missed you too, sweetling."

Memory surged: The girl could almost smell burned wood, spilled blood, and the reek of death. The last time that she'd held her mother, Sarra had been stone cold, and Daine had been trying to yank out the arrows that had killed her. Tears rolled down her face.

Gentle hands stroked her hair and back. "There, there," Sarra whispered. "I am sorry. Never would I have left you willingly, not for *all* the gods in these realms." Softly she crooned until Daine's tears slowed, then stopped.

"Forgive me." The girl pulled away, wiping her eyes. "It was — remembering . . ."

"Me too." Sarra drew a handkerchief from a pocket. Tugging on it until two handkerchiefs appeared, she gave one to Daine, and used the other to dry her own eyes.

"Grandda?" asked the girl. She blew her nose.

"In the realms of the dead. He's happy there. Well, you know we never got on well. We like each other better now that I only visit and—" Sarra cocked her head, that odd, listening expression on her face. "Someone needs me?" she asked, her smile wry. "Two in one day—I must be getting popular." Her voice changed, as it had in the garden before. "Yes, Lori Hillwalker. The Green Lady hears you." Turning, she walked away, crossing the stream on the log bridge.

Daine wasn't sure if she ought to follow. Looking around, she saw Queenclaw trotting toward her.

"Don't just stand there," ordered the cat goddess, "pet me. Did she get another call?"

Daine knelt to obey. "I don't see why they *would* call on her. They liked her well enough when they needed a healer. The rest of the time, they thought she was silly, and odd . . . and shameful." Queenclaw looked up, and Daine answered the unspoken question. "Well, there was me, and no husband, and there was—*were* always men around Ma."

"Cats have more sense," Queenclaw said. "We don't

keep toms or kittens about any longer than we must. Mind, your people don't know it's her they pray to. They call on the Green Lady, who started to appear over the town well in Snowsdale. She told them to summon her for help in childbirth and sickness, or for matters of the heart."

"I'll be switched." Daine was impressed in spite of herself.

The cat's eyes followed something in the grass that only she could see. "You'd better go do something with the stew," she remarked, tail flicking as she crouched low to the ground. "It hasn't been stirred in a while." She pounced. A mouse squeaked and ran for its life, Queenclaw in hot pursuit.

Grinning, Daine went inside. The stew smelled wonderful. Stirring it, the girl realized that she was half listening for a courier to arrive, wanting her or her friends to arm themselves and come quickly. There were no horns calling for riders to mount and ride out. There was no thunder of message drums, pounding signals to those who had no mages to pass on the latest news. Her parents' house breathed rest and quiet.

I wish I could stay, she thought wistfully. I never realized how tired I've been, till now. And I can't stay—neither of us can.

3
DREAMS

As she moved the stew off the fire, she heard an assortment of sounds from one of the other rooms. She grinned: Numair had a habit of talking aloud as he fixed information of interest in his memory. Walking to an open door, she looked inside. Bent half double, the mage stood at the window as he tried to shave, using a mirror propped on the sill. That's the trouble with being so tall, she thought, not for the first time. The things most folk can make use of, like windowsills, are that much farther away from him.

When he took the razor from his skin, she asked, "Need help?"

His dark eyes lit in welcome. "It's good to see you on your feet."

"It's good to be on them." Getting the mirror, she held it for him. "Have you talked to Da or Ma about sending us home?"

He smiled crookedly, and wet his razor again. "Let us say rather that I have *attempted* to do so. They are amazingly elusive on the subject. The best I've gotten so far is that we may discuss it once you have recovered."

"I've recovered," she assured him. She knew that wasn't entirely true, but the images she had seen in the sunbird's display worried her.

"Daine," he said, then stopped. She waited. Something was troubling him; she could hear it in his voice. "Perhaps—perhaps you should stay here when I return. This is your home. You'd be safe here."

She put down the mirror, outraged. "How can you say that? *Tortall* is my home!"

"You'd be with Sarra—I know you've missed her. You'd get to know your father." He put the mirror back on the sill and scraped the remaining bristles from his chin. "Look at it from my perspective." He wouldn't meet her eyes, but his soft voice was pleading. "I was powerless against the Skinners. There are so many foes in this war, and too many are strange. I would like to know that *you*, at least, had a chance to survive."

"I'll make my own chances, if you please." Standing, she fought sudden dizziness. Carefully, she sat on the bed as Numair rinsed and dried his face.

"Will you at least consider it?" he asked, draping the towel over the window ledge.

"No."

"Daine . . ." Picking up the mirror, he examined his face. His dark brows twitched together; he shoved the mirror under her nose. "What do you see?"

Instead of her reflection, the glass showed battle. Sir Raoul of the King's Own, Buri of the Queen's Riders, and a mixed company of the Own and Riders fought in a temple square. Ranged against them were Carthaki warriors in crimson leather. Overhead, creatures swooped down to attack the Tortallans with long-handled axes. Daine gasped: These were some kind of bat-winged, flying apes, their long black fur streaked with gray.

The image vanished. Numair put the mirror down with fingers that shook. Quietly, the girl described what she had seen in the sunbirds' dazzling flight.

"In the Divine Realms, we observe mortal affairs,"

said Broad Foot, waddling into the room. "Liquid is the most reliable, but flame and mirrors work. Mortals who visit tell us that in their sleeping, just before they wake, they hear what is said as well."

"Is it possible to observe specific people and events?" inquired Numair.

"Yes," replied the duckmole. "It is how Sarra could observe you, Daine. With practice, you could master it in a week or so, and hear as well as see what goes on in the mortal realms."

Numair picked up the mirror and sat on the bed.

"We'll finish our chat *later,*" Daine told him, standing. "I'm not done with you!" He was not listening. With a sigh, she left him, trying not to use the furniture for support.

The animal god followed her into her room. "Are you well?"

"Just tired is all." Sitting on the bed, she rubbed her face. "Maybe climbing that bluff wasn't the cleverest thing to do my first day out of bed."

The duckmole vanished from the floor, reappearing beside her on the coverlet. Careful not to bump him, Daine lay back. "Of all times for him to go protective on me. Maybe he ate something that was bad for him." She closed her eyes.

"Maybe he loves you," Broad Foot said.

She didn't hear. She was already asleep.

In her dream, a pale wolf approached. Instead of the plumed tail that her kind bore proudly, the wolf's was thin and whiplike. "Rattail!" Daine ran to meet the chief female of the pack that helped to avenge Sarra's murder. It didn't seem to matter that Rattail was dead, or that a nasty female named Frostfur had taken her place in the pack.

When she was close, the wolf turned and trotted away.

"Wait!" Daine shouted, and followed.

Rattail led her down a long, dark hall, stopping at a closed door. When the girl caught up, the wolf held her paw to her muzzle, as if to say "Hush!" Daine knelt and pressed her ear to the door.

"Gainel, Uusoae's power worries you too much." While Daine had never heard that booming voice before, she knew that the speaker was Mithros the Sun Lord, chief of the gods. "We have always contained her. She has not the power to break through the barrier between her and us."

"If she's got no power, how is she holding her own against you for the first time in a thousand years?"

Daine stifled a gasp. That was Carthak's patron, the Graveyard Hag. "She's using tricks we've never seen before, and I don't like it. You're fighting her the way you always have. What if she's found a new way to overset us—a way that we've never encountered and don't know how to defeat?"

"She will not consume us," Mithros said flatly. "She cannot fight us all, and she has no allies in any realm but her own."

The dream faded as Daine opened her eyes. She was still tired; her legs and back felt limp. Her nose worked as well as ever, though. She breathed deeply, enjoying the flood of good smells in the air. One was stew, the other bread. She was *hungry*.

Her dress should have been wrinkled from her nap, but when she flapped her skirts, the creases vanished. Quickly she splashed water on her face and combed her hair, then went outside, hearing voices from the garden.

There was a bit of sunlight left, but globes of witch-fire hung over the table, growing brighter as night fell. Three men stood when she arrived. Sarra, Broad Foot, Queenclaw, and the badger nodded to her. Weiryn gestured to the new male. "Daughter, this is Gainel, Master of Dream, and one of the Great Gods. Gainel, my daughter, Veralidaine."

The girl looked up into a pale face framed by an unruly mane of dark hair. The eyes were shadowy pits that stretched into infinity. Staring into them, she thought that she saw the movement of stars in the distance—or was it Rattail? Cold hands took hers, jolting her back to the present. The god brushed Daine's fingers with a polite kiss.

"He says it is a pleasure to meet you," Weiryn told her. "You must excuse him—as the Dream King, he's only permitted to speak to mortals in dreams. We gods hear him"—Weiryn tapped his skull—"but you won't."

Daine curtsied to the god. "I'm honored, Your Majesty."

Gainel smiled, and took a seat at Sarra's right. Numair was at Weiryn's left; a place had been left for Daine between the mage and the duckmole. She stumbled trying to climb over the bench. Numair caught her and braced her arm until she was seated.

As utensils clattered and plates were handed around, there was no way to avoid noticing that the company included a duck-beaver creature, a man crowned with antlers, and a lanky, pallid man who seemed to fade into the growing shadows even while his face shone under witchlights. More than anything Daine had observed since she and Numair were yanked out of that orchard, that dinner table said that Sarra Beneksri was not the Ma she had lived with in Galla.

The animal gods, her parents, and Gainel spoke mind to mind—she could see it in the way they turned their heads, moved their hands, or leaned forward. Daine concentrated on her food. She was fascinated by the variety. She hadn't seen a cow, a wheat field, or a grape arbor, but there was wine, bread, and cheese as well as the hare. Even knowing that the hare god lived on in a fresh body, she couldn't bring herself to have its meat. When the wine pitcher came to her, she passed it to Numair without pouring any for herself. If the food and water of the Divine Realms made her senses reel, she didn't want to think what liquor might do.

Numair asked Weiryn a question, keeping his voice low.

"Petition the Great Gods, for all the good it will do." Weiryn's reply could be heard by all. "They are too busy fighting Uusoae to ferry mortals back home. They won't even reply to mind calls from us lesser gods."

Numair looked at Gainel. "Forgive me," he said, "but our friends are hard pressed. Might *you* send us home? You are one of the Great Gods, and you don't look as if you are locked in combat with the Queen of Chaos."

Gainel smiled, shadowed eyes flickering, and shook his head.

"He says you forget your myths," Sarra told them. "Of the Great Gods, the Dream King alone cannot enter the mortal realms. He can only send his creatures to do his work there."

"Forgive me," Numair said politely. "I *had* forgotten."

On Daine's foot, caught in a beam of light that fell between her and Numair, something moved. Reshaping her eyes to those of a cat, she looked harder. An inky shadow had thrown a tentacle over her bare foot. Was it the darking that Weiryn had shot?

"Pass the cheese?" asked Broad Foot, nudging her with his head. She obliged, forking slices onto his plate. As the duckmole happily mashed cheese in his bill, she glanced at her companions. Queenclaw mildly batted a piece of bread to and fro. Her mother seemed to be conversing with Gainel, while Numair tried to learn from Weiryn if a human mage might have better luck in approaching the rulers of the Divine Realms.

"I don't see why you fuss about it so," Weiryn

snapped. "Come the fall equinox, *you* at least will be dragged back to your wars, and I wish you joy of them!"

"They don't *give* me joy, and I didn't ask for them," Numair said, voice tight. "Would you prefer we let Ozorne and his allies roll over us?"

Daine palmed some cheese. Breaking off a piece, she let her hand drop to hang beside her leg, and offered the tidbit to the creature. Tentacles grabbed the cheese and pulled it into the shadow. Daine offered another morsel. The darking made that vanish, too.

"By the way," Sarra told Gainel, "I think one of your servants might have escaped somehow and wandered here. It called itself a darking."

Daine flinched. The shadow flinched, too, and slipped off her foot to hide in the darkness under the table.

The woman fumbled with her apron, then sighed, exasperated. "Look at this." She lifted her hand. Her fingers stuck out of the hole in the pocket. "It got away."

The pale god covered Sarra's pocket with one hand. White light shimmered, and an image of the darking appeared. Immediately the Dream King shook his head.

"He's never seen its like," Weiryn told the humans. Gainel's light faded; he withdrew his hand from Sarra's apron.

"I *told* them you are strict with your subjects," said Queenclaw, grooming her tail.

Rising to his feet, Gainel nodded to them all, and vanished.

"He's terrible at good-byes," remarked Broad Foot. "Worse than a cat that way."

"I prefer to think he's as good as a cat," retorted Queenclaw.

Sarra got to her feet. "Well, no amount of wondering and chatter will see that the dishes are done. Let's get started, Daine."

The girl looked up at her mother, surprised. It had been a long time since anyone had told her to assist with cleanup. She wanted to say that she was tired, but if she did, her mother would fuss, and no doubt feed her nasty-tasting potions. With a sigh, the girl rose. Accepting a stack of plates from Sarra, she bore them inside. A washtub sat on a table in the common room, steaming faintly.

Daine set her burden next to it and turned. Sarra blocked the garden door, a bottle in one hand, a cup in the other. The girl winced—so much for fooling her ma.

"You overdid today, and you know it." She poured dark liquid into the cup. "Drink this, and off to bed with you."

Daine took the cup, but didn't drink. "Ma, why am I so weak? Are you sure it's because I'm half mortal, or might it be something worse?"

Sarra shook her golden head. "You came here long before it was time," she said firmly. "The balance between your mortal and divine blood is delicate— a crossing like yours usually causes problems. They're only temporary, I promise you. Now, drink, miss."

It tasted as vile as she had feared. She kissed her mother's cheek, went into her room, and closed the door.

A dull hiss filled Daine's ears. Darkness covered her eyes.

Light dawned far ahead. It was impossible to tell if the scene that she now saw moved toward her, or if she flew to it. Within moments she was close enough to see two-leggers standing in a ring, arms overlapping, hands clasping their neighbors' shoulders. In the middle of their circle a lump of material shifted and pulsed in the same colors as the Chaos vent had done. Daine turned her face away.

"It's all right." Rattail appeared beside her. "You can look. You *must* look."

Daine obeyed.

At first the ring of men and women, and the thing at the hub, stood on black, empty space. One by one stars winked into being around them. With the added light, she could see the faces of those who formed the circle. Their names sprang into her mind as if she'd always known their true appearance: the Black God in his deep cowl and long robe, the Great Mother Goddess. Daine identified Kidunka, the world snake, lord of the Banjiku tribes, and even the K'miri gods of storms and fire. The large, powerful-looking black man in gold armor was Mithros himself. Looking from face to face, she saw that all of the Great Gods but one formed the ring.

The lump in their center began to rise, changing color swiftly. When it halted, a person stood there, bent nearly double. The hunched figure straightened. At first it was a gold-skinned woman with stormy gray hair and a simple gray dress. Within a breath, she changed. Her skin went yellow, her hair became twigs, her body sprouted a mass of tentacles. That, too, lasted briefly. She never kept one shape for long, but shifted constantly from patchwork to patchwork in combinations of things that lived and things that did not. Pincers grew on a cheetah's forequarters; a cow's head and a man's legs were attached. Just to look at the changing thing made Daine's stomach roll.

The creature lurched to the side, diving for the opening between the Wave Walker and the Black God; white fire appeared, to form a dome between gods and their captive. Half lion, half crone, she dropped and crawled for the gap between the Thief and the Smith, only to retreat howling after she touched the barrier.

"Why don't they kill her?" Daine asked. "They just wear themselves out holding her in their circle, and she doesn't seem to weaken at all."

"They are forbidden to, as she is forbidden to slay them," Rattail explained. "They can imprison and enslave each other, but Father Universe and Mother Flame, who made them all, will not let their children murder a sibling."

The scene rippled like pond water and dissolved before her. Daine was flying backward now, over a broad, perfectly flat plain. Looking around, wondering what had happened to the circle and the shifting monster, she discovered a long figure, Gainel. A gale whipped his shirt and breeches. He reached one hand out to her. A balance hung from his white fingers.

A crack opened under the Dream King's feet. His left foot rested on that flat and barren floor. His right was planted to the ankle in gray-green muck that boiled and twisted.

Gainel vanished when Daine opened her eyes.

"I have such peculiar dreams here," she complained to the ceiling. "Seemingly the Dream King wants me to know something, but why? Given my druthers, I'd druther have a good sleep." She sighed and rolled out of bed, to hit the floor with a bang. The floor was comfortingly solid.

Her old strength was returning faster than it had the day before. She tried to puzzle out the rest of her dream as she made her bed, cleaned her face and teeth, and brushed a multitude of tangles out of her hair. At least she felt like her old self for the first time in days, even if she couldn't decide what Gainel meant.

The items in her room had been added to during the night. She found boots and a belt. On a chair lay neat stacks of folded breeches, shirts, loincloths, stockings, and breast bands, all in her favorite colors. Unlike her dream, Daine could read Sarra's message easily. Her mother had provided as if Daine would spend the rest of her life here. She would not be happy when Daine insisted upon leaving.

Daine needed to clear her head to prepare a campaign against her parents. Putting on yesterday's dress, she gathered clean garments, towels, and brush, and went into the main room. Broad Foot was there, nibbling a bunch of grapes on the counter.

"Is there a place I can swim?" she asked. "My head feels like mush."

The duckmole's eyes lit. "There's the pond where I stay when I am here," he replied eagerly. "It's clean and quiet, and not too far. Come on."

Daine followed. After a few minutes' walk along a forest trail, they reached a very broad pond, almost a small lake, set just below a ridge crowned with brambles. Her guide plunged in as soon as they reached the water. Finding a cluster of broad, flat-topped rocks on the pond's rim, Daine put her things on them and began to strip off her clothes.

The duckmole surfaced, a frog sticking out of his bill, and swallowed his meal. "Hurry up," he urged. Daine wondered if the meal that he'd just eaten was a god, too. Would it be reborn, as her father claimed the hare had been?

As if to answer her, a small frog, identical to the one that Broad Foot had just eaten, rocketed out of the water to land on the duckmole's head. It gave a rasping trill, then leaped on the path and out of sight as Daine giggled and the duckmole glared.

"Some gods always have to comment when they're being eaten," he grumbled, and dove once more.

Wearing only a loincloth and breast band, Daine slipped into the water. It was *cold*, drawn from mountain streams. She yelped with the first shock, then took a deep breath and submerged. Long experience had taught her to keep moving until she warmed up.

Opening her eyes, she could see most of the area around her—the water was crystal clear. Broad Foot swam up and ran his bill over her face; his eyes were closed. Spinning, he sank to the bottom and glided snakelike over it, passing his bill over everything in his path. Soon he was gone from sight, questing for prey.

The gods of bass, minnows, sticklebacks, and brook trout fled Daine's approach, then returned in small groups to nose her. She squirmed—they tickled—and dropped to the bottom. There she sat, looking around as the fish continued to examine her. A snapping turtle, bigger than those she knew in the mortal realms, eased out of the mud and glided over. Daine watched him uncertainly, not liking the idea of those formidable jaws closing on any part of her. Instead the turtle circled her twice, inspecting, then swam away.

Thrusting herself to the surface, she filled her lungs with fresh air, then submerged again. A black, inky blob rose to meet her as she swam farther out. She stopped, treading water. Before her, the blot spread out until it was plate-sized. Gently she reached out and touched it. Was it a darking? She felt warmth and a slippery resistance.

Against the darking's blackness, a face she knew far too well appeared: Ozorne the Stormwing, once called the Emperor Mage. He was perched on a wooden fence above her, staring into the distance.

Suddenly he looked down; he seemed to be staring directly at her. His mouth stretched in a savage grin. Throwing his head back, he voiced a screeching call that she heard even underwater.

Gasping her shock, the girl choked as the pond filled her mouth and throat. With a kick, she drove herself to the surface, trying not to breathe more water before she got there. She broke into the air, liquid pouring from her nose and mouth.

Was that another darking, or the one from yesterday? she wondered, treading water and coughing. And how could a darking show her a vision of Ozorne? How—

A low, grating hum filled her magical hearing. It

was faint to begin with, but swiftly turned into a roar. Frantic, she looked around for the source. Only an immortal would affect her magic like this. The sound was new, which meant that she'd never met this kind of immortal. She hated that; she hated surprises in general.

Her things lay on rocks on the beach of an inlet that opened onto the rest of the pond. On the far side of the inlet, air bent and rippled. From its warping center came a reddish brown arm, with a black-nailed hand, and a powerful, shaggy leg tipped with a splayed hoof. Daine caught her breath as the owner of the arm and leg finished his crossing between the mortal and divine realms. It was a tauros.

Her skin crept. She had seen drawings and heard tales, but they had never frightened her as much as looking at one did now. The immortal was seven feet tall with short, strong horns. He had a bull's broad, powerful neck and slablike shoulders, but the large eyes pointed forward, like a predator's. His nose was almost human, but squared off and flat. The jaws were large, the teeth nearly too wide for them. Most of the remainder was human, though built on a large, powerful scale to support his massive head. Since he wore nothing like clothes, she could see that he was quite definitely a male. As he turned to one side, she glimpsed a bull's tail at the foot of his ridged spine.

She held very still, treading water lightly. The stories claimed their sight was poor. Smell was the thing to worry about with a tauros. Could it smell her?

The creature swayed, eyes shut, nose lifted. He snuffled wetly.

If he catches me, he'll rape me, she thought, scalp prickling. The stories were far too detailed about the fate of women who met these particular immortals. Quietly, without lifting her arms or feet from the water, she thrust herself to shore, mind fixed on her clothes. She always left her bow with them when she swam. Then she remembered, her strength evaporating. She had no weapon. Her bows were in the mortal realms.

She heard a bone-rattling bellow and looked back. The tauros had her scent; it was wading into the pond. The need for quiet was over. Making for the rocks, she swam in long, practiced strokes. She had a head start on the thing; she'd outrun it to her ma's.

Too busy watching the tauros to see where she was going, she plowed into the mud at the water's edge. Gasping, she lurched to her feet and ran the few steps to her clothes and towels, grabbing them. The immortal was a third of the way across the inlet. He was an ungainly swimmer, wallowing like a bull, but wise enough to use his arms to pull himself through the water.

She turned and ran three steps, then halted. If she escaped—

He would find her mother.

Nearly four years of protecting others from immortals fused with a lifetime of looking after Sarra. Weiryn was forgotten. Her frightened mind seized on one thing: If he didn't get her, the tauros would go after her ma.

The tauros bellowed. Daine spun. She had to do *something*—in a minute he would be on her. Hands shaking, she dropped what she held. If only she had a bow! Even the sling she'd used as a girl—

The towels lay across her fallen clothes in a pair of clean white stripes.

She grabbed both, slinging one over her shoulder, keeping the other in hand. The brambles grew to the pond's edge on her left. Even if she had seen ammunition there, it would be impossible to get. She'd have to go to her right, around the open edge of the water. Trotting around the cluster of rocks where she'd left her things, she scanned the ground. In a heap of stones and gravel, she saw five rocks the size of hen's eggs.

The tauros moaned, a sound that made her own throat go tight. He was two-thirds of the way across the neck of water between them.

Daine seized a rock. Fumbling slightly—it had been years since she'd used a sling—she folded the towel into a sling and placed the stone in the cradle. Cloth and rock felt awkward, even wrong, as she began to twirl her makeshift weapon. Her body protested the large, strong movements required for a sling.

When she felt the best moment, when the weight of the stone and the speed of her arm seemed right, she released one end of the sling. The rock shot past the immortal's head, skipped over the surface, then dropped from sight.

The tauros watched her missile sink. Horrified, Daine could see that he stood on the bottom. The water was up to his chest.

When I was little, I would've been *glad* to skip a rock four times! she thought, grabbing a new stone. She neatened the towel-sling, keeping an eye on the tauros. He decided that her first missile was not worth his interest. He plowed into the shallows, drooling as he stared at her.

"Goddess, help me," she whispered. Bringing the sling up higher, she twirled hard. The motion felt better. She let fly.

It struck the tauros on the shoulder, opening a large gash. He roared with pain and fury; silvery blood coursed over his chest. Frantically he scooped pond water to splash on the wound, flat nose running.

Daine seized two more stones—all she could hold—and backed up, putting the cluster of flat rocks between her and the immortal. It was hard to neaten the sling one-handed. Still retreating, she took the time to do it right; sloppy work now would kill her. When the tauros advanced, she loaded a rock and began to twirl. The circles of her wrist and elbow were broad now; her sense of when to release was exact. She let fly.

Her stone hit the tauros in the throat. His bellow was a strangled croak; he dropped to his knees with a splash, scrabbling at his neck. Dripping sweat, the girl flipped her sling into place and loaded her final rock.

The tauros lurched to his feet, wheezing. He stumbled forward, flat teeth bared.

"Don't," she called, lips quivering. She didn't want to kill a beast who could no more help his nature than she could. "Give up, please!"

He roared and came on, the ground quivering

under his weight. When he was six yards from her, she loosed her final shot with all her strength. It slammed between his eyes and stayed, embedded in his skull. The tauros gasped, flailed blindly, and toppled into the mud. There he thrashed, and choked, and died.

"I'm sorry," she cried, eyes overflowing. "I'm sorry, I'm sorry. . . ."

Broad Foot surfaced nearby, plainly upset. "What happened? If I'd known that a tauros was about, I wouldn't have brought you here! Where did it come from?"

"It crossed between realms," she replied, still trembling. "I think it may've been sent. I had a vision of Ozorne, anyway, right before it came."

"But how did he know where you are?"

"I've no idea."

"And why do you weep? You've killed before."

"And I hate it!" she cried. "Especially when this poor, idiot thing couldn't do no different!" She tried to gather her things, and dumped them into the mud. "Look at him—what else is he made for but to prey on females? *Are* there any lady tauroses?"

"No. No, there aren't."

"Wonderful! No one cared enough to give them mates of their own kind. All they know to do is grab two-legger females. They either kill them or get killed themselves. It's wrong!" Pulling her belongings from the mud, she ran to her parents' house.

Broad Foot eyed the dead tauros. "She has a point," he told it. "Someone ought to bring the matter to the Great Gods' attention—once things quiet down a bit."

Halfway to her parents' home, the girl paused: A Stormwing awaited her there. She hesitated only for a moment, then re-formed her towel-sling and grabbed stones for ammunition. If that Stormwing was an enemy, he or she had a surprise coming!

Emerging from the cover of the trees, she saw that her father and Numair were seated on the slab of rock that served the cottage as a doorstep. The immortal she had detected stood on the ground before them. He turned as she approached, his movement setting the bones that were braided into his long blond hair to clicking.

Daine relaxed and tossed her rocks aside. She wouldn't need them for Rikash Moonsword.

"What happened to *you*?" asked the green-eyed Stormwing as Broad Foot appeared on the path between him and the men. Numair got to his feet, frowning.

"Broad Foot will explain," Daine said, weaving between the mage and her father. "I need to clean up."

She scrubbed, then pulled on clean garments with hands that still trembled. As she was combing out her hair, Sarra knocked on the door. "We're having lunch in the garden," she called. "If you're decent, come take a perch out for your Stormwing friend to sit on."

Quickly the girl finished. Feeling calmer now, she did as she was told. Once she'd set up the perch by the outdoor table, Rikash glided down from the rooftop and took his place. For the moment they were alone. Numair and Weiryn were nowhere in sight.

"You let me down," the girl told the Stormwing. "We thought your Queen Barzha would finish Ozorne once he was a Stormwing. Instead, he shows up in the spring with our enemies, and hundreds of Stormwings at his back."

"Two hundred and forty-eight Stormwings to be exact," Rikash said bitterly. "Those who did not care that he held a queen and her mate captive. Those who ignore the fact that he took his Stormwing crown by killing Jokhun from behind. Those without regard for Stormwing law. *They* are the army that followed him to the mortal realms." He laughed. "Queen Barzha and her followers are fugitives, Daine. We stayed in the Divine Realms when the barriers fell. Here, at least, we are partly safe from Ozorne and his flock."

Ignoring his pronounced odor, Daine put a comforting hand on the Stormwing's shoulder. "I'm sorry to hear it. How *are* Queen Barzha and Lord Hebakh?"

"Tired," replied the immortal. "As am I. Ozorne sends groups back to harry us. It is not enough to have most of us as followers—those who will not follow, he wants dead."

"How many are on your side of it?"

Rikash shook his head, making the bones in his hair clatter. "Sixty-three, in all." He tried a smile; it was half bitter. "Don't take us to task for not killing him. We've tried our best."

Daine sighed. "We humans haven't done so well at it, ourselves."

Sarra, Weiryn, and Numair came out, carrying their lunch, as the three animal gods materialized at their places by the table. With Rikash positioned downwind so that his odor wouldn't spoil their meal, the plates and bowls were passed.

"Has anyone thought of a way that we can go home?" asked Numair.

"There is none," growled Weiryn. "The Great Gods are speaking to no one as long as Uusoae fights them."

Daine moved the food on her plate. "What about the animal gods? I came here last fall, while I was in Carthak. *You* took me back to the mortal realms then, Badger."

"Not possible," replied the great animal. "You were dead then. All I had to do was put you back into your mortal body. With both of you still alive, not all of the animal gods together could move you between the realms."

"You are far better off here with your mother," said Weiryn. "If you insist on leaving, then wait until the fall equinox, when the gates open for the likes of us and you. And there's one of those *things* again!" he cried as the darking oozed onto the table, having climbed up Daine's leg.

"Leave it be, Da," she told him. "It's not hurting anyone."

Stretching to make itself taller, the darking changed. Up came a serpentlike neck, supporting a wedge-shaped head. The body the darking made was long and slender, with powerful hindquarters and long fore-paws that were as nimble as hands. Two great wings unfurled out of the blot's shoulders.

"Dragons," Rikash said. "This creature is right, whatever it is. They might very well take you back. You *have* been looking after their young one."

87

"You mean for my daughter to journey to the Dragonlands? Absolutely not," Weiryn snapped. "It's too risky."

"They might refuse to help," Queenclaw pointed out. "I never met a dragon that wasn't perverse—they're worse than we cats. Even the Great Gods can't force a dragon to do *anything* it doesn't wish to."

"I'm almost positive they will do it," said Rikash, baiting. "Don't forget, we Stormwings know them best—our eyries border on the Dragonlands. They are proud. One or two of Skysong's kin will feel they *must* repay you for what you've done, and one is all you need to go home." He looked at Numair and grinned. "Well, it may take two. There's so much extra of one of you."

The girl smiled, then asked, "How do we find them?"

The Stormwing looked at Weiryn. "I'm sure a map can be drawn—unless you plan to cage them?"

"Da, Ma, please listen," pleaded Daine. "Humans and People *need* us. I've friends that would risk their lives for me and Numair. If you won't help us, then we'll muddle along on our own—but we can't just sit here, seeing them in visions, and laze about."

The god sighed and rubbed his antlers. "No—no, I won't cage them."

Sarra wiped her eyes. "Not even a day I've had to talk to you. But I know you can't sit idly by when them you care for are in trouble."

"Lord Rikash," the house cat said, "they will need help to cross the Sea of Sand."

The immortal sidled, digging into his perch with steel claws. "I will see what can be done. It will take persuasion." He looked from Daine to Numair, frowning. *"Be careful,"* he told them. "The Divine Realms are perilous. Maybe Queen Barzha is right, and I am getting sentimental, but I would hate to see anything happen to either of you." Jumping into the air, he took flight, blowing waves of stench over the table.

4

TRAVELERS

"Forget sentimentality," the badger grumbled. "*I'd* like to see him lose that *smell.*"

"And from a badger, that's saying a great deal," quipped Queenclaw.

"I will go with them," said Broad Foot. Everyone stared at him. "I can't transport them, but I can act as guide and protector. The three of us should manage."

"The *four* of us," the badger told him. "I will come as well. I haven't put so much time into looking after this young one to stop now."

"Lord Weiryn, will you and Sarra come with us?" Numair asked.

Daine's mother smiled wistfully. "As a new goddess, I'm bound to Weiryn's lands for a century."

"As am I, for requesting her admittance here," added Weiryn. "You will do well with the badger and Broad Foot."

"If we're to leave today, I'd best get a little extra hunting done," commented the duckmole, and vanished.

"I will join you tomorrow morning," the badger said. "There are a few things to deal with at my sett before I go." He, too, vanished.

"Ma, Da," the girl said thoughtfully, "are there horses we might trade for, or buy? We'd go faster than afoot."

"No, dear one," Sarra replied. "Every horse in the Divine Realms belongs to itself, or its herd. They do not serve anyone." She rose. "I'd best pack your things—No, Daine, I don't need help. You'd only be in my way."

"Besides," added Weiryn, also getting to his feet, "I need you both to come with me." He led Daine and Numair inside.

"What about making horses?" Numair asked. "Could you—"

"No," Weiryn said flatly. "Any being created in the Divine Realms belongs to itself and serves no one else. You would be lucky if such a horse only dumped you in the dirt. It *might* take you for a ride that would last a century of mortal time."

In the main room, he opened a door that the girl was positive hadn't been there the day before. It gave onto a small, dark chamber that was more like a shed than a room. Here, to her surprise and delight, she saw a woodcarver's tools, staffs, boxes of feathers, boxes of arrowheads, coiled strings, and completed bows.

Weiryn ran long brown fingers over the finished weapons, checking the feel, rejecting this one and that. "These are my gifts to those I favor." He selected an ebony-colored bow with startlingly pale horn nocks over both tips. "And if my own daughter isn't one I favor, who is?" He laid the stave across his palms, and offered it to Daine.

It was air-light in her grip at first, but it got heavier, until it reached the exact weight she looked for in a bow. Weiryn offered a string. Fitting the loop over the lower nock, she braced that end against her instep. She drew the upper nock down and slipped the other loop over it in a flash. "She's sweet, Da," she told him, smiling.

The god offered her a quiver full of arrows. "I should have given you a proper bow long before this," he told her, wrapping extra strings in a square of oiled cloth.

Handing that to Daine, he went to the staffs in the corner. "Here, mage." Weiryn selected one that was six feet of thick, knotted wood. About to hand it over, he frowned. "A moment." He looked at Numair, then cupped the top of the staff in one hand. White fire shone from his palm; when he drew it away, a fist-sized crystal knob sat on top of the staff, embedded in the wood. He gave the staff to Numair.

The mage took it and stood for a moment, one hand wrapped around the wood, the other around the crystal. Daine saw no magical fire but knew he examined the staff with his Gift, looking for its secrets. When he looked up again, his eyes were filled with respect. "Thank you. I've never had something that was so—attuned—to me."

Weiryn scowled and went to a wooden counter along one wall. "Come here, both of you." An ink pot and brush appeared on the surface next to him. The god wet the brush, and began to paint symbols directly onto the wood. "Here we are," he said, tapping the brush against a painted square. "Here's the stream, and the pond where Broad Foot stays. And this is the path you must follow."

Daine, following the brush, thought for a moment she saw trees and streams along the dotted line of ink. When she blinked, she saw only glossy black dots sinking into the stained wood.

"If you walk steadily, you will spend the night beside Temptation Lake," Weiryn informed them, drawing that body of water close to the trail. "Do *not* drink from it—unless you desire to be tempted, of course."

A vision of Numair reclining among three naked, lovely women who fed him grapes, or rubbed his feet, or finger-combed his hair, filled the air over the counter. From Numair's deep blush, Daine could tell that he saw it, too.

"Not funny, Da," she told her father, her voice very dry.

"Neither of us is in the mood for temptation, Lord Weiryn," the mage added quietly.

"Hmpf," snorted the god. "Well, just don't drink the water there. It's a good place to stop—no dweller of the Divine Realms may harm another within a league of Temptation Lake." He rewet his brush and continued to draw. "The trail will carry you to Long Drop

Gorge, which you will cross on the First Bridge."
Briefly Daine glimpsed a wood-and-rope bridge in
the air over the counter, like the bridges that filled the
mountains of Tortall and Galla.

Weiryn continued the line of the path for an inch
or two, then stopped to create a blurred area around
it. "This is Mauler's Swamp." The vision in the air over
the map showed a pair of yellow, slit-pupiled eyes
sticking out of murky water. They moved. A ripple of
passing square ridges like those on a crocodile's back
cut through the image of water, followed by the snakelike curving of a long tail. "Give no offense to Mauler,
if you can avoid it.

"Here is the Stonemaze." The vision was one of
rocky canyons and a distant, small river, as seen from
high overhead. "Watch your footing, never leave the
path in the maze, and harm no stones."

"Lord Weiryn," said Numair, "it would help if you
were to explain what will happen if we make a mistake
in these places."

Weiryn looked at him, leaf-colored eyes glinting.
"Who can tell?" he asked. "The gods in most places
never punish a trespass in the same manner twice.
Mauler once ate the mortals who disturbed his afternoon nap, but that was a while ago. He may not choose

to eat the next intruder. Of course, he may have young to share his swamp, and they always need a meal. Just use caution. Cut no green wood. Take no fruits without asking the bush or tree. If you don't, you might spend a century with wild pigs trying to dig you up by the roots. Blackberries in particular have a very nasty streak."

"Wonderful," Daine whispered.

"Where was I?" asked her father. He rewet his brush, and sketched another blurred area on the wood. "Oh, yes. At last you will come to the Sea of Sand." The vision revealed dunes; for a moment Daine's face was hot and painfully dry. "If the Stormwing can't find help, the winds will strip your body of moisture in the time it takes your mother's pan bread to bake. Don't you see what folly this is?" he demanded, eyes on Daine. "The Divine Realms are too dangerous for a pair of mortals!"

"We will have Broad Foot, and the badger," Numair said. "And we have protected ourselves, from time to time. Mortals have survived in the Divine Realms before."

Weiryn sighed. "That's what I thought you would say." His brush and ink pot disappeared. Palms down, he tapped the inked surface of the wood. "At least I can tell Sarra that I tried." Like bark that was barely attached to its parent tree, the surface with the map cracked away from the wood, thinned until it could have been heavy parchment, and rolled itself up. Weiryn gave it to Numair. "You need not fear that it will go to pieces, or that water will smear the marks," he said grumpily.

Daine leaned over and kissed the god's forehead. "Thanks, Da."

When the three returned to the main room of the cabin, Broad Foot, dripping, was on the table. "Are we ready?"

Sarra offered them cloaks—a blue one for Daine, a black one for Numair. Once the two mortals had donned them, she handed over their packs.

"How do you want to do this?" Numair asked Broad Foot. "You can't use your power to move us, and—forgive me, but—I doubt that you can walk at our pace."

Broad Foot looked at the mage; Numair jumped. Visible through the opening of his cloak, his cream-colored shirt twisted. When it stilled, a deep pouch had formed in the cloth over Numair's belly. The duckmole vanished, than reappeared in shimmering fire, tucked into the pouch. He looked back and up at

Numair. "The view from here should be very nice," he said as Daine and her mother giggled. "Mind you don't bump me."

Sarra hugged Daine. "You'll come and stay a bit when your war is settled?" she asked. "Please?"

"I will, Ma—I just don't know when that will be."

"We'll know. We'll come for you on the holiday that's closest." The woman scanned her face intently. "You'll visit for a season, or two?"

"I'll come, Ma."

"Promise?"

Daine hugged her mother hard, tears in her eyes. "I promise. We—we'll catch up on the time them bandits took from us."

Sarra gave her a last squeeze, then turned to Numair. Daine slung her pack and quiver over her shoulders, then looked at her father.

Weiryn leaned down and kissed her gravely, first on one cheek, then the other. "We shall see you again, so what's the point of goodbyes?"

"None at all," she said, and brushed a hand along his horned crown.

Weiryn opened the door; they filed outside. "Straight down the path," instructed Broad Foot. "We've a couple of hours of light still."

Daine let Numair take the lead. She glanced back only once, to see her mother crying in the circle of Weiryn's arm. They both waved. She waved, too, and didn't look again as the path led her into the woods and out of sight.

They walked quietly, descending into a mountain forest on a much-used track. Listening for the voices of the People, as she did in walks at home, Daine once more had that odd sense of being deaf. Her physical ears picked up the rustle of small creatures moving on the forest floor and the many calls of local birds. Magically she heard nothing. She had no way to know what was said in conversation between a squirrel and a jay—though she could guess from the rage in the squirrel's voice and the mockery in the bird's. Far in the distance, her sense for immortals registered a small herd of killer centaurs on the move. About to warn her companions, she realized that the centaurs were traveling in the opposite direction. Soon afterward, they faded from her awareness.

"Goddess bless," Numair said, coming to a halt. They were in a dark hollow where only slivers of light touched the ground. The cause of the early twilight grew beside the path: a white oak tree, or what Daine thought *might* be an oak, except that it was the largest that she had ever seen. If she and Numair stretched out their arms, together they still could not reach all the way around the bole.

"She is the First Tree," Broad Foot explained. "From her acorns, the first mortal white oaks were born."

"*Her?*" asked Numair, looking down at his passenger.

"She is a god," the duckmole said. "She is aware. All of the First Trees are."

Daine snatched her hand from the bark.

Stepping back, with Broad Foot held away from him, Numair bowed deeply, sweeping an arm before him as if the tree were a queen. Straightening, he frowned. "What's that noise?"

"What noise?" chorused Daine and Broad Foot.

Numair approached the girl, hand cupped around one ear, and bent. "Easy, there," the animal god cautioned. Giving Daine a half turn, Numair put his ear close to her pack. Now Daine heard a thin, high shrilling.

Numair opened one of the pack's side pockets and reached inside. When he drew it out again, he brought a small clay pot with a wax seal, and a darking.

"Now where did *you* come from?" he asked, holding the blot up to eye level.

"Is it the one that's been following me about Da's?" inquired Daine.

Shaping a head for itself, the darking nodded.

"Were you in my pack by accident?"

The inky creature shook its head.

"You *wanted* to come?"

The darking nodded.

Daine shrugged and held open the breast pocket of her shirt. "Pop it in here, then." Numair hesitated, then dropped the creature into its new residence. "Now we've each got a passenger." She smiled into his face, so close to her own just then. Briefly, his eyes changed; a strange, burning excitement filled them, and made her catch her breath.

He straightened abruptly. "We shouldn't dawdle," he said, striding off down the path. "We've a lot of ground to cover."

Puzzled, confused—feeling as if she'd glimpsed something important, only to have it vanish—Daine trotted to catch up.

They walked long after dark, stopping only to eat a brief supper. As night drew down, Numair called light from the crystal on his staff to illumine the way. At last the path emerged from under the trees. They had come to the rim of a stretch of water—a large pond, or a lake.

"Temptation Lake?" asked Numair, looking out over the water.

"Yes, indeed," Broad Foot said. "And I could do with a swim."

Daine sighed her relief and let her bow, quiver, and pack slide to the ground. The thick, lush grass that grew almost to the water's edge looked better than the softest feather bed at that point.

Numair first lifted the duckmole from the pocket in his shirt, putting him on the ground, then removed his own pack. "Broad Foot, if I bespell our camp for protection, will it inconvenience you?"

Broad Foot clapped his bill in a laugh. "No, not in the least. Though you don't *need* to spell it— Temptation Lake is sacred. No one of the Divine Realms would harm anyone here. If anything *does* happen, mind," he added, looking at them soberly, "just call or think my name, and I'll come. And remember—don't drink the water!" He vanished in a cloud of silver light.

Numair gave his pack to Daine. She pulled out folded squares of cloth and spread them. There was more cloth in the folds than she had expected. Laid flat on the ground, they were big enough to wrap each of them completely.

Exhausted, Daine stripped off her boots, dagger, and belt, and freed the darking, who vanished into the shadows. "Don't let me step on you," she warned, and heard a squeak in reply. "I hope that means 'yes,'" she muttered. Rolling herself in her blanket, Daine watched as Numair gathered rocks, placing them in a circle around their things.

Once the stones were placed, he walked counter-clockwise around the rim of his circle. She couldn't hear what he said, but when he finished the first circuit, all noise from outside the barrier stopped. He walked the circle again; this time, when he was done, the rocks began to glow faintly. To Daine's surprise, they warmed, throwing off a mild heat without scorching the grass. The third time that he walked his route, black fire glittering with white sparks flowed behind him. When he completed this circle, the magic blazed, then vanished. The only sign that he had done anything was the glow and warmth that came off the stones.

"We're shielded from sight and sound." He tugged off his boots.

"And the rocks?" she asked.

He smiled tiredly. "We only have one blanket and a cloak each. You know I don't like to get cold." Using his cloak as a pillow, he rolled himself into his blanket and turned on his side, his back toward her. "Good night, magelet."

Dreams brought Daine once more to that vast, empty space. There were the Great Gods, standing in a wheel of linked arms. Their focus was the changing thing that wore the colors of the Chaos vent. Daine got queasy as she watched its constant shifts—did others feel ill when *she* shape-changed?—but this time she kept her eyes on circle and captive. The creature leaped for a gap between Kidunka and the Thief, and was blocked by the white barrier that made a dome between gods and it. The creature shrank into the center of the ring and fell in upon itself until it was a heaving mass.

Lightning fast, that mass split into a star, shooting its many arms toward all of the openings between its captors. Each arm of the changing thing sprouted a wide mouth with outsized, jagged teeth. The Great Gods shifted, and the fiery barrier shone more brightly than ever. The mouths shrieked and retreated into the central mass, smoking where they had made contact with the white fire. In the meantime, unseen by the ring of Great Gods, small puddles of multi-colored liquid appeared behind them. The puddles grew, spreading to the left and right, until they formed a ring at the backs of the Great Gods.

The scene dissolved. Daine was back on the plain, seeing the Master of Dream as he stood poised, one foot on each side of a great chasm. He still held a scale in one hand. The foot that rested on the flat side of the crack skidded. He fought to regain his balance on that polished surface without taking his other foot out of the wriggling muck. At last he was steady again. A bubble grew in the strange liquid. When it burst, thousands of exotically colored butterflies swirled around Gainel in a spiral dance.

Daine thought that she'd opened her eyes, but although she could see clouds drifting over a pink-and-gray sky, it felt as if her dreaming was not over. The sound of oddly muffled voices, coming from somewhere close by, met her ears. In case the voices weren't part of a dream, she wrapped her fingers around her dagger and grew bat ears to hear every word.

"—you ordered what is left of the Razor Scream nation to attack those mortals in the harbor. Eleven Stormwings were killed out there—*eleven*!"

"That is the cost of battle, Qirev. Everyone takes casualties."

Daine stiffened. It had been six months since their last meeting, but there was no mistaking that cold, distant voice. It was Ozorne's.

"The cost of *mortal* battle! When the kings chose to ally themselves with you, it was your promise that while we might *harry* two-leggers, we would kill *only* to sow fear!"

"I lied." There was bleak disinterest in the former Emperor Mage's tone.

"We are no army for mustering. We *feed* on armies," said a cracked and aged voice. "You promised feasting to glut us—not to throw our kindred against archers and mages. Mortal wars are not Stormwing wars."

"Jachull?" inquired Ozorne. "Do *you* feel Stormwings have no part in mortal wars?"

A third, female voice replied, "What does it matter if we kill a few or many to sow the fear we dine on? Whether they shoot us for eating the dead, or for attacking the living, what difference does it make?"

"There, sires. Jachull of the Mortal Fear nation does not disagree," announced Ozorne, and *her* subjects number more than your—sadly reduced—nations combined."

"Humans attack on the north road!" someone cried. "Warriors come!"

"Fellow Stormwings, I would love to chat all day, but as you can hear, business intrudes." Ozorne sounded friendly and false. "If you don't mind?" He paused briefly. Then in a cold, direct voice, he continued, "Number fourteen, report your position. Where are you? I can see nothing!"

Daine's bat ears filled with a voice both closer and louder than her enemy's. It sang a bizarre tune that sounded like nothing on earth. She sat up.

Numair's things were packed. The rock circle around their camp had grown cold; two stones had been moved to open the last of the protective spells on the camp. There was no sign of Broad Foot, either. The sun was clear on the horizon, but not by much. It was time to get moving. If she could just find Numair . . .

She spotted him nearly a hundred yards away. He was striding into the lake, without even bothering to roll up the legs of his breeches.

"Numair!" she called. He gave no sign that he'd heard. *"Numair!"*

He never even looked her way. The water reached his belly; still he walked on.

Bespelled! she thought. Jumping up, she raced

across the grass and waded in after him. Closing the distance fast, she lunged and grabbed air. He'd gone under.

She dove. He was speeding away. Worse, she could see he was not swimming: His arms were flat against his sides; his legs fluttered. Something was towing him.

Daine surfaced and gasped, filling her lungs with air as she filled her mind with sea lions. Her body shifted. She dove and arrowed after her friend. She was gaining on him when she realized that she was now a saltwater animal in a freshwater lake.

Too late to fret, she told herself. I just won't eat or drink here.

The thing that towed Numair picked up speed. Daine poured her strength into her rush through the water and drew even with the man. Now she saw his captor. A naked blue female with hair like silver tentacles, she dragged her prize on a gold rope as she sang the weird tune that had captivated Numair.

The song pressed on Daine's ears; she flattened them and did her best to ignore it. Lunging, she clamped a sea lion's sharp teeth on the gold rope. Acid pain seared her mouth, making her cry out. The leash dropped from her jaws.

Muddled and dizzy, she almost slammed into

Broad Foot, missing the duckmole by inches. She's got Numair! Daine cried, speaking mind to mind.

The duckmole took up the chase, easily keeping pace with her. —*That's no she.*—

Of course it's a she, the scheming wench! A—a river god, or lake god!

Broad Foot fell back slightly, letting her slide by. Rising above Daine, he swept his bill over her eyes.

The thing that had stolen Numair bore right in a broad arc, trying to get by its pursuers. It clearly *was* a thing now, a blobby mass of burned orange and pale lilac that towed the mage not with a gold leash, but with a tentacle of its own flesh.

Daine shot across the arc, slamming into Numair. She knocked him aside, but not free—the tentacle was wrapped around his throat.

—*Again,*— urged Broad Foot.

Speeding at her friend, Daine prayed she wouldn't break his ribs, and crashed into him. Broad Foot opened his bill and shouted in a voice that filled each drop of water around them. The blob shrieked and dissolved. The peculiar song was cut off.

Numair came out of his trance, to find himself in deep water. He tried to yell, and inhaled liquid. Daine shook her head to clear it of Broad Foot's cry and dove under the man, pushing him to open air. Taking on her own form, she looped an arm around the choking mage and struck out for the shore. As soon as the water was shallow enough that he could manage, she left him. Racing onto dry land and into a clump of tall reeds, she threw up, rejecting every trace of whatever she had bitten.

Wiping her face in wet grass, she saw Broad Foot go by, sweeping his bill over the ground as if he looked for breakfast. Nearby, she could hear Numair doing what she had just done, and decided to give him privacy. Hardly aware that she wore not a stitch, except for the badger's claw on its chain around her neck, she caught up with the duckmole. "Where are you going?"

"I want to look at something." Now that they were on land, he spoke as the other animal gods did. "Why didn't you call me?"

She stopped, horrified. Why *hadn't* she summoned him? Red-faced, she said, "I forgot. I'm used to it being just him and me, and I had to move so fast . . . I'm sorry!"

The tall reeds opened onto a broad, flat stretch of clay. In it, spilling into the lake, was a pool of shifting tan, pale gray, and blood-red light. Nothing stayed the same for more than a breath; she thought that she saw images, but they changed the moment she focused on them. She leaned closer, drawn by the play of colors.

"Wake up!" cried Broad Foot.

The girl straightened. She'd come to within a few steps of the pool—and pieces of it had risen in the air to meet her. When she moved back, the raised goo collapsed with plopping sounds, like boiling mud. Weakly she asked, "Is—is that a Chaos vent?"

"It is, and an active one, too. Activity I don't mind. That's Chaos for you. But this . . ." He waddled to the water's edge, where the fluid ran to mingle with the lake. "*This* worries me. It means the whole lake is tainted—and Chaos bile is dangerous to us."

"Numair's been poisoned?" she gasped, suddenly dizzy with panic.

"No, no. It affects only immortals and gods," said Broad Foot. "Mortals are half Chaos naturally. He is completely safe, and it sounds like you rid yourself of it before any entered your blood. But . . ."

He paused so long that Daine thought he might have forgotten her. "Broad Foot?"

"It doesn't poison gods or immortals as *you* would think of poisoning. It brings them closer to Uusoae. They go from enemies to—to potential allies. I wish we knew all those who've drunk here. This lake is very popular."

Even though he'd said Numair would take no harm from the water he'd inhaled, she wanted to check on him and make sure. Leaving the duckmole beside the Chaos vent, she picked her way through the reeds and returned to their camp.

There she found the mage, looking the worse for his experience. He sat with his back to her, talking to the badger, who must have arrived while she was off with the duckmole. "I think I hear—" Turning, he blushed scarlet and looked away.

She had forgotten she wore only the claw necklace that stayed with her each time she shape-changed. "Oh, for—!" she cried. Getting her pack, she went behind a tree. Fumbling with her garments, the girl shouted the details of her talk with Broad Foot.

When she emerged, stockings in hand, Numair was close by, ready with her boots.

"Are you *sure* you didn't drink from the lake?" she asked quietly, fixing him with a stern eye. "That creature looked to me like a blue, naked female with a big chest, until Broad Foot changed my vision. She looked like *just* the kind of female you might want to be tempted by, Master Salmalin."

He blushed. "I give you my solemn word that I did not drink the lake water and request temptation," he said, combing his wet mane back with his fingers. "I tested it with my Gift, and sensed there was something very wrong with it. You know, magelet, the gods may be losing ground against Chaos."

Broad Foot had arrived and was talking softly to the badger. Hearing the mage, they broke off their conference and came over. "What makes you think so?" asked the badger, dark eyes sharp.

"I know my legends and myths," explained the man. "The creators of the universe ordained that the gods, who stand for order, and Chaos, who stands for—"

"Chaos," Daine interrupted with a smile.

Numair tweaked her nose. "They must stay in balance. The only problem is that it's the nature of each to fight the other. It's written that a day will come when the Queen of Chaos will break free of the prison made for her by her siblings, the Great Gods."

"When that day comes, the mortal and divine realms will melt into Chaos. The gods—all gods—will perish, as will mortal life." Broad Foot's voice was grim.

"You know your legends well, human," remarked the badger.

"I have to report this," the duckmole told them.

"It's more than just the lake being poisoned. The creature that had you captive was no part of this place. It was a Chaos-dweller, masked as a lake being. How one of *them* managed to escape into the Divine Realms . . . You start without me—I'll catch up." Without another word, he vanished.

Packing, Daine filled Numair in on what he'd missed while bespelled, as the badger went to examine the vent. Once she was ready, the girl realized that she hadn't seen the darking.

"We have to go," warned Numair. "We can't spend the day searching for it."

"I know," replied Daine, scanning the grass around them. "I think it does, too. I just hope it didn't fall into the lake."

When the badger rejoined them, the humans shouldered their packs and returned to the path. There, stark against sandy dirt, was an inky pool. "Is that you?" she asked it. "Did you come back?"

The ink split. Half flowed over to her and reached up with a pair of armlike tentacles. The other half thrust up a part of itself shaped as a head, cocking it to one side.

Daine stooped and picked up the one that clearly wanted her to do so. Cupped in her hand, the darking was light, but still had weight and a presence against her skin—like a bubble filled with water, she thought. "You brought a friend?" The darking on her palm grew its own head and nodded.

"More of those?" grumbled the badger. "Don't they have anything else to do?"

Both darkings shook their heads.

Daine smiled. Giving her bow to Numair to hold, she lifted the newcomer in her free hand. "I don't know where you two will sit, though."

The first darking trickled up her arm and curled around her neck, a bit of coolness on her skin. The other flowed over her wrist until it could drip into her belt pouch.

"I guess we're set," she told her companions. Numair returned her bow. They set off briskly, mage and badger in the lead, Daine bringing up the rear. It was something she and Numair did automatically: She could trust him to pay attention to what was ahead; he knew that she would guard their backs.

The duckmole rejoined them as they stopped for their noon meal. "Not good, not good," he said, pacing the clearing where they sat. "They have placed a ban on the lake, but they won't be looking into the matter of those who have been tainted. I think—" He came to a halt and sighed. "I think it is all they can do to hold the barriers against her."

"Then if we can do nothing here, let's be on our way," suggested Numair. "Daine and I would like to go home, where we *can* do something."

5

THE BRIDGE

THEY MADE GOOD TIME THAT AFTERNOON. BLACK mountain pines gave way to maples, chestnuts, and paper birches, and larger clearings. Flashes of bright color darted through the tree canopy as the sunbirds began their afternoon's homage to the sun.

Suddenly the travelers emerged onto a long, wide grass shelf. Ahead the land fell into a vast gorge. Approaching the edge, Daine looked down and whistled. Far, far below lay a thin silver curl: a river.

"Long Drop Gorge," the badger told them. Nodding at two splintery logs planted upright in the ground at the cliff's edge, he added, "And there's the First Bridge."

Daine gulped. What had looked like a sturdy enough wood-and-rope construction in the vision over Weiryn's map was in reality fraying, twisted hemp and ancient slats. Twin ropes, as old and unreliable-looking as the rope of the floor, were strung as rails at waist height and attached to the logs. The whole structure didn't look as if it would support even one of them, let alone their whole group.

"The first rope-and-*wood* bridge," corrected the duckmole. "The first rope bridge is farther up. We didn't think you'd like that."

"First Bridge or First Wood-and-Rope Bridge, it won't break," snapped the badger. "It was set here after the first humans were done with it, and it's been here ever since. No force in the Divine Realms may break it, until the realms themselves are broken."

"Is there an easier way to cross?" Numair asked. "Anywhere?"

Both gods shook their heads. "Long Drop Gorge extends several days' march in both directions," explained Broad Foot. "You *did* say you are in a hurry."

"Would you be able to carry our belongings if you

and Broad Foot transported yourselves across?" the man wanted to know.

"No," said the duckmole. "Weiryn and Sarra both put some of their power into what you carry to help you. Those things are bound to you. If we tried to take them, they would not come."

Numair eyed the crystal in his staff and said dryly, "I didn't know Weiryn cared."

Daine looked at the canyon floor again and winced. It was just too far down. First Bridge or no, the thought of seeing that distant ribbon far under her toes made her sweat. I could take eagle shape, she thought. Heights never bother me when I fly.

That was no good. Numair carried his staff; she couldn't burden him with her belongings, not when he'd need a free hand to grasp one of the ropes that served as rails.

An arm slipped around her shoulders. "Are you all right?" Numair asked. "Heights don't bother you."

"It's the bridge as much as the height," she replied.

"I will carry our things, if you want to shift," he told her softly. "A shape change is out of the question for me. We must keep our food and weapons, for one. For another, I would hate to use my Gift to fly across, then need it to handle trouble on the other side."

"If we are going today, let us begin," urged the badger. "I would like to be across before anyone, or anything, else comes by."

The thought of being caught on that bridge by an enemy made Daine's stomach roll. "He's right." She tried to smile at Numair. "We'd best start walking."

Numair put down the duckmole and stood back. Silver fire bloomed, shrank: The gods vanished, to reappear on the far side of the canyon.

Daine insisted that Numair go first, and tried not to watch as he carefully moved away from the cliff. When he was well ahead, she bit her lip and stepped onto the first plank. It shuddered beneath her weight; the whole structure shook with her friend's movement. Trembling, she seized the rope handholds: firmly with her right hand, awkwardly with her left, the one in which she carried the bow.

Numair slipped, making the bridge rock. Like Daine, he'd managed the barest hold on the left-hand rope, hampered by his staff. "It takes getting used to," he called to her.

"It's stood for time out of mind!" The badger's voice came from the air near them.

"That's what I'm afraid of," they both chorused.

Numair glanced back at the girl, and grinned. She

had to smile as well. Carefully, he walked on, eyes on the planks before him.

She'd meant to keep her eyes forward. Instantly she discovered that would be impossible. Gaps lay between the wide boards. To avoid putting a foot through an opening, she had to look where she stepped, and was treated to a view of the river as it wound between tall, jagged rocks far below. She forged ahead, a step at a time.

Away from the cliff, she walked into a brisk, playful breeze. "Of course," she growled. "What would a First Bridge *be* without its own plank-rocking first *wind*!"

Movement pulled her attention to her chest, rather than her footing. Shimmering with light, the darking that had been tucked into her belt purse now hung by a tentacle from her belt. The other darking had flowed off her neck to swarm over the belt darking, hitting it with tentacles shaped like hammers. She heard small plops as each blow landed.

"Here, you two, stop it! This isn't the time—"

"What's wrong?" The breeze was strong enough that Numair was forced to shout. He was more than forty yards distant, a third of the way across the bridge.

"I don't know!" she yelled. "It's the darkings!

Enough!" she told her passengers. Clutching the left handhold with fingers still wrapped around her bow, she released the right-hand rope and grabbed the top darking. She pulled it away from the one on her belt and stuffed it down the back of her shirt. Seizing the belt darking, she held it up.

Examining the darking, she gasped and nearly dropped it. Its center was filled by Ozorne's face. He grinned and waved, then vanished. The darking was solid shadow once more. Daine stuffed it into her belt purse and tied the pouch shut with one hand. As she seized the right handhold again, her magical senses prickled. Wind made the bridge jump. Clinging to the rails, the girl looked for the disturbance. Far overhead, the sky rippled.

"Uh-oh," she whispered. Like the tauros, something, or someone, was crossing from one realm to the other.

Winged shapes came into view, as if they flew through a waterfall or beaded curtain. Please let them be friendly, Daine thought, shaping her own eyes to those of an eagle. Now she saw the new arrivals clearly: horse-shaped, with powerful, batlike wings and a predator's talons and fangs. They were not at all friendly.

"Hurroks!" she yelled to Numair, pointing. "Eleven of them!"

The immortals drew their wings in and dropped, coming for the bridge like plummeting falcons.

Numair planted his feet and raised his staff, holding the rail with his right hand.

The girl couldn't afford a handhold. Kneeling, spreading her legs to balance herself, she grabbed two arrows. One she put to the string; the other she held in her teeth. She refused to think about the rocking bridge, or the gaps on either side.

Five hurroks formed the first attacking wave. Carefully Daine selected a target. Black fire shot from the crystal on Numair's staff even as the girl loosed; the hurrok struck by the mage burst into flame and dropped. Another screamed in rage: Daine's arrow had grazed its chest and punctured a wing. With her second arrow Daine shot the next hurrok coming in. It shrieked and fell, her shaft through one eye.

She yanked two more arrows from her quiver, putting one between her teeth, one to the string. Sharp pain dragged across her scalp: A hurrok had come from behind to rake her with his claws. As momentum carried him far below, into the gorge, the impact of his strike knocked Daine forward. The arrow in her bow fell as something ink-colored hit the board in front of her. Daine flinched.

It was a darking. Keening, it clamped onto the board, locking itself down with a half-dozen tentacles. She couldn't believe it might attack—something in its shrill cries told her it was too busy keeping itself from dropping into the gorge to do her an injury.

Rolling, hampered by her pack and trying not to crush her quiver, she put her second arrow to the string. Carefully, she turned over, tracking the hurrok with her blood on his talons; correcting for wind, she loosed. The arrow soared across the air below to plunge into the hurrok's belly. Shrilling, he tried to claw the missile from his flesh as he dropped. Two more attackers plummeted, one set ablaze by Numair, another fighting silver fog wrapped around its muzzle. The animal gods had joined the fight.

Daine sat up, holding the bow at an angle to keep it from tangling in rope or boards, and groped for her quiver. Two arrows met her fingers. Glancing back, she saw that the darking she'd put into her shirt was spread over the quiver's top. It had saved her arrows from the chasm; now it handed them to her. "Thank you," she whispered, getting to her knees again. She touched the back of her skull: Wetness trickled through her curls. "Hope you don't mind getting bled on."

Other hurroks, including the one that she had first wounded, spiraled down to the attack. Daine shot and killed the injured hurrok. A sparkling black net enveloped a pair of immortals and exploded, leaving nothing. Two more hurroks, one nearby, one higher up, dodged frantically, trying to evade the badger's deadly silver fireballs.

Coldly, Daine drew the bowstring back to her ear. Silver fire overtook the hurrok farthest from her. It turned black and charred, dissolving as it fell. The last hurrok, screaming its rage, plunged toward Daine, claws outstretched. The girl shot.

The arrow flew as neatly as if she were in the practice yards of the palace. It slammed into the hurrok's throat, cutting off its scream. The immortal beat its wings to stop, and flew right into sparkling fire. Instantly transformed into a charred skeleton, it broke up, raining into the canyon.

Carefully Daine put down her bow. "I want to go home," she whispered. "I've had enough excitement for a while."

A darking head peered over her shoulder.

"*You* have some explaining to do," she told it. "The one in my pouch was spying on us, wasn't it?"

The darking squeaked and hung its head.

Daine pointed to the darking that clutched the plank. "What about this one? Is it coming with us?"

The darking on her back squeaked at the newcomer. It trembled like jelly, and finally shrilled a reply. Her passenger nodded to Daine.

"Is it a spy, too?"

The small, inky head shook emphatically. The newcomer was no spy.

"Well, it's certainly a deserter from Ozorne's army, at the very least." Carefully the girl reached forward to peel the newcomer off the board. Quivering, it pooled in her hand. "Why did you come over to my side, hm?"

"Daine," called the mage, "may we move on?"

"Sorry," she yelled. "Just a moment." To the darkings, she said, "You'd better come up with some answers that make sense, and soon." She dropped the newest of the blots inside her shirt. The darking on her shoulder stuck its head under her collar. Their soft, peeping conversation was drowned out by the creaking of the bridge as Daine carefully got to her feet. Gripping the rope handholds, she caught up to Numair.

"You're hurt," he said, touching the back of her

head, when she reached him. The girl winced. "I'll tend it later, though. Let's get off this thing!"

"I don't know," she remarked, following. "It seems like a nice little bridge." He looked back at her, eyebrows raised. "It never dumped us, now, did it? And it could've."

"Yours is a happy nature," the mage answered, wry. "I confess, this is too much like excitement for me."

"It could be worse," Daine said, and giggled. "It could be raining."

Numair shook his head, then returned his attention to crossing the bridge. "I wonder if that hurrok struck your head a little too hard."

"Nonsense," the girl retorted. "I couldn't have shot straight if it had."

When they stepped off the bridge, Numair swept her into a tight hug, and examined her scalp as he held her. Daine rested gratefully against him. He'd sounded calm on the bridge, but his heart pounded; his shirt was sweat-soaked.

"We should clean this," he remarked over her head. "Didn't Sarra give you ointment for injuries?"

"Mm-hm." Daine rubbed her nose in the patch of chest hair that peeked through the V of his shirt collar.

He drew back. "Stop it," he said sharply. "I can't think when you do that."

"You think too much," she retorted, but she stopped anyway.

"I smell water," said Broad Foot. "Fish, and frogs, too."

"Let's find it," the badger ordered. "Before something else happens."

They found their way down into a valley. It was cut in two by a lively stream that flowed out of a deep pool. Broad Foot plunged in. Seconds later, Daine saw him on the bottom, riffling through sand and rocks with his bill.

On Numair's orders, Daine washed out her cuts. The darking that had deserted the hurrok remained inside her shirt, clinging to her waist, enduring without complaint the cold water that dripped onto it. The darking that had protected her arrows helped the man to gather firewood. The third darking remained in Daine's belt purse. She ignored its bumping as she dipped water and poured it over her aching head. The badger hunted for his supper among the ground-squirrel, snake, and mice gods nearby.

By the time he returned, the fire was burning well, and a pot of tea water was heating. Daine submitted patiently as Numair examined her scalp wounds, made sure they were clean of grit, and rubbed ointment into them. Neither he nor the girl were much surprised when the cuts healed as the ointment was applied.

"She said the herbs she finds here are more powerful," Daine remarked when Numair patted her shoulder and moved to another seat, one not so close.

The badger settled across the fire from the two mortals. Broad Foot was there already, half tucked under a fallen log.

"Daine, what in the name of all the gods was going on at that bridge?" the badger demanded. "It looked as if you were dancing!"

The girl rubbed an aching temple and sipped her tea. She felt weak and watery, a bit like tea herself. "It's these darkings." She explained what had taken place, while the darking that had saved her arrows nodded vigorously. Somewhere it had acquired a faint streak of gold through its body, color that filled the tiny head that it fashioned for itself. "Seemingly they were fighting, or disagreeing," the girl finished. "And then I saw Ozorne." She bit her lip. "There was another time, when the tauros almost got me. A darking was in the water—was that you?" she asked. The gold-smeared blot nodded. "I saw Ozorne then, too, inside *him*." She pointed to the darking.

"You never mentioned this," Numair remarked, eyes glittering dangerously.

She stiffened. "I had other things to worry about! I *thought* maybe I saw Ozorne because the darkings are liquid, kind of, but they aren't, are they?" Her gold-streaked companion shook its head.

"We need answers," said Broad Foot. "Where is the spy—in your pouch still?"

The leather purse thumped at the girl's belt, the creature inside trying to free itself. "Oh—and I've another one."

"Another—?" asked Numair, his brows coming together in a frown.

"It dropped off the hurrok that cut my head. I think it deserted to our side."

Broad Foot waddled over to Daine and cut a circle in the earth with a claw. Before he closed it, he told the gold-touched darking, "Inside, you." The shadowy thing cowered away from him.

"It won't hurt," the badger said. "Getting answers in other ways takes too long."

"But Ma tried that," protested the girl. "She only got its name."

"Because that was what she asked for," Broad Foot replied. "We're doing something else. Stop dawdling!"

Flattening itself like an anxious dog, the gold-streaked darking trickled across the ground unwillingly. It hesitated outside the mark in the earth, then flowed into the circle. The duckmole looked up at the girl. "Where's this new darking?"

Daine fished out the deserter. "Go with your friend." She put it on the ground, and the darking rolled into the circle.

"Now the third," said Broad Foot.

Quickly the girl upended her belt purse over the circle. Her captive fell out with a plop; Broad Foot closed the circle. The darking from the pouch surged against the line in the ground, and flattened as if it had met a wall of glass.

"Stand back," ordered the duckmole. Opening his bill, he uttered a strange noise, half croak, half bark. Silver fire bloomed over the darkings, who shrank away from it. The glittering light stretched; deep within, a picture began to form.

There was Ozorne, streaked with soot, cuts on his face and chest, a clump of braids singed. At his throat he wore a black, glassy stone on a frayed cord. His lips moved as if he talked to himself. The view spread: The former Emperor Mage stood alone in a cave, a pool of water at his feet. Outside the entrance, snow fell in a thick veil.

An image formed in the water. It showed Daine as she read a book. Ozorne reached for her. When his outstretched wing touched the water, she disappeared. Though the image was soundless, they could see him shriek, baring sharp silver teeth. Veins in his chest, neck, and face stood against his skin. He spun, and came to an abrupt halt, a look of sudden cleverness on his face.

His lips moved. A thick worm of gold-edged scarlet fire appeared before him.

"So he'd mastered Stormwing magic by winter," murmured Numair. "Possibly even before the barriers between the realms collapsed."

"This is months ago," said the badger. "I remember this blizzard. We don't have that many, even here in the colder climates—it was the first full moon after Midwinter, the Wolf Moon."

Neatly, Ozorne cut his cheek on a razor-edged feather. The fiery worm flew to the cut, battening on it as a leech might. Ozorne spoke again. The tube fell away, turning into a bowl as it moved back. It brimmed with dark blood.

Lurching to the pool, Ozorne drank. When he straightened, his eyes were bright; he grinned. Returning to the magical bowl, he breathed a red-gold mist on its surface. It sank into the depths of the blood and swirled, making wavy patterns. Quickly the Stormwing cut both lips, flicking the blood drops into the bowl.

"For speaking," guessed Numair, engrossed. "Blood also for life, and to bind the fruits of the working to him. He couldn't have done it as a mortal, but here—"

"Here magical laws are what you make them," Broad Foot said. "He seems to have learned that better than most who are *born* immortal."

Numair raised an eyebrow. "I doubt that he learned that at all," Ozorne's one-time friend replied. "He merely wanted to do the thing, and so he forced it to happen. Subtlety has never been his strong suit."

Again that delicate flick of a feather edge, this time across each ear. The blood went into the bowl. Closing both eyes, Ozorne raised the same wing feather. Even more carefully, he just nicked the skin of his eyelids, producing two scant drops to add to what he'd already gathered.

Slowly, he raised his wings, pointing at the cave's ceiling. As he did, the liquid surged upward. Ozorne lowered his wings; the bulge remained. Twice more he repeated the motion; each time the liquid in the bowl rose higher. After the third raising, it formed a red-black column nearly eighteen inches tall.

Ozorne was sweating. Now he shouted; the bowl vanished. Its contents dropped, breaking into a myriad of blobs. Each turned black. The Stormwing's face was mirrored in each newborn darking.

The vision dissolved. Only the trio of darkings remained.

"There you have it," said the duckmole. He broke the circle to release the captives. "Your enemy made them to serve as his voice, eyes, and ears."

Free, the darkings did not try to escape. Instead they created heads for themselves so that they could nod. Again Daine noticed that one still contained a streak of gold. Somehow, while in the circle, another had picked up a small leaf. This it wore on its head, like an absurd hat. She was nearly positive that the third—the plain, shivering one—was the darking that had dropped from the hurrok.

"So you *are* Ozorne's spies," she said.

The answer was a head shake, first on the gold one's part, then on that of the one that bore a leaf. The third blot shrank lower to the ground, trembling.

"You showed Ozorne that we were at the bridge," Numair reminded them.

Gold-streak pointed an accusatory tentacle at Leaf.

"You'll do it again when he summons you," growled the badger.

The answer was emphatic head shakes from the gold-tinged and leaf-wearing blots. The third shrank against the other two.

"But he *created* you," Numair said.

Gold-streak began to tremble.

"Don't be afraid," Daine said. "You needn't—"

"I don't think it's fear," interrupted Numair.

"It's trying something new," added the duckmole. "Wait."

The streaked darking's companions leaned against it to somehow give it strength. An image formed in Gold-streak's depths, growing to cover its surface. There was Stormwing Ozorne: He glared at a darking on the ground before him.

"*Obey,*" whispered Ozorne. Its victim began to shrill; the darkings with Daine and her friends shrilled, too, tiny voices rising and falling. When the image vanished, they stopped.

"He hurts you," Daine said. "Is that why?"

Gold-streak showed a fresh image: a red-clad female giant—a blot's-eye view of Daine—as she tugged an arrow shaft away from the onlooker's vision. That picture blurred, to form a fresh image.

"Your leg, isn't it?" asked Numair, grinning. "From the foot up?"

A large hand came into view, cheese in its fingers. It dropped the scrap and pulled away.

"You fed it." The badger sighed. "Sometimes I think you'll feed *anything*."

"You were trying to warn me, in the pond?" asked Daine. The visions disappeared. The tinted darking nodded. "And on the bridge? Your friend here—Leaf, and you're Gold-streak, and this little fellow—" She scratched her head, looking at the trembling creature. "You'll be Jelly."

The darking's shivers slowed, though they didn't stop. It rose a bit in the middle, no longer trying to merge with the ground.

"So on the bridge, Leaf was reporting to Ozorne. Gold-streak, you tried to put Leaf in the pouch to keep Ozorne from seeing where I was, but it was too late— Ozorne had already sent the hurroks. You hadn't told Leaf not to do as Ozorne bids you."

Both Gold-streak and Leaf nodded.

She looked at Jelly. "And you abandoned the hurrok when you saw I had Gold-streak?" A bump that might have been a head lifted in Jelly's mass. Stiffly it shook its new head.

"Or did Gold-streak call to you?" inquired the girl. Jelly nodded.

The badger chuckled. "Ozorne mastered Stormwing magic," he remarked, "but he created the darkings *here*."

"Are you sure?" inquired Numair. "That cave may have been in the mortal realms."

"He did it here," Broad Foot said firmly. "We gods can always tell the difference."

"Here, life is forbidden to remain a slave of its creator," explained the badger. "It's why so many children and servants of gods act against the interests of those who gave them life. The darkings are forming their own ideas and ways to communicate, and they're getting names."

"They're his *blood*," argued Numair. "Blood will bind anything. How can they refuse when he commands?"

"I don't know, but they can." Daine looked at the gold-tinted blot. "This morning I heard Ozorne say, 'Number fourteen, report.' I thought I dreamed it, but I didn't. Gold-streak was still in my pack then, so Ozorne couldn't see where we were. Gold-streak refused to tell him!"

Gold-streak nodded vigorously.

"That's why Ozorne sent Leaf, because he couldn't make you tell, and Jelly chose to be with you, not Ozorne."

Both Leaf and Gold-streak nodded.

Daine picked up Jelly. "You were brave to jump off that hurrok," she told it gently. "Why don't you talk to Leaf and Gold-streak a bit, and hear what they have to say?" The darking nodded, then—abruptly—rubbed its head against her thumb before she put it down. The three came together in a shadowy pool. Daine realized that she was exhausted.

"We'd best turn in," Numair said, eyes on her. "We've had a long day."

"Doubtless tomorrow will be longer still." The girl dug in her pack for her blanket.

"We will stand guard," the badger said. "Broad Foot and I have things to discuss."

Daine's last awareness was of the badger and the duckmole rocking to and fro, their heads together as they conferred mind to mind.

Rattail, who Daine was now sure spoke with the Dream King's voice, awaited her when she fell asleep. Again she called the girl's attention to the changing

creature that was Uusoae, the Queen of Chaos, sur-
rounded by the Great Gods who kept her captive.
The fiery barrier between her and them blazed. Daine
couldn't see her under that bright light, but she could
feel the creature's changes, and wished very much that
she could not.

Behind the Great Gods, multicolored liquid ran,
not as puddles that spread and merged, but as a stream
that whirled in a circle, seeming to flow both right
and left at the same time. Watching it made the girl
feel giddy. Suddenly columns leaped from the stream,
rising and curving over the gods. If the columns met
at the peak of the circle, the gods would be under a
bowl of Chaos light, just as Uusoae was under a bowl
of light.

White fire winked into existence at the backs of the
gods. Instantly the columns turned to spinning drills,
trying to bore their way through. The second barrier
flickered.

"I hope you don't expect me to get excited over
all this," Daine remarked, finding that she could speak
for the first time. "*Or* that you mean the gods want my
help." Part of her quivered at speaking so lightly of the
gods; she rudely stepped on that fright. "I can't help
the gods against Chaos—I have troubles of my own,

back home. It's not as if they came to *our* aid when the barrier between us and them gave way at Midwinter."

"Why in the name of Father Universe would they meddle in that?" demanded Rattail. "The barrier was made by human mages, who never asked permission to do it."

"I still don't understand why you're showing me all this," the girl told her stubbornly. "It's like I'm being asked for help. Forget it. I've none to give."

A paw cuffed her soundly on the ear, knocking her over. Suddenly she was pup-sized; Rattail towered over her as she had over her own wolf pups. "You cannot have been attending to the duckmole, then," the wolf told her sternly. "Look there!" Planting her nose on Daine's behind, she scooted the girl forward.

Before them was the image that Daine had just seen, with the columns of shifting light connecting over the heads of the gods. They spread to cover the outer barrier. Mouths, distorted with jagged, sharp, and weirdly angled teeth, opened throughout the cover of Chaos light, and sank within it.

Suddenly everything sagged inward; Daine felt the white-light barrier evaporate within her very bones. Shapes thrashed under the rippling, glimmering Chaos stuff as it fell inward. At the center was Uusoae, born from the muck that she commanded, her eyes—when she had them—shining with triumph. She opened a mouth with swords for teeth and sprouted a hundred arms. They lashed out, seizing animals and two-legger gods from seemingly empty air, carrying each to the Chaos queen's jaws. She ate, and ate, and ate. Blood of all colors streamed over her chin and body and was soaked up, to add its colors to the muck in which she stood. The last two struggling figures she raised to her lips were Sarra and the badger.

With a gasp, Daine sat up, eyes open. Her curls and skin were dripping sweat. Sometime in the night she had thrown off the cover. It lay beneath her, dragged into folds and ridges. Her back and head ached.

"Numbers eleven, twenty-seven, fourteen, report!" That voice was Ozorne's; the girl looked around for the darkings. "How *dare* you defy me!" The commands issued from Daine's pack, where the blots had spent the night. "If you will not show what I wish—"

Crimson light shone through openings in the pack. The darkings keened, tiny voices shrill. He was hurting them! She yanked the flap open, furious; black tentacles streaked with red veins reached out to pull it shut again. The darkings wanted her to stay out. Rather than listen, she went to the pool to clean up. It took her longer than usual; she was trembling with rage, and dropped things. The sky in the east was just turning pink.

"Did you hear me?" Numair stood on the rise near their camp, wearing only his breeches, hair tousled. "It's how our enemies seem to know every move!"

Daine rubbed her face with her hands. "I didn't hear."

"It's the darkings. *They're* the answer."

She felt a powerful urge to yank him into the pond, just for being awake and chatty, let alone for having poked up the fire and set tea water on to boil. Mastering the urge—barely—the girl returned to her pack.

The darkings came out. She cuddled them, asking if they were all right. All three nodded, but Jelly quivered more than ever, and even Gold-streak and Leaf were trembly.

The badger waddled over to her. "Did you dream?"

Daine glared at him. "I dreamed, all right," she said grimly. "Amazingly clear dreams, like all the ones I've been having here. Amazing and *long*, since I don't remember sleeping much!"

Numair scooped up the darkings. "It's these little fellows," he said. "Or ladies," he added, squinting at them. "It's impossible to tell if you have a sex."

There was a splash; Broad Foot climbed out of the pool, a small fish in his bill. The resurrected fish god that had supplied his breakfast leaped from the water, splashing him. "What about the darkings?" he asked.

"They don't just spy on *us*," Numair said. "I *thought* Ozorne had created a number far in excess of his needs, if they were solely to keep an eye on Daine or me. Your kinfolk are with our leaders, aren't they?" he asked the darkings. "The king, the queen—"

"In the north," Daine said, realizing what he meant. "I heard in a dream that the Scanrans got away clean. Somehow they knew the Yamani fleet was coming."

"As I woke, I heard that yesterday the Seventh Riders tried to use a secret exit from Legann," Numair added quietly. "The enemy was waiting. Three of the Riders are dead."

Daine clenched her teeth. She had friends in the Seventh Riders. Their commander, Evin Larse, had pulled a roll from her ear the first time she'd eaten in the Rider mess. She looked a question at Numair.

"I don't know who they were, magelet," he said gently, smoothing a wet curl off her forehead. "No one mentioned names."

She nodded, and made herself think about the immediate problem. "The darking spies tell Ozorne.

And other darkings with his commanders pass it on," she whispered. "That—dung-fouled, mold-eating—" She faced the badger, eyes blazing. "You could put an end to it!"

"The Great Gods don't like the People's gods to intervene in human affairs," the badger replied. "We are to keep to doings of our own children."

"You've always said I mean as much as your own kits." She knelt beside him. "Badger, please! I can't help them at home whilst I'm here—but *you* can! *Please!*"

The badger fluffed out his fur, snorted, and stamped.

"What good is knowing that your friends have eavesdroppers?" asked Broad Foot. "The darkings are very good at hiding."

"There are general spells to make an area secure," Numair said hesitantly. "I would hope that the darkings aren't immune to their effects. Of course, chances are that our friends are using such spells now, to hamper the enemy's spy-mages."

Colors rippled over Gold-streak's skin. The other two blots flowed into it to form a single, quivering mass. They seemed to be conferring.

Movement in the pot where Numair was brewing their tea caught Daine's eye. On top of the curtain wall at Port Legann, Tkaa the basilisk stood by Kitten. Yellow fog was drifting through the air over their heads: The wyverns were on the attack once more.

A burning log snapped, throwing up sparks, and the image dissolved. Mute, Daine pulled off the silver claw that hung around her neck, the symbol of the tie between her and the badger. She held it out to him. "I'm asking you now, by this symbol of the bond that's between us: Please help my friends."

The badger whuffled, wet nose quivering.

"If it helps, I will take them as far as I can," the duckmole told his fellow god.

"What is it, Gold-streak?" Numair asked. The three darkings were surging up and down beside Daine, reminding her of children trying to get an elder's attention. Gold-streak had stretched until it stood taller than Leaf and Jelly.

To her surprise, a slit opened in the knob that served Gold-streak as a head. The opening moved; a squeak reached the girl's ears. Quickly she bent down so that her ear was close to the blots. "I go," repeated Gold-streak. Its voice was tiny.

6

CHESS GAME

Numair touched her shoulder. "What's the matter?"

She looked up at him. "It's Gold-streak. It—it talked."

"But they *don't* talk, do they?" he asked. "My impression was that they only communicate what is said *to* them, or *near* them."

Gold-streak stretched a bit more and said, "Now talk." It was louder this time, enough so that everyone heard. "I go. Talk to darkings. Teach them—" It returned to its huddle with Leaf and Jelly. They vibrated together until Gold-streak's head rose out of the mass. "Freedom," it said clearly. "Choosing."

"Do you know where your brethren are—who they spy on?" asked the badger.

All three blots nodded.

"And I can transport a darking from place to place, here or in the mortal realms," the badger commented. He sighed, and pointed out, "It will take us a while, even going from spy to spy by magical means. Transporting all over the mortal realms, I will need to rest. Numair Salmalín, look after my kit. Put that back on your neck," he ordered Daine crossly, meaning his claw.

She obeyed. Gold-streak ended a last conference with Leaf and Jelly, and rolled up the badger's leg to his back. The god looked at it. "Ready?" he asked. Gold-streak nodded. Silver light exploded, and they were gone.

Numair straightened their camp. He filled their fire pit and the trench that had served as a privy, scattering leaves and stones to make the place seem untouched. Daine packed, rapidly stowing their belongings. Broad Foot, Leaf, and Jelly watched from a safe distance.

"It's as good as the courtship dances of cranes," the duckmole remarked. When they finished, he created a pouch in Numair's fresh shirt, and materialized in it. "You never bump into each other, and you never try to do the same tasks."

Daine smiled up at her tall friend. "We've been doing this for a while," she explained. "I've lost count of the camps that we've put up and broken down."

Numair reached, as if he wanted to stroke her cheek, then dropped his hand. "Where do the darkings ride?"

Leaf coiled around Daine's neck. Jelly, still aquiver, tucked itself into a pocket of the girl's breeches, letting only its makeshift head stick out.

Today Daine set the pace. She knew exactly how fast she and Numair could walk together, just as she knew how often they had to rest. The man and Broad Foot talked quietly; Numair had a great many questions about the home of the duckmole's mortal children. Daine and the darkings watching their surroundings. The small blots were fascinated. Wary, the girl carried her bow in her free hand. She wanted no surprises.

Their trail led downhill, through a less heavily forested land. It was almost noon when they came to the narrow arm of a swamp. "Mauler's Swamp?" asked Daine, seeing that Numair was looking at their map.

The mage nodded. "There should be a bridge ahead."

Daine pointed. The bridge was a low one, rising a handful of inches over the water's surface. Fashioned of sturdy-looking logs, it would hold them clear of the murky water until they were completely across.

Mosquitoes and biting flies came for them as soon as they stepped onto the bridge. Killing the insects did no good: They were gods, and restored themselves instantly; their dead bodies fell into the mouths of waiting frogs and fish. Their bites raised welts that itched crazily. At last Numair spun a fiery magical shield to keep the things at bay.

The insects buzzed outside, on a level with the humans' faces.

"The bears and the deer let us feed off them!" protested a horsefly.

"Muskrats," a tiny voice said; Daine couldn't see who spoke. "Don't forget them."

"They are gods," Numair said calmly, undisturbed by a chat with insects. "No doubt they replace their blood instantly. *We* are not gods."

"Mortal blood tastes best," added the small voice. "It has life in it. The blood of gods doesn't."

"I can't begin to tell you how sorry I am to deny you such a treat," Numair said.

"You know very well we could break that shield, if we wanted to," cried a blackfly. "We are *gods,* after all."

"What good is blood that's given so grudgingly?" the horsefly grumbled.

"What good indeed?" inquired the mage, voice mild.

"Selfish," a mosquito snapped.

"I hope that Mauler eats you! It would serve you right!" the invisible bug told them. The insects left as abruptly as they had come.

Daine wiped her forehead on her sleeve; it was hot and close in this marsh.

"Broad Foot, what is this Mauler?" Numair asked. He kept his staff—its crystal charged with his Gift— raised before him in case something larger than insects came to feed. "He looked like a crocodile in the image that Weiryn showed us."

"Lord Mauler is an older god of the People," said the duckmole. "He is a link between crocodiles and the dinosaurs. May we move faster?"

"Why?" asked Numair. Daine paused briefly to string her bow. When she reached back to her quiver, an arrow met her fingers—Leaf had gotten it for her.

"Mauler isn't entirely friendly to trespassers," Broad

Foot told him. "He puts up with them on his good days, of course."

"You're afraid today may not be one of his good ones?" suggested the mage.

"Exactly."

Daine watched their surroundings closely as they followed the low bridge around the bole of an immense cypress. Below, in murky water, she saw an oddly regular pattern that ran under their bridge to emerge on the other side.

The pattern moved; water heaved and rolled. A hollow tree boomed like a giant drum. The bridge shook, then settled. The thing underneath headed for open water, pulling skeins of vines in its wake. Daine's jaw dropped. At best guess, the creature was over thirty feet in length; any three of the crocodiles she'd seen in Carthak, lined up head to tail, could fit inside its skin comfortably. It curved back around, then stopped.

Twin yellow rounds popped through the surface.

A tiny voice just under the girl's ear—Leaf's—said, "Uh-oh."

Dark shutters slid down over the orbs, then lifted. They were eyes. Daine gulped, sweating. It was one thing to see a creature in a vision over her father's map; such a vision was very misleading as to size. One of those eyes alone was larger than Broad Foot. If she used her bow, would her arrows do more than tickle him?

"What the—?" Numair stared at those two immense yellow eyes.

"Lord Mauler," Broad Foot whispered. "Greetings to you, cousin!" he called.

"And good day," muttered Numair. He broke into a trot, Daine behind him. To their relief, solid land was a few yards ahead. Mauler thrashed as they stepped off the bridge. The surface of the swamp rolled, and crested, and splashed the travelers. The great creature dove, leaving only surging water to mark his passage.

Broad Foot shook a clump of plants off his bill. "I don't know which is worse—when he's cross, or when he's trying to be funny."

Numair wiped his face on his sleeve. "If it's all the same, I won't stay around to study his moods."

Now the way led slowly uphill. The trees thinned. Clearings expanded; streams flattened and slowed. The air was warmed and dried. They kept going after sunset, using the lights overhead, fired by the war with Chaos, to see by. At last they made camp beside a lazy, wide stream.

After eating, Broad Foot volunteered to stand watch until dawn, since he didn't always need to sleep. The two humans curled up under their blankets. Daine had thought she would sleep instantly. Instead she watched the war lights bloom and fade.

I know my da, she thought. I could change my name. No more looks from them that know I'm Sarrasri because Ma was my only family—that I'm a bastard. I s'pose Da acknowledges me now. It's my right to change my name. Weirynsra. Veralidaine Weirynsra.

It didn't sound right. When all was said and done, she was Veralidaine Sarrasri, really. She'd been that for sixteen years. Changing now would be—uncomfortable.

That settled, she closed her eyes. What did the Dream King want to say tonight?

She had the answer almost instantly. Rattail appeared next to her; they were seated on clear air that had turned solid, enough so that Daine could hear her friend's tail slapping the invisible floor in back of her.

"So now we get down to it," said the wolf. "There is one thing that Father Universe and Mother Flame have forbidden Uusoae to do—*meddle in the affairs of mortals*. All of Chaos gets half of its strength from mortal creatures, because *they* are half Chaos by nature. My lord Gainel thinks that someone is helping Uusoae to tap into the other half of mortal fire, the half that does not belong to her. He thinks that she is playing this game, which she is forbidden to do."

Below them appeared a great chessboard in red and gold. Uusoae was the red queen, her appearance for the most part that of a woman in an orange gown, with tangled black hair. Only her eyes and hands changed shape, constantly. Her king was an empty shadow that tried to draw all that was nearby into it. At last a pincer-handed Uusoae ringed it with multicolored fire to save her other pieces from being gulped by her consort. The leftmost rook was a yammering, three-headed ape: "Discord," said Rattail when the girl pointed it out and asked. Uusoae's other rook was a lean, blue-skinned youth with six arms, each one holding a weapon. Smiling at Daine, he pulled a seventh arm from behind his back—it held Numair's dripping head.

A hand rested on her shoulder; she jumped. The newcomer was Numair, well and whole. "Violence," he said, pointing to the blue youth. "With Discord, the gatekeeper of Chaos." Daine glanced at the rook Discord and saw that it juggled her own head.

"Charming," she murmured dryly.

"It's their nature," said Rattail, with an unwolf-like shrug. "They can't help being what they are."

Numair took his hand from Daine's shoulder and looked at the wolf. "Daine, would you introduce us?"

"I dunno," said the girl, looking at Rattail. "Are you Rattail, or are you the Dream King?"

The wolf's shape puddled, curved, and straightened into a rail-thin man with inky, tousled hair and bottomless eyes. —*I thought perhaps you would be less unnerved by hearing of these things from a friend.*—

"Maybe," she replied, looking at gold's ranking pieces. These were the Great Gods: Mithros and the Goddess as king and queen, the Black God and a white-eyed female—"Shakith, goddess of seers," whispered Numair—as high priests, the desert god Jihuk and the Smith god as knights, Kidunka the world snake and the Wave Walker as rooks. "Where are you?" Daine asked Gainel.

The Dream King smiled. —*Like you mortals, I have one foot in the Divine Realms, the other in Chaos. Lately that's been a most uncomfortable position.*—

"Understandably," replied Numair. He pointed to Uusoae's pawns as they materialized on the board all at once. "*Now* we have some answers!"

The central pawn was the Stormwing Ozorne. His

closest neighbor was a blond Scanran mage who used a ruby in place of a lost eye.

Numair whistled softly. "Inar Hadensra. *That* explains far more than it doesn't."

"He's very powerful?" asked Daine.

"Yes, indeed. And he serves only the Council of Ten in Scanra, not whomever they have as king that week. The Copper Islander to his right? That's Valmar, the third of King Oron's sons, carrying a general's baton. And next to him is Deniau, the high admiral of the Copper Isles, and Valmar's brother. Ozorne has powerful allies."

Daine wasn't sure how mere two-leggers might compete with the spidren—a giant, furred spider with a human head—hurrok, dull-eyed female Stormwing, and winged ape that filled out the number of red pawns, but she kept that to herself. Looking to the row of gold pawns, she saw a piece that looked like her at the far end of the board, and one like Numair at the end closest to them. Between their pieces stood a gold-skinned, almond-eyed Yamani who carried a spyglass, Tkaa, King Jonathan, Queen Thayet, the King's Champion, and Kitten.

"I don't like being so far apart from you," she told Numair.

Pieces vanished and reappeared. Now the Great Gods struggled with the Chaos beings, neither side appearing to have the advantage. Ozorne and his allies, holding swords, spears, and axes that rippled with the constantly changing colors that filled the sky and Chaos vents in the Divine Realms, attacked the gold pawns. Gold's pieces were armed, but the attack took them while they were staring at the Great Gods' fight; red's pieces swiftly cut them down. When Daine, Numair, and the other gold pawns were dead, Ozorne and his allies slumped to the board and dissolved, blending with their weapons. Their melted selves flowed around the outside of the ring of struggling gods, to become the Chaos stuff from Daine's earlier dreams, flooding over, then eating, the Great Gods.

"I don't like that game," said Numair, his grin a bit forced. "Can we play a new one?"

In the blink of an eye, the whole board twisted. When it straightened, all the pieces had been returned to their original places. This time, as the gods and lords of Chaos struggled, gold's pawns led the attack. The Scanran mage threw fire at them; King Jonathan blocked it. Alanna the Champion locked blades with an armed spidren. Daine's pawn went straight for Ozorne, Numair's for the Copper Islander Deniau.

All over the board, opponents were locked in desperate battles.

The spidren was the first killed; Alanna raised her sword with a triumphant cry. Uusoae appeared, shrieking as she charged the King's Champion. Gold's pawns were swept out of harm's way as the Great Gods appeared in a circle around the Queen of Chaos. Red's pawns vanished.

—If she is behind this, she will come to avenge her servitor, the one who found a way for her to use mortal power without Father Universe and Mother Flame knowing. Once she reveals herself, they will enter the matter, and end the fight. Gods and mortals will be safe again, at least for another thousand years.— Gainel, who had stayed beside the girl and Numair all along, looked at them. Daine could no more read the emotion in those shadow eyes now than she had been able to the last time she met their gaze.

He disappeared, and was replaced by tree limbs and leaves. It took Daine a moment to realize that she was now awake and that Gainel's soft voice was in her mind, not her ears. *—Her ally may not be a spidren. It may be another immortal, or a human. Whoever it is, for the sake of your parents, humankind, and the Beast-People, you must kill him, or her. It is the only way to end the war.—*

"Why didn't someone just tell us what the problem was?" demanded Numair. Daine looked: He, too, was awake and sitting up.

—*Because the Great Gods believe that no problem exists. They say that no mortal would risk the destruction of his or her own realm by helping Uusoae to break the walls that keep her contained. I no longer argue with my brothers and sisters. They only laughed, so I gave it up. Farewell then, mortals. Good luck.* —

Though he was nowhere to be seen, Daine knew the Dream King had left as surely as if she'd seen him walk away.

Later in their travels that day, as they ate lunch by a stream, the ground shook. Two sounds tore through the air. The first, Daine and Numair agreed later, was that of an iron door being slammed. The other, hard on the heels of the first, was undeniably that of a draw-bridge being slowly, ponderously lowered.

Daine and Numair covered their ears, to no effect. When the booming echoes faded, she checked Leaf and Jelly. Both were shrinking, shivering blobs.

"Oh, my goodness," Broad Foot remarked sadly. "So it's come to that."

"Come to what?" Daine asked, rubbing her abused ears.

"Follow me." Broad Foot waddled to the stream, Daine, Numair, and the darkings right behind him. Leaning over the water, he breathed on it. An image—or rather, three images—grew on the surface.

The first, before Numair, showed the walls and ramparts of Port Legann from high overhead. A colossal spotted hyena gnawed on a tower, then on a siege engine outside the walls. Under her, around her, even through her, humans surged in battle. Was the hyena a ghost? Raising a muzzle that dripped blood, she gave the stuttering, eerie cry that made her kind so feared. Pricking cat ears forward, Daine also heard a distant, dim roar: human voices shouting and the clang of swords, shields, and armor.

In the water before the duckmole, Daine saw wheat fields. Cattle and sheep grazed nearby, herded by children and dogs. Over everything, in a form as sheer as the hyena's, slunk a yellow, mangy cur dog. He was little more than a skin-covered skeleton, as unhealthy an animal as Daine had ever seen. He took bites from everything: grapes, wheat, apples, herd animals. As he bit, things began to shrivel.

Daine looked at the water image in front of her,

and shivered. It showed Corus, the Tortallan capital, with its crowds, rich marketplaces, and temples. A giant, ghostly rat crept through the streets, thrusting his nose into windows and doorways. He licked a man who was making a speech in front of the stocks: The man began to cough. A woman brought him a dipper of water; he could barely drink it. Two men helped him to sit. The ghosts of tiny rats flowed from his mouth, landing on those who had gathered around him.

"Slaughter has been out since May," Broad Foot said. "Malady, though, and Starvation—what you heard were the gates to their dwellings being opened."

"The Three Sorrows," whispered Numair, making the Sign against evil on his chest.

Daine copied him in the Sign; her skin prickled. Leaf curled around her neck to see. Now it rubbed its tiny head, with its green hat, against her cheek. Jelly had vanished into Daine's pocket when the three images had appeared in the water.

"They are the siblings of the gods," the duckmole explained. "Their appearance causes great changes, many for the good—"

"I doubt the ones they kill think so," murmured Daine. She looked at the duckmole, thinking hard. It was one thing to ask the badger for help, another to ask the duckmole. Broad Foot had nothing to do with her, really, or with humankind—there were no two-leggers in the lands where his mortal children lived.

"You know," said the mage casually, "the more disorder that is created in the mortal realms, the more power that Uusoae will have to use. Or so it appears to me."

Daine took her cue from the man. "I bet that Chaos will feed on this. How can she not, when all three Sorrows are wandering loose?"

The duckmole sighed. "So that's it. You want me to halt the Sorrows." He scratched himself. "I can't stop them all," he warned them. "They are strong. They ought to be, with humans feeding them for centuries. I can only hold one, and I'll have to remain in the mortal realms to keep it from breaking loose. The Great Gods themselves could do no better. Some powers cannot be ruled, even by the mightiest."

Daine and Numair traded worried looks. *Choose* between Slaughter, Malady, and Starvation?

"Who are we to say which roams free?" whispered the girl. "If we ask to hold Slaughter, Malady and Starvation will kill hordes of folk—but if we hold Starvation, which kills slow, the other two will wipe out large numbers . . ." Her throat closed.

"Armed humans can defend themselves," Numair said, thinking aloud. "Hopefully Starvation can be held at bay through food imports. But Malady . . ." He shuddered. "Malady doesn't care who it takes, or how many. Malady can wipe out armies and leave no one in the Yamani Islands or Carthak to farm the land."

"And it's just out," added the duckmole. "It's weak still."

Daine shivered and tried not to think of friends killed in battle or dying slowly of hunger. "Malady," she whispered. "If it can be only one, let it be that."

Broad Foot rocked from side to side, muttering. At last he stopped. "Stay on the path," he ordered. "It is a fixed thing, even on the Sea of Sand. It will lead you to the Dragonlands. Getting in, of course, is *your* affair."

"Of course," murmured Numair.

Daine knelt to face him. "I'll owe you for this, Broad Foot."

"So will I," added the man.

"It *is* only fair. If you can force Uusoae to reveal herself, and save the divine and mortal realms, *we* ought to do some things for *you*. Be careful, then." Silver fire gathered around his small body, and he vanished.

"What will we do if the dragons refuse?" Daine asked Numair.

"Fret about them later," he said, gathering their things as she quickly finished her lunch. "I'm worried about crossing the Sea of Sand, if Rikash doesn't help us."

Daine stowed her pack and quiver on her back. "What's wrong with the Sea of Sand?"

"I keep forgetting that we haven't both made a study of myths and legends," remarked Numair, shrugging into his own pack. "The Sea of Sand is more than a desert. It's said the Great Gods take mortal heroes there—although Alanna the Champion never mentioned such an experience. If the hero survives, it is a sign that his—or her—mortal impurities have been seared away."

Daine winced. "Please, Goddess," she said, looking up. "Send Rikash with help." She led the way to the path. "I'm fair confused," she told Numair. "If I'm in the Divine Realms, why do I look up to pray to the gods? Shouldn't I be looking somewhere else?"

"Thinking about things like that will give us both headaches," he replied. "Although I believe that Shuiliya Chiman had visions of the dead praying by looking down. Now, in the lost books of Ekallatum . . ."

Daine smiled. As long as he could talk of learning, Numair would forget anything else, including future dangers. At her belt and on her shoulder, two heads craned toward the mage: The darkings were fascinated.

The path ahead climbed; they stopped often both to rest and to get out of the sun. To the east, the ground fell to a broad river with a sea of grass on its far bank. To the west, the thinning forest gave way bit by bit to scrub and short grasses. Finally, as the afternoon sun beat down without mercy, they stopped near a spring tucked in a rocky cleft. First they ate a meal of bread and fruit, then curled up to sleep until the sun went down.

"What do you mean, 'no reports'?" The voice was young, male, with the accent of the Copper Isles. "All through this campaign you have been able to say exactly where the enemy is! Now, suddenly, you have no information from your spies? There is a Yamani *fleet* north of us—what if it is coming here?"

"I have but two spies there, as you know! If there is some way that they have been detected—Put your own idle mages to the task!" Ozorne's voice was twisted by fury. "You want everything handed you as a gift. But for me, you would have neither courage nor allies to take on Tortall, for all your vows of death to King Jonathan's line! If you want news, scry for it!"

A hoarse voice added, "General Valmar—if you think perhaps to take your fleet and slip away tonight, or tomorrow, or ever, know this." From a childhood spent too close to that harsh land for comfort, Daine recognized a Scanran voice. "Every skin of liquid fire that you possess will burn, should I touch it with my Gift. If you throw them overboard, our allies among the merfolk will fasten those skins to your hulls, and I will burn them then. We will not have the Copper Islanders act as they have so often, and forget their vows of allegiance."

Footsteps—hurried ones—receded. Daine heard metal claws digging into wood.

"The centaurs, too, grow restless," the Scanran remarked.

"I have hairs from every tail among them, to bind them to me. They'll sing a very different tune, should I scorch even one." Ozorne's voice was sullen.

"Sometime you must tell me how you first had information so detailed that one might think you perched on the shoulders of the northern defenders, and now you have nothing. I look forward to hearing."

* * *

Daine opened her eyes and smiled. The badger and Gold-streak had visited the darkings in northern Tortall, then, and talked them into breaking contact with their creator.

Wanting Numair to sleep a bit more, she wandered over to the spring. On its glittering surface, she looked for news of home. An image formed immediately. In it, Broad Foot clung to one of Malady's feet. The rat-Sorrow tried to shake him off; the duckmole jammed venomous spurs into Malady's transparent flesh. Malady stiffened; his reddened eyes went blank. He froze.

Daine blinked. Now she was over Port Legann, so high that men and the ships that blockaded the harbor looked like toys. In the distance to the southwest—the direction of the Copper Isles—she saw the bright flare of torches. The image moved closer and brightened, so that even though it was night, she saw the shapes of ten ships. With the strange, clear sight granted by the water image, she easily read the flags that crowned the masts.

Numair said softly, "Daine?" He was sitting up, frowning.

She began to stuff things into her pack. "The Copper Isles is sending ten ships—they're flying battle flags—north. I think they're making for Legann."

The sun had set. Quickly they packed; before they set out, Jelly changed its seat from Daine's pocket to Numair's shoulder.

The land was changing, turning to desert in the west. The path headed that way, gleaming silver under war light and the light of the newly risen moon, sloping down through huge clusters of rock. In the distance a bird leaped from a pinnacle, flying as if it meant to reach the moon. When it pulled in its wings and tail, Daine grabbed Numair's arm and pointed.

The bird opened itself, spinning on its tail. Lances of silver, blue, and gold light shot from its feathers, an explosion of color over the desert. Within seconds, more dark forms took wing. Each opened itself to the light in a shimmering dance of colors. Unlike the sunbirds, these did not drop back to earth. They spiraled around one another, winding like a river across the scrublands, more of their kind falling in behind them.

"Beau-ti-full," whispered Leaf beside Daine's ear.

She had been holding her breath. Releasing it, she sighed. "Beautiful," she agreed, stealing a look at Numair.

Petting Jelly with a finger, he watched the spectacle, eyes glowing with awe. "I wish I could stay, or come back," he whispered. "So many wonders."

The way grew steep. Lizards that glowed pale blue or yellow darted across the path, or crouched in stone hollows, tongues flicking out to taste the air as the two mortals went by. The path led among stone formations that looked like cracked and broken pillars tightly jammed together. Wind and grit had cut the soft rock into laddered, fantastic shapes. They made Daine nervous: She had an odd feeling that some hollows in the columns were eyes that tracked her.

She tried to meet one pillar's gaze. Half hypnotized by it, she searched for the flash of intelligence that she *knew* was there. Numair and Jelly, far up the trail before they realized she wasn't behind them, returned for her. "I feel it, too," the man said quietly, drawing her away from the stone. "I don't know if this place is dangerous, but I will be happy to get out of here all the same."

For the next two miles the path followed a narrow slot between deep rock cliffs. Numair's crystal blazed with light, creating shadows within shadows, turning long hollows into mouths that screamed. The sense of eyes on her was almost unbearable. The hairs at the nape of her neck stood on end.

"Can you—put the staff out?" she asked. "I—I think it makes things worse."

169

He nodded. The crystal went dark. She took the lead, making bat ears and cat eyes for herself. Numair saw well in the dark; he also had the moon and the rippling battle flares to light the path.

A fresh breeze hit their faces, air from an open place being funneled into a narrow one. Looking up, Daine could see the edges of rock formations. It was nearly dawn. Just ahead, a stone pedestal rose into the air. On top of it, a massive boulder had been cut by the elements into the shape of a question mark.

"Well, *that's* fitting," Numair remarked.

Daine grinned, her mood lightening. Behind the question rock lay open air and, she hoped, an end to those frozen screams.

To their right, at the edge of a cliff, lay a drop; to their left, stone heights reared. They were on the side of a mountain. Sage clung to the pale soil of the shelf; junipers thrust twisted limbs into the sky from rock clefts above their heads. Across the path, in a swath too wide for them to jump, a Chaos vent had overflowed, its shifting yellow, green, and gray liquid a yard from the cliff's edge. To get around it and back onto the path, they would have to walk that narrow strip of bare earth between rim and air, then pass a massive clump of odd gray stones.

"Now *that's* curious." Numair frowned. "The indigenous stone is lava rock of the brown variety. These are different. They could be granite." He walked closer, eyebrows knit, halting a few yards from the spill.

Daine strung her bow and put an arrow to the string, then trailed him. "Indi—what?"

"Indigenous," he replied quietly. "Local."

"Why couldn't you just *say* local . . . ?"

He chuckled as the black, sparkling fire of his Gift flowed out of his hand to wind around the gray rocks. "I'm sorry. I'd meant to do better than my university friends, and not upset people by talking in that abstruse fashion. Then my *father* complained. He asked how did he know that I even *went* to those expensive teachers when I spoke just as I always had?"

Daine grinned. "You never told me that. I s'pose once you get used to doing it at home, you forget the rest of the time."

His magical Gift returned to him. "Those rocks *seem* all right."

Impulsively, she cast her magic over the stones. A chasm tore through her magical self, just as it had done with the Skinners. At the edges of her perceptions, the world shifted and rolled; she was drowned in odors and sounds like nothing that could, or should, exist in the natural world. She tried to cry out, but dripping hands closed her mouth.

A sharp pain lanced through her ear. The magical assault ended. It was her *own* hands that had closed her mouth. Tears ran down her cheeks.

"What happened?" Numair had one arm around her as he fumbled for his handkerchief. She took it with gratitude. "You're white, you're—"

"They're touched with Chaos, those stones," she replied, wiping her eyes. "If I try to use my wild magic to look at something like that, it—it pulls me in."

"You shouldn't generalize from one experience—"

"But it *wasn't* just one. This made me remember the *last* time!" She finished wiping her face—particularly her mouth, where she'd felt oozing fingers—and told him what had taken place with the Skinners.

"Then how did you break free this time?" Numair demanded.

"Leaf, you bit me, didn't you?" she asked, raising a hand to her right ear. Tiny spots of blood came off on her fingers.

"Sorry," the leaf-wearing blot replied, hanging its head.

"Don't apologize," she told it. "Do that whenever

you think it's needful. You just saved me from maybe walking off a cliff." The darking rubbed its head on her finger.

"For now, we shall delay the question of where it got teeth," Numair remarked. "Let's get away from here. Can you walk by those rocks, Daine?"

"Chaos mostly gets me through my magic. I just won't use it. And it's not likely they're *alive,* after all." She looked at the way around the Chaos vent and rocks, and gulped. Three feet was a small margin between her and the long drop. "You go—I'll come after."

Resettling his pack, Numair took the lead as confidently as if he had ten yards, not one, in which to move. Once he cleared the vent's spill, before he passed out of sight behind the rocks, Daine followed. Watching her feet, she skirted the vent, backing away an inch or two as the shifting-colored substance threw a tentacle in her direction.

Numair cried out. She looked up: A gray stone arm was wrapped around him, lifting him off his feet. Rocky, grinding sounds filled the air as the other stones began to move. Fumbling to get her bow up, Daine stepped back to get a cleaner shot.

The rim of the canyon broke under her weight. With a shriek, she dropped, bow tumbling out of her grip.

7
FALLING

THE FIRST TREE DIDN'T EVEN SLOW DAINE DOWN. Branches, gnarled by the fight to get their share of sun in the narrow canyon below, snapped easily when she hit them. She pulled Leaf from her shoulder and tucked it into her middle, curling into a ball around the darking. Panic swamped her; she could think of nothing but the rush of air and the sickening drop.

The second and third trees that she struck held her a bit longer as they raked her back and legs. The quiver caught on something, nearly dislocating her shoulder. She screamed, and hauled her arm out of the strap. The fourth tree was full of thorns. It kept her for almost a full breath, and ripped her skin.

She clutched at the branches of the fifth tree, thorns or no, missed her grip, and fell into deep, ice-cold water. Down she and Leaf plummeted, dragged by the pack. Yanked along by a heavy current, she dumped her belongings and shot to the surface, choking.

White water swept her along. Battered against the stony riverbed, she fought to reach the shore. At last she was swept into a calm pool, out of the undertow. Gasping and cursing, she dragged herself and Leaf into the shallows, and looked up.

The sky was a distant blue strip. Earth and rock soared on either side of the canyon. Nowhere in those forbidding walls did she see the trail of broken trees that would mark where she'd come down.

"Not a problem," she told Leaf, slogging for the rocky shore. "I'll just take hawk shape and find him—once I catch my breath. Are *you* all right?"

The darking's leaf hat was soaked; Leaf itself trembled as devoutly as Jelly had. "No," it told her flatly.

"Me neither. At least we're alive." Daine waded onto dry land.

Had she been herself, she would have seen the odd

regular pattern under scattered dirt and stone. Instead, the trap closed on her the moment that she stepped into it.

Heavy, stick ropes clamped around her. One strand fell over her eyes; when she opened her mouth to cry out, two more dropped over her lips and nose. Suffocating, she tried to claw at them, only to find that her hands and legs were bound. She tossed her head, fighting to breathe.

Whatever covered her nose peeled back. She sucked in air, ordering her lungs to be happy with what came through her nostrils alone. Her instinct was to feel the gag in her mouth and panic. Sweating, she forced herself to calm down, and breathe slowly.

There was a new movement on her forehead. Slowly, a hair at a time, her blindfold slipped up. At last it was over her brows. Her left eyed filled with a small, inky head. The bonds that wrapped *her* so well apparently had no effect on a darking.

"Thank you," she tried to tell Leaf.

Whatever sealed her mouth kept the sound in.

"Badbad," Leaf replied.

Yes indeed, she thought. Badbad. I must've stepped into a snare laid for anything big and edible that came down here to drink.

Turning her head, she examined her bonds, and began to shake. Not rope, but dust-gray web, gripped her. She knew what it was, having seen enough webs in both sunlight and in the dark, when they glowed. They were the creation of spidrens.

She trembled. Of all the immortals that she had battled over the last three years, those were the worst. They had furry spider bodies, at least five feet tall; the females were mottled, males black. Their heads were human, with sharp, predatory teeth. They leaped amazing distances, and preferred human blood to any other food. She had lost count of the times that she had found humans caught in their webs.

Immediately she listened, listened *hard,* for the web spinners. There was no telling which could be worse— that they had laid the trap and then left the area, or that they might be close by. At last, on the outer fringes of her magical range, she felt something immortal. If it was a spidren, perhaps she still had time to escape.

Taking a breath, the girl became a great jungle snake. Her clothes drooped around her scaled form. Gathering herself to crawl away, she ran face first into a shrinking web. As she fought to get her skull free, it closed so tightly that it pinched her coils together.

She changed: swan shape. The web fitted her new body perfectly, binding her. That sense of immortals on the fringes of her awareness was stronger, and familiar: spidrens for sure, three of them.

She wanted to scream, but stopped herself. They were very close now, moving fast; they must know they had a prize.

Perhaps small's not the best way, she thought. Focusing on the great bears of the north, Daine shed her swan shape. The web, instead of bursting, stretched. She was as captive as before.

It she had to face them, she needed clothes. No one could feel brave when naked, and all she wore now was a silver claw. Somehow she didn't think she would feel dressed, meeting spidrens with only the badger's token to wear. Eyes closed, she reformed her true self, easing human limbs into breeches and sleeves, recovering her back and hips, until she was properly dressed. That done, she sank back. What now?

Her dagger. She twisted, looking for it. Her forearms were plastered against her sides, but if she could reach it . . . The hilt at her waist was covered by web. She couldn't even touch the weapon.

"Look, dears, we have a guest!" taunted a voice from above.

Daine looked up. Three spidrens—two males and a larger female—descended a rock face on threads of web. Her stomach rolled as they jumped away from the cliff to land near her.

"Only think," said a male. "All the realms know that King Ozorne of the Stormwing Alliance will heap rewards of whoever brings a certain female mortal treat—"

"Or a long-shanked mortal mage," interrupted the other male.

"Quite right," said the first. "So everyone else searches—and the treat falls right into our nets. The gods must love jokes like these; they tell them so many times."

The female minced over. "Greetings, Veralidaine Sarrasri. How are we today? We look *terrible*." She bared silvery teeth in a grin.

"Eat my loincloth," retorted the girl, sweating. "It's bad enough *looking* at you, without hearing your blather."

"Oh, tut." The female patted Daine's cheek lightly with a clawed leg. The girl winced—even a light spidren tap hurt. "That empty-headed mother of yours should have taught you manners."

"Keep your mouth off my ma!"

The spidren crouched to bring her face closer. "You're in no position to dictate the rules of conversation."

"Where's the long man?" the male who'd spoken first wanted to know. "He's always close to this little morsel."

"Can we kill her even a little bit?" asked the second male. "Can we eat her?"

The female spun. Pink web flew out of the spinneret under her belly, plastering itself over the hungry male's face. He screamed and fell back, clawing at it.

"Remember Ozorne's reward!" she cried when he'd gotten most of the pink strands off. Unlike the gray webbing, the pink left thick, raised welts. "He'll give us human slaves for centuries! He—"

One of the two male spidrens exploded. The female spidren shrieked and kicked Daine to the ground behind her. The girl squinted. What had happened? One spidren was gone, blown to pieces. In the splatter of black blood that was his remains stood Numair. Livid with rage, he raised his staff as the female spidren reared.

Jelly raced over the ground to plaster itself over the spinneret on the female's belly, and bulged as the spidren tried to force liquid web through it. Leaf jumped from the top of a nearby boulder to cover the female spidren's face. Her shriek was muffled; she could neither see nor breathe. Numair pursued the remaining male, beating him with his staff.

Slowly the female spidren collapsed. When she stopped moving, Jelly dropped away from her spinneret. The liquid web that the darking had bottled up spilled to pool uselessly on the ground. The female's head fell back; Leaf peeled itself away from her face. Daine saw lumps on the hatted darking, pieces of it that had been sucked into the spidren's nose and mouth. Leaf had suffocated her.

Numair's opponent was the last to die. When the immortal sank to the ground, head crushed, the webs on Daine turned liquid and flowed away. She was free.

"Numair?"

He stood motionless, his back to her, leaning on his staff. He appeared to be staring at the dead spidren.

Frightened, the girl dragged herself to her knees, then to her feet. Upright, she swayed. "Please . . . are you all right?"

He turned. "You—you're alive. I thought . . ."

She staggered over to him. "I hurt too much to be dead."

Dropping the staff, Numair swept her up in his

arms; hers went around his neck. He stroked her back; Daine buried her fingers in his hair. Pulling away, she tried to get a proper look at him. Their eyes met for a breathless moment as heat surged through her body. Then his mouth was on hers, his breath warmly mingling with her own.

She had been kissed before, over the last two years. Perin the clerk, the most persistent of her swains, had done it a number of times since Midwinter, before the war broke out. A moment ago, she would have said that she liked kissing well enough.

This was different. *Liking* did not begin to describe the thunder in her body and heart. Hot sweetness raced from his lips through her body, making her tingle, making the breath come short in her tired lungs, making her knees watery. Powerful awareness of all the places their bodies touched—from his palms on her back to her breasts, belly, and thighs crushed against his—made the blood pound in her veins.

Numair took his mouth away. "No," she whispered, and pulled him back. He was gentler this time, easing his lips carefully over hers, pulling away briefly, then returning.

A good thing he's holding me up, she thought giddily. *Elsewise I'd fall down.*

He pulled away with a strangled laugh and scooped her up in his arms, carrying her over to a large rock. There he sat, cradling Daine in his lap. "Goddess bless," he whispered, smoothing her curls away from her face. "Magelet, I thought I'd lost you."

On top of her recent experiences, it was too much. She buried her face in his shirt so he wouldn't see the tears that trickled from her eyes. He seemed content to simply wrap his arms around her, lips against her hair. The darkings on the ground observed the humans, small, eyeless heads cocked to one side. Noticing them, Daine smiled.

"We need to rest and eat," Numair remarked after a while. "It'll soon be too hot to travel, and there is the path to relocate as well. If I remember correctly, this river is on the map. It parallels our route and emerges from this canyon near the path. Once you feel better, perhaps you could fly up and locate it. What do you think?"

She didn't answer.

"Sweet?" Craning to see her face, he realized that she was asleep. With a sigh, he got to his feet, cradling his student, friend, and love. Daine's only reaction was to snuggle closer. To the darkings Numair said, "Let's find some shelter."

* * *

"—if I have this straight—no disrespect, Lord Badger, but I confess to some confusion."

Daine smiled in her dream: Queen Thayet of Tortall was never confused.

"You and this—"

"Gold-streak," a tiny voice said.

"Tell me that these two creatures—"

"Darkings," Gold-streak corrected.

"These darkings are made of Ozorne's blood, and they were created to be his spies. Now they think for themselves, and they claim they will help us, not him. Is that correct?"

—*It is.*— That was the badger's mind voice, the one he used in the mortal realms. —*Now these darkings who spied on you will tell you where your enemy is.*—

"The possibilities are dazzling," murmured the queen.

Daine turned over, and realized that she was awake and thinking already: Reinforcements from the Copper Isles were approaching Port Legann.

Numair had brought them to a hollow under a rock shelf in the canyon wall. The river thundered nearby. Outside their shelter, heat rose from the flat, unshaded stone on either side of the river. It would be mad to start walking for several hours, unless they wanted to lose more time still to heat exhaustion. She also ached and stung from top to toe, as if she'd been pounded with a hammer and dragged through thorns. Which I have, she admitted to herself.

The mage leaned against the wall, dozing. Leaf and Jelly, seated on rocks by the fire, watched a small pot of soup. When she sat up, Jelly reached out a tentacle to grip the long-handled spoon and stirred. Creating a head, the darking squeaked, "Food done."

Numair woke up. "Very good," he told the blots. Glancing at Daine, he blushed and looked away.

"How in the name of Shakith did you find me?" the girl demanded.

The man fidgeted. "It was merely a simple magic, Daine—"

"Mouse manure," she replied. "D'you think I've lived all this time with mages without *knowing* what it takes to find somebody *and* go to them?"

"I had a focus," he mumbled.

"A focus? Something of mine to connect us?"

"Yes—and I'm glad I had it."

"Yes—but—may I see it?" She wouldn't like to find that anyone but Numair had a focus, something

that had been hers for a long time, in his or her posses-
sion. There were all kinds of magic that could be done
with focuses, including control of her body and mind.

For a moment he looked grave; she thought that
he might refuse. Then he reached across the distance
between them. A bracelet appeared on his left wrist: a
gold chain with an oval locket. This was the first time
that she had seen it.

The locket fell into her palm opened. Inside one half
was a miniature painting of her face, perfect in every
detail, from blue-gray eyes to stubborn chin. Tucked
behind a gold clip in the other half was a smoky brown
curl. It seemed more like a lover's token, not a magical
device to find an errant student. She returned it to him.

"I thought you might laugh if I asked you to sit for
a portrait." He attached locket to chain—both vanished. "The painting was done by Volney Rain." He
was a court artist they knew. "The hair I got when you
were delirious with unicorn fever six months ago."

Going to the fire, he took charge of the soup, filling three bowls. One he gave to Daine; one he kept
for himself. The third he placed on the ground. The
darkings flowed over their bowl.

Daine blew on a spoonful to cool it. "What happened to you? What about those rock things?"

"They carried me off. I used my Gift to shield myself, but it took them some time to learn that *I* was the source of their pain. Once they did, they fled. When I returned to the Chaos vent, and realized that you had gone over the cliff—" He swallowed hard.

"You can thank a number of trees and a deep part of the river that I'm reasonably alive." She sat next to him, inching over until he was forced to raise his arm. Flinching at the bite of her cuts and scratches—she'd have to tend them soon—she tucked herself into the curve of his arm, then rested her head on his chest.

"You're trembling," she murmured.

"I'm only tired." He was lying, she knew. "*I* used my entire Gift to reach you."

"You shouldn't have," she told him. "You need it to defend yourself—and we still have to reach the Sea of Sand."

Numair's arm tightened. She looked down so that he couldn't see her wince. "If I'd lost you and kept my power, I would hate myself. Eventually magic returns, even after a draining. I had no way to know if *you* would."

She looked into his face, and smiled. "It would take more than falling off a cliff to keep me from you."

Numair kissed her again, his mouth lingering. The

flooding heat of desire nearly swamped Daine before he broke the kiss. "I'd hoped you felt that way," he whispered. He kissed her eyelids, and the tip of her nose, then found her lips again. When he stopped, Daine was limp within the circle of his arm; now she too was trembling.

He sighed regretfully. "I should look at your cuts."

Daine sat up as he drew the pack over. Gingerly— even her bones ached—she lifted her shirt hem.

"Daine!"

"What?"

He had turned crimson under his tan. "You—We aren't—You should be clothed!"

"I've a breast band on, dolt. Besides, this shirt's in shreds. Like the rest of me."

He shifted slightly. "It just doesn't seem *right*. I feel that I'm . . . taking advantage of your innocence. A man of my—years, and reputation—"

"'Taking advantage of'?" she repeated. "And *what* reputation?"

"You of *all* people should know that I've been involved with ladies of the court."

"What has *that* got to do with the price of peas in Persopolis?"

"It's easy for an experienced man to delude a young

woman into believing herself in love with him. It is the basest kind of trickery, even when the man does not intend it."

"Do you love me or not?" she demanded.

"That is *not* the topic under discussion." He fumbled, getting Sarra's ointment from his pack. Jelly and Leaf trickled over, carrying a bottle of water between them. "Thank you," Numair told them as he took charge of it.

Defiantly the girl stripped off her shirt, turning her back to him. Her breast band was in little better condition than her outer clothes, but she didn't care. *He* was making the fuss, not her! "We're not talking about love?" she demanded, wincing as he began to clean the cuts on her shoulders and back. "What are we talking of, then? Canoodling?"

"Daine! Is that what you think I want?" he demanded, outraged. "*Sex?*" Despite his dismay and fury, the hand that smoothed ointment on her was gentle.

"It isn't?" Rising to her knees, she stripped off what remained of her breeches. She heard Numair move away.

Swinging to face him, she searched his eyes; when they met hers, she knew that she'd hurt him. But how? she thought, baffled. Why? Perin only wanted to bed her, as a few Snowsdale men had bedded her mother.

Then she knew. Grabbing the hand with the bracelet, she held the locket. A lover's token, she'd thought before. She had been right. "You're in love with me?"

He looked away.

"Love's fair wondrous. Where's the harm?"

"I was 'canoodling,' as you so charmingly put it, when *you* were four. You're so young, Daine. I knew that if I spoke, you might think yourself in love with me; you might mar—" He stopped.

"*Marry?*" she sqeaked. "*Marry* you?"

He wouldn't look at her. "One day you'd turn to me and see an old man. You'd want a young one." He got up and walked out of their shelter. She watched him go to the river and crouch there, a big shadow against sun-bleached rock.

She rubbed her face. Love was well enough, but *marriage?* There was so much to consider. All her life she'd heard that no respectable man would marry Sarra's bastard—though she wondered if the Snowsdale gossips would think Numair respectable.

All those things he'd said of her waking up some-day could be turned to fit him. She had managed to get a look at all of the women whose names were linked with his. They were typically in their thirties or late twenties, buxom, well-groomed, beautiful, mature.

What if *he* woke up, later on, to see a baby where he wanted to see a woman?

If they married, they would be trapped. Daine had seen enough bad marriages to know a life sentence when she saw one. Some of those marriages had involved men whose marriage proposals her mother had turned down.

Unrolling one of Numair's shirts, she wrapped it around herself—the scrapes on her back were healing fast, thanks to her mother's ointment—and walked down to him.

"Can't we just go on as we have?" she asked. "This is a fair weight to solve when things are so—mad."

He looked up and smiled, just barely. "That is certainly true."

"I know I love you. Maybe I always have—"

"Which is what I was afraid of."

She ignored his frivolity. "Once we're home—once the war's done—we can work it out. We'll talk then."

Standing, he cupped her face in his hands, and kissed her gently. "Indeed we will."

Her mother's ointment made small work of her injuries. As Numair cut his spare clothes down to fit her, she took advantage of the powerful thermals in the canyon, letting them carry her in hawk shape above the rim. There she flew upstream until she found the path of destruction that she'd left in her tumble down the cliff.

Here was the trail they had been on, minus the cluster of gray rocks. She followed it through winding stone alleys, keeping high enough to see the river as well. Numair was right. If they kept to the water's course, they could find the path where the river met open scrubland. Beyond that lay the desert—the Sea of Sand.

She returned to him, and donned the clothes he'd cut down for her. Once the worst heat had passed, they set out again, pacing themselves to avoid heatstroke. After dark, nearing the spot where they could pick up the path again, Daine sensed Stormwings. Rikash was there for certain; she also thought she knew at least two of his companions.

Spying on the waiting immortals through a crevice between two rocks, Daine sighed with relief. She *did* know two of the others. One crowned female had the appearance of a mortal in her fifties. Her nose was prominent and forbidding over a mouth carved by a master sculptor, her dark eyes commanding under perfect black eyebrows. The girl thought that Queen

Barzha of the Stone Tree nation of Stormwings must have been a beauty in her youth; age had added majesty. Her younger consort, Hebakh, had a pale, intense face lit by slightly mad gray eyes over an aquiline nose.

Daine walked into the open. "Hello."

Some of the immortals idling near the path jumped, caught by surprise. The air was filled with metallic clicks as steel feathers ruffled and fell into place.

"Don't you make *noise*?" one of them demanded crossly as Numair came forward.

"You dine on fear, but you don't care to feel it yourself?" the man asked innocently.

When the immortal opened his mouth to reply, Daine said, "Enough, both of you." She bowed to the crowned female and her mate. "Queen Barzha and Lord Hebakh. May I present Numair Salmalín?" He had seen the Stormwings in Carthak last fall, but she didn't think they had been properly introduced. "This is Leaf." The darking nodded its hatted, knobby head. "And that's Jelly." The darking under Numair's shirt thrust out a tentacle, waved, then disappeared into its refuge.

"It hasn't met royalty before, that we know of," Numair explained. He bowed elegantly to Rikash's queen and her consort. "May I say that it is good to see you again?"

"As long as you don't get downwind of us, right, *mortal*?" taunted a male voice from the rear of the flock.

"Do you challenge my decision, Vekkat?" Barzha asked without looking away from the humans. "Have you questions left unanswered?"

There was no loud reply, though Daine could hear voices whispering, "Shut up!" and "Aren't you in enough trouble?"

Rikash came up beside his queen, green eyes glittering. "I confess, the most amusing part of our association is that I am not sure who is more puzzled by it—you or me," he said wryly. "I'm shocked Sarra let you go out dressed that way."

Daine looked at her clothes. "My things got lost. I fell off a cliff."

"You take such a fall well, Veralidaine," Barzha said, her voice wry. "Rikash tells me I should apologize for not killing Ozorne while I had the chance."

Daine smiled. She hadn't thought the formidable Stormwing queen *had* a sense of humor. "He's good at survival," she remarked. "I know you gave it your best."

Hebakh bated. He was a nervous creature, always shifting his weight from one clawed foot to another. "We have not put the matter aside yet. There will be other chances to explain to Ozorne how things are done *properly* among our kind."

"In the meantime," Rikash said, "Queen Barzha has agreed that we shall carry you over the Sea of Sand, to the portal of the Dragonlands."

"We are in your debt," added Barzha. "You freed us from Emperor Ozorne. We shall feel better if we may repay you."

Hebakh whistled. Two Stormwings flapped over, bearing some dark substance coiled in their talons.

"Your mother helped us to make these slings," explained Rikash. "It won't be an easy ride, but it's the quickest way to cross the desert."

Numair and Daine nodded. The pair with the slings, assisted by Rikash and one of the other immortals, spread their materials on the ground.

"I heard something that might be of interest to you, if you didn't hear it yourselves," Daine told the Stormwing queen. Briefly she related the conversation she'd heard by Temptation Lake, before she had known the darkings were Ozorne's spies.

The queen dug into rock with her claws, eyes glittering with malice. "So Qirev—"

"The other must be Yechakk," interrupted her mate. "He's the only old one left."

"They are finding mortal warfare a bit rich for their stomachs," said Barzha. "Perhaps Mogrul of Razor Scream also feels the pinch, after losing eleven. Perhaps—"

"You'll never turn Queen Jachull," Hebakh said, bating. "She is empty. There isn't a Stormwing inside of her, only a void. But the others—they might yet listen to reason."

Their conveyance was ready. After the humans secured their things and sat in the rope webs, Barzha croaked a word; shimmering with gold and crimson fire, the slings rose. On Hebakh's command, five Stormwings took flight, the ropes that cradled the humans in their talons. Three carried Numair; two bore Daine. Belatedly, she said, "You know, I could shape-shift and fly my own self."

"Save your strength for the dragons," replied Hebakh.

The Stormwings began to climb. The magic that had lifted the slings to a level where their porters could grab them released. Daine and Numair dropped an inch, then rose, borne by Stormwings.

The scrubland came to an end and was replaced by sand dunes. Like all deserts, this one was cold after sunset. Daine shivered, but was resigned; at least the cold laid the Stormwings' odor.

Barzha flew close to Numair. Mage and queen spoke, but Daine couldn't hear; the wind bore their words away. Jelly was nowhere to be seen. Leaf, to the contrary, was looped around Daine's neck, its small, eyeless head stretched forward to take the full brunt of rushing air. It was talking softly. She had to bring an ear close to the darking to hear, and when she did, she laughed. Leaf was saying, "Funfunfunfunfun."

For a while, she was content to sit, shivering, as she watched the immortals. There were sixty-three Stormwings present, all of the queen's allies. These were the ones that Rikash had spoken of, those who took honor and tradition seriously.

There's a thing to boggle the mind, she thought, rubbing her shoulders to warm them. Stormwings with honor!

Rikash had been flying in the van, watching the sky. Now he fell back, gliding into position near Daine. A female Stormwing behind them called, "Mortal lover!"

The green-eyed male looked at her. "Repeat that on the dueling grounds at the next full moon, Zusha." The female shut up, and Rikash turned his attention to Daine. "A feather for your thoughts."

"Hm?" she asked, startled.

"Mooning over Long Lankin?" he inquired, jerking his head toward Numair.

Daine blushed, and glared at him. Long Lankin was the villain in a ballad, a tall bandit who lived for slaughter. "He's no more Lankin than you are a songbird," she retorted. "Besides, he's not what I'm thinking of"—which wasn't entirely a lie.

Rikash laughed. "What *were* you thinking of, then?"

"I heard somewhere that immortals are born in dreams. Or our dreams give them shape—something like that. Now, I can see folk dreaming winged horses and unicorns. Even dreaming that a winged horse or unicorn would go bad makes sense. Haven't we all thought something's a joy, only to find that it's evil inside? But—forgive my saying it; no offense intended—how could *anyone* dream a Stormwing?"

His smile was cruel. "Ages ago, a traveler in the mortal realms went from place to place and found only the leavings of war—the starving, the abandoned, the dead. It was the work of armies, fighting over ground they soon lost again. That traveler sickened of waste—of death. She wished for a creature that was so repulsive, living on war's aftermath, that even *humans* would think twice before battle. That creature would defile what mortal killers left, so that humans couldn't lie about how glorious a soldier's death is. *She* dreamed the first Stormwing."

Daine shivered. "But it doesn't seem to make a difference, most of the time." Leaf, who had trickled down to pool in her lap, nodded.

"That's humans for you," said the immortal cheerfully. "Nothing slows them down for long. *But*—if one person asks himself—or herself"—he nodded politely to her—"if the matter to be fought over is worth his corpse being ripped to pieces and smeared with our dung, and decides it isn't, that's all we need to justify ourselves. You'd be surprised how many people changed their minds, knowing that we'd come to live on their pain and play with their bodies. The barrier changed that. Humans forgot us. We've had to start all over. It will take a century before we'll make a difference again."

Daine shook her head as she stroked Leaf. "Am I a bad person, then, for wanting to fight to protect what I believe in?"

"I'm only a Stormwing, not a philosopher. For that, you must talk to Salmalin—if you don't mind the headache he'll give you."

She smiled. "Have people tried making offerings

and sacrifices to you, to keep Stormwings from coming down on them?"

"Very good. You know human nature almost as well as we do." The Stormwings who carried Daine had been listening. They cackled their amusement, making the girl's hair stand on the back of her neck. "Of course humans have tried to buy us off." Rikash grinned, his sharp, silver teeth glinting. "We go after them first."

Hebakh called. "My master's voice," Rikash commented with a sigh. He winked. "Sweet dreams." He rolled in the air in front of her, and caught up with Hebakh effortlessly.

Daine thought long and hard about his words, curling up into a ball within the ropes of her sling. She was afraid to sleep, but she must have done so anyway. The next thing she heard was a voice in her ear. "Wake up!" it said. "We're setting down!"

She opened her eyes to dawn. They were indeed descending, bound for a flat expanse of sand. Before it roared a curtain of white and red fires, like a flaming waterfall.

The slings touched the ground; their porters dropped the ropes. Daine landed with a gentle thump, untangled herself, then lurched to her feet. She was stiff all over. Numair, too, winced as he straightened.

Barzha, Hebakh, and Rikash landed in front of them, while the other Stormwings remained aloft. "Our debt to you is paid," the queen informed them. "We are going now. If the dragons are unhappy with your presence, we prefer not to be nearby."

"Thank you," Daine said. "If you see Ozorne before we do, give him our regards."

Barzha and Hebakh nodded and took flight, the rest of the flock behind them. Rikash gently tapped Daine's arm, then Numair's, with his wing. "Be polite to the dragons, and watch your step." He leaped into the air, and soon caught up with his brethren.

Girl and mage surveyed the fiery curtain, standing well back from a heat that made them sweat. "Now what?" Daine asked her companion.

A voice chimed in the air around them. "Go away, mortals. You will not be admitted to the Dragonlands. We wish to know none of your kind."

"On the contrary," Numair said, voice mild. "One dragon knows a great deal of us. My companion is the guardian of the dragonet Skysong."

"The true guardian of a dragon is brave. You are shrinking, cautious beings."

"Oh, really." Daine stalked toward the curtain, feeling its heat grow to unbearable levels. Just when she thought she might scream with pain, she was through a hair's breadth of fire. On the other side of the portal lay rolling, sunny hills.

Numair burst through the gate behind her, glistening with sweat and gasping. Before Daine realized what he was doing, he'd dropped his staff and grabbed her by the shoulders. "Don't you ever— *ever*—frighten me that way again!" He shook her for punctuation, then wrapped his arms around her so tightly that she thought she might just pop. *"Ever,"* he added, and kissed her thoroughly before releasing her.

"I don't know," she said impishly, smiling up at him. "I like this particular kind of tantrum. Besides— at least now they know we're brave enough."

"Speak for yourself," the mage said weakly, fumbling for his handkerchief. He wiped his face with hands that still trembled.

"The darkings?" asked Daine, suddenly worried. "What if they—"

The darkings popped their heads out of their hiding places. Jelly had dropped inside Numair's shirt. Leaf had trickled into Daine's belt purse.

"Warm," Leaf told them. "Fun."

Nervously Jelly crept up to Numair's shoulder.

"I know it wasn't fun for you," the mage said comfortingly, stroking the darking with a finger.

The darking stretched until it could look Numair in the face, if it had possessed eyes. "Fine now," it assured him. "Get stick." Grinning, Numair picked up his staff.

"Wait," the portal's voice instructed. "Guides will come for you."

8

DRAGONLANDS

SOME TIME LATER, LEAF TUGGED ONE OF DAINE'S curls, pointing at two creatures who trotted toward them. Like Kitten, they had long, reptilian snouts, slender paws like hands, and colorful scales. They were also like Daine's friend in that they were young dragons—the wings on their backs were tiny, incapable of bearing them in flight.

The smaller one reached them first. Snow white in color, it had black shoe-button eyes. It was four feet long from head to rump, with an extra two feet of tail. Its companion was as tall as Daine, with steel-gray and black scales intermixed. Unlike the white dragon, this one was more sedate, and walked with slow, deliberate steps.

—*We're to take you to our grandsire,*— the white dragon told them, speaking to their minds, not their ears. —*You're the first mortals we've ever seen. It's very exciting! I'm Icefall, only the elders call me Scamp. My cousin—well, she's really a third cousin twice removed—her name is Steelsings, only I call her Grizzle because she's so old.*—

—*Welcome to the Dragonlands,*— said Grizzle, mind voice grave. —*Ignore Scamp. She has only two centuries. She doesn't know very much.*—

—*You've only one more century than me!*— accused Scamp. —*You don't have your wings yet either!*—

Numair hid a smile behind one hand. Daine sighed. Perhaps it was just as well that Kitten still could not speak mind to mind, if all young dragons chattered.

—*Children should be seen, not heard.*— Grizzle cuffed Scamp, then looked at Daine and Numair. —*Follow us, please.*—

She led the way with composure. Scamp frolicked around them, asking questions nonstop, in spite of Grizzle's frequent orders to leave their guests alone. Scamp was convinced that humans spend their time fighting, and—sadly, Daine thought—she knew enough of the present state of things that it was hard to persuade her otherwise. Finally, Leaf stuck its head out of Daine's shirt and chittered angrily at her. The shock was so great that Scamp actually held her tongue for a moment before pelting them with questions about darkings.

"Is your grandfather the, um, king?" the mage asked as they turned downhill to walk beside a deep stream.

—*King?*— asked Scamp, distracted from her pursuit of a butterfly. —*What's a king?*—

—*They rule mortals,*— Grizzle replied smugly. —*The male ones, that is. The female rulers are queens.*—

—*Oh,*— was Scamp's comment. —*But you'd always have to change them, wouldn't you? Since they're always dying?*—

Daine bit her lip to keep from grinning. "It's true," she said gravely when she'd gotten herself under control. "Mortals must forever change leaders because they die. That's why we're called mortals."

—*I wouldn't like to be mortal,*— Scamp remarked wisely. —*Uncle Moonwind has been teaching me about mortality. It sounds uncomfortable.*—

—*He's not really our uncle,*— said Grizzle. —*Just like Grandsire isn't our grandfather, exactly. He's our great-great-great-* . . . *I don't remember how many* greats. *There are a lot of them. Grandfather. He's the oldest—*

—*No,*— interrupted Scamp. —*Moonwind, Rainbow, and Cometfern are older.*—

—*He's the biggest* . . . Now *what are you looking at?*— demanded the older dragon: Scamp was staring at the sky. When she did not answer, Grizzle looked up. —*Uh-oh.*—

An enormous blue-green shape crested the winds over a hill. Regally it glided toward them on huge, bat-like wings boned in silver.

"Is there a problem?" asked Numair. Daine saw that both dragons' scales bristled.

—*It's Jewelclaw,*— replied Grizzle. —*He's not very nice.*—

—*He can't do anything,*— Scamp told them, but she trembled. Waves of pink, the color that Kitten turned at those rare times when she was afraid, washed over her body. Grizzle, too, had acquired a rosy tinge, harder to see against her darker scales. —*They're here to see Grandsire, not him.*—

The mature dragon lit on the ground and advanced, wings half extended. Until now, the only adult dragon that Daine and Numair had seen was Kitten's mother, a young female who had measured twenty feet from nose to hindquarters. This dragon was nearly forty feet long, with a tail that was half again as long as he was. His scales were a deep, almost glowing shade of blue-green on his back, then emerald green on his belly. Like other dragons, this one had silver talons and teeth, in addition to the silver bones that gleamed inside the delicate hide of his wings. His eyes, emerald around slit pupils like a cat's, were cold indeed. Sparks and threads of fire similar to lightning jumped over his scales; his head crest was raised.

—*Who let* mortals *into the Dragonlands?*— His voice was a roar in Daine's mind. —*You two will find this to be far more serious than your usual pranks!*— He bridled, scales ruffling. The grass under his talons began to scorch.

Grizzle jumped between Jewelclaw and the humans. —*You can't touch them!*— she cried. She was now an eye-smarting shade of pink, with no trace of gray, but she stood her ground. Scamp, also entirely pink, scrambled to stand next to her. Tiny sparks flared on both youngsters. —*They are under Grandsire's protection.*—

—*Then Diamondflame will answer to the Dragonmeet! Out of my way!*— Jewelclaw ordered, wings fanning. —*They will be my captives!*—

—No!— Scamp's voice was shrill, but firm. *—She's the one who's raising Skysong!—*

—Raising? Or imprisoning?— demanded the adult.

Numair crossed his arms. "If you know anything about the young members of your race, you know that captivity is not an issue," he said mildly. "I do not believe there is a cage that could hold Kit—Skysong—if she wished to get out."

Leaf, still on Daine's shoulder, extended its head to chitter angrily at Jewelclaw. After a moment's pause, Jelly thrust its head through Numair's collar and chimed in.

—Must we tell Grandsire you took them from us?— Grizzle asked.

—The old newt has gone senile!— snarled Jewelclaw. *—And I'm not the only one to object! I'm not finished with this!—* He took to the air, the back draft of his wings making both humans and dragonets stagger.

—He is not senile!— Scamp shouted. If Jewelclaw heard, he gave no sign, flying off with hard, rapid beats. In a small voice she added, *—I bet his mother was a wyvern.—*

—Scamp!— cried Grizzle, shocked.

—I don't care. He's rotten. He's always rotten.

Come on,— she told Daine and Numair. —*Before anyone else comes after us.*—

When they reached a bridge that looked as if it had been spun from glass, the two young dragons raced ahead as if it were rough and sturdy wood. Daine and Numair, certain that mere humans might just slide off, were testing the bridge with their feet when crackling filled the air. Grizzle and Scamp halted in midspan, raising themselves up on their hindquarters as Kitten so often did. Jelly retreated inside Numair's shirt, while Leaf raised its head, looking for the cause of the disturbance.

—*There has been a change.*— The voice boomed in their minds all around them.

—*Grandsire, Jewelclaw came and yelled,*— cried Scamp.

—*I know it. He and the other Separatists have been dinning my ears since our guests came through the portal. They have called the Dragonmeet.*—

Scamp shrank inside her skin.

—*Uh-oh,*— Grizzle whispered softly.

—*Take them to the amphitheater,*— ordered the voice. —*Do not enter the floor with them, mind. Sit among our people.*— Voice and presence faded from their surroundings.

—Turn back,— Grizzle told them, dropping to her fours. *—At least it isn't far to go.—*

Daine and Numair exchanged glances. They needed to talk. "May we get a drink?" asked the girl as they stepped off the bridge. "And *I* need to relieve myself." The dragons nodded. Daine stepped into a cluster of bushes to empty her bladder, first making sure her urine wouldn't run into the water. Finished, she joined Numair. They crouched beside the stream to drink and wash their faces.

"What do you think?" asked the mage softly.

"We have to go. We can't force dragons, only persuade," she reminded him.

Scamp and Grizzle looked down at them from the top of the stream bank. *—Are you finished?—* Grizzle inquired. *—It's a bad idea to keep a Dragonmeet waiting.—*

Grizzle led them uphill from the bridge, following a broad track through knee-high grasses. When they crested the hill, they stood on the uppermost edge of a deep, tiered bowl in the earth. It was too regular to be natural, though grass flourished on the tiers. The floor of the amphitheater and the long ramps that cut it into eighths were bare earth, beaten and gouged by centuries of pressure from dragon paws and talons. At the far end of the giant oval was the only other exception to the grass carpet, a heap of glistening blue stones that was piled about the arena's rim.

Each tier was dragon-sized, big enough to contain even the largest of them when they crouched on all fours. A number of dragons were already present. Jewelclaw, for one, was installed near the western ramp. Miniature lightnings still played over his blue-green scales. He glared at them and returned to whatever he was saying to a sixty-foot dragon whose scales had the white glimmer of pearl. As Jewelclaw spoke, bursts of fire—Daine thought of heat lightning—came and went along the bigger dragon's hide.

Grizzle saw what the girl was looking at. —*The pearly one—that's Moonwind,*— the dragonet explained. —*She's one of the oldest. Her grandson Summerwing was the last dragon to willingly visit the mortal realms. That was before the Dragonmeet put a ban on visits. Um . . .*—

—*Stay away from Moonwind,*— Scamp said bluntly. —*She isn't even nice to people she likes.*—

"Just how old *is* this dragon?" asked Numair.

Scamp cocked her head, blinking. —*Fifty-five centuries, I think.*—

—*Fifty-nine,*— Grizzle corrected her. —*Come on.*

This way. — She started down the ramp, headed toward the arena floor.

"Your grandsire said you weren't to come with us," Daine said quietly, watching the adult dragons. They were huge creatures whose scales blazed with color, some of them twenty or thirty feet longer than Moonwind. The girl didn't know if their kind formed lynch mobs, but there was enough mob feeling here that she didn't want to take any chances.

Busy watching the larger dragons, she didn't see the seven young ones until they swarmed around the humans, curiosity in their eyes. One was nearly as small as Kitten, still unable to use mind speech. Others were as big as, or bigger than, Scamp and Grizzle. Behind them, walking majestically, as befitted their age, came a handful of dragons fifteen and twenty feet long, the length that Kitten's mother had been—adolescents.

— *We'll* all *escort you,* — Grizzle announced proudly. The humans were swept along by young dragons, unable to protest, across the beaten earth of the arena floor.

The price of their escort was a hail of questions about the mortal realms. Daine left Numair to answer. She was counting the adults present—thirty-three thus far—when the air exploded to her right. Where there had been nothing but empty space a moment ago, a sixty-foot black dragon crouched.

—*Aunt Nightbreath!*— cried Grizzle. —*You're not supposed to materialize so close to everyone else!*—

—*Oh, tut,*— the dragon replied, coolly amused. —*I haven't fouled anyone in a materialization since I was* your *age.*— There was more than a hint of wicked glee in her eyes as she added, —*I was in a hurry. This may be my only chance to see humans before these two are made into fertilizer for Moonwind's rosebushes.*—

The young dragons protested her cynicism. Daine reached out instinctively, and Numair took her hand. He kept it as they reached the center of the Dragonmeet floor. Their escort remained with them when they stopped at last.

Three dragons appeared on the highest part of the arena. The blast of air caused by their arrival made the humans stagger. Daine gulped, and clutched Numair's hand tighter. All of the newcomers were over a hundred feet long. The biggest, whose scales were a pale, delicate green, was fully a hundred and twenty feet in length.

—*That's Wingjade,*— Scamp whispered, seeing where Daine looked. —*My father.*—

"Biiiig," commented Leaf.

"Too big," squeaked Jelly, its head protruding from the V of Numair's shirt.

— We start, — boomed a golden dragon directly across the amphitheater from the mortals. — Diamondflame is charged with ignoring the will of the Dragonmeet, and with permitting humans to enter the Dragonlands. Humans, the question is asked: Why have you come here? —

"You should do the talking," Numair told Daine softly. "You are Kitten's guardian."

Daine was about to reply when a mind voice yelled, — No one cares what they want! Kill them! — Looking around, the girl saw a mottled black-and-white dragon who sat up, balanced on his back legs. — Kill them, and bring Skysong home! — Slowly he fell back to his fours.

Nearby, a second dragon reared onto its haunches. — Our law bids us to first hear what they have to say. —

Moonwind sat up. — They and their defenders lost their right to claim justice under our law when my grandson was murdered by their kind. Look at them. Already they cause trouble here. Already they try to seduce our young away from us. —

— We aren't seduced! — cried a younger dragon hotly. — They're new; they're different. We could learn

215

from them—except you *and* your *crowd have closed minds!—*

—Silence!— roared Moonwind. Daine and Numair cringed away from the force of her rage, while the young dragon who had spoken clawed at his muzzle.

—Now you've done it,— whispered Grizzle to the gagged youngster. *—You'd better hope that she takes the Silence off you before you get too hungry.—*

—If you felt that humans were not to be treated with under our law, Sister Moonwind, you should have amended the law in the four centuries since your loss,— snapped a new adult. *—You know as well as I that all changes in law must be reviewed, debated, and considered. You cannot demand that it be changed here and now.—*

"Excuse me," said Daine, wanting to answer the initial question. The dragons continued to argue about legal issues. Red tinted the scales of most present; lightning, in sheets or threads, danced over more than a few. "Excuse me!"

"Try again," murmured Numair. Black fire glimmered around the hand he placed on the nape of her neck.

She took a deep breath. *"EXCUSE ME!"* she cried. Her voice, amplified by the mage's spell, thundered in the bowl of the arena. Daine winced, and used a quieter tone. "All we want is to go home—that's it. We don't like being here any more than you want us. So, if you could take us back to the mortal realms, we're quits."

—*No one asked you.*— Jewelclaw did more than sit up. He stepped onto the ramp and began to walk down toward them. Balls and rails of lightning raced around his hide as it turned a deep crimson, the color of dragon rage. —*You* humans. *How could we have allowed you to continue to exist, with your murderous hearts, your waste, and your noise? It's time to scour the mortal realms clean. We can start with you.*—

"You *dare.*" Numair took his hand from Daine's back. Suddenly it was hard for the girl to breathe. She stepped away from him and the sudden bloom of his power.

—*Do you think we fear you, mortal?*— the black-and-white dragon asked as he stepped onto the ramp behind Jewelclaw. —*No human can face down a dragon!*—

A burst of wind threw Daine back. Moonwind had vanished from her station, to reappear on the beaten earth of the floor.

Numair handed Jelly to Scamp, ignoring the

darking's unhappy cries, and advanced on Moonwind. With each deliberate step that he took, fresh power shivered the air around him, as if he gathered magic like a cloak.

Daine gave Leaf to Grizzle and unlaced her over-large shirt, looking at the pair of smaller dragons on the ramp. Her skin was clammy and tingling with fear, her knees weak. She wished passionately that she knew more about dragons. Swiftly she reviewed forms she could take: A big one might slow her down, make her an easy target. A falcon's claws and beak could make an impression, and she would be fast.

—*There are mortals who may battle us on an equal footing.*— The speaker was a lean, knobby dragon who sat in the lowest tier. He did not bother to rise on his haunches. His green, red, blue, and yellow scales were pale, as if coated in dust. The two on the ramp halted; even Moonwind looked at him. —*Not many, but some. Your coterie has chosen to ignore that which does not add to your overweening selfishness in regard to which species have importance, and which ones do not... Or are you merely stupid? I never could decide which it was, though perhaps I should have.*—

—*You do not understand the matter, Ancestor Rainbow!*— snapped the black-and-white dragon.

Pale eyes swept over Daine as the elderly dragon looked in the direction of Jewelclaw and his companion. Seeing no pupils, she realized that Rainbow was blind.

—*Do I not?*— he asked, voice mild. —*Well, you are entitled to your opinions, Riverwind, however foolish they may be. I too am entitled to my opinion, which is that I grow weary of your bad manners. Leave the Dragonmeet.*—

The black-and-white dragon reared. He clawed at the air with his forepaws, screeching so high and so loudly that Daine felt a pressure like thumbs in her ears. His screech dwindled rapidly, as did he, until he vanished from sight.

For a long, still moment, there was no sound in the arena.

Daine was taking a deep breath when all of the dragons spoke at once, mind voices blending into a wordless roar in her mind.

She heard one voice clearly: Jewelclaw's. —*The humans are mine!*— He trotted down the ramp. Moonwind raised a forepaw and unfurled her immense wings. Numair faced her, the air rippling and bending visibly where it touched him.

Daine jumped, taking goshawk shape as her feet

left the ground. Her clothes dropped, empty. With a screech, she sped toward Jewelclaw.

—*Enough,*— said the crackling mind voice that had spoken to Daine and Numair near the bridge. Jewelclaw froze in his tracks.

—*When did my* personal *invitation to guests of my clan become a matter for every wing and claw in the Dragonlands to discuss, and interfere with?*— What Daine had thought was a huge pile of blue stones uncoiled, and walked leisurely to the amphitheater floor. Diamondflame—Grandsire—was a dragon over eighty feet in length from nostrils to rump. While she could see larger dragons, none had a presence that made the air hum as he approached Moonwind and Numair.

Daine kept a wary eye on Jewelclaw as she drifted overhead. Diamondflame's scales were a shiny blue so dark as to be nearly black, picked out with flecks of gold and violet. A golden crest rose from his broad forehead and swept down to his shoulders, lending him a stern, crowned aspect. His large indigo eyes glittered with intelligence.

—*I understand your grief for your grandson, Moonwind, but only to a point. With no law passed by the Dragonmeet, I am entirely within my rights* to welcome my grandchild's guardians to my home. It should not matter if they are human, dragons, or dragonflies. They are my guests, and no business of the Dragonmeet!—

—Ancestor Rainbow, I demand a ruling,— hissed the pearl-scaled dragon. —Humans in the Dragonlands are no matter of personal choice, as Diamondflame has said, but of the will of the Dragonmeet. I vote to dump them into the Sea of Sand and let them cook.—

—Will the Dragonmeet now tell each dragon what guest to have, what to read, when to have children?— Diamondflame wanted to know. —I am within my rights, the ones granted to me and to every dragon by the Golden Dragonmeet, to accept the visit of the guardians of my grandchild, without certain meddlers getting involved.—

—Now he calls "meddlers" those who wish only to see dragonkind return to power in all the realms!— cried Jewelclaw. —Have you old and conservative ones turned to wyverns and salamanders?—

—Humans or no humans, I must say that I have not heard such insolence from the young in the last thousand years as I have heard today,— said the one called Rainbow. Slowly he lowered himself from his grassy seat and walked over to Diamondflame. —*I will judge now.*— He sat on his haunches and rose up, many-colored scales tightening over his knobby, fragile-looking skeleton. Slowly, as gracefully as a dancer, he stretched out enormous, nearly transparent, bat wings. The sun glinted off the silvery bones within them, and painted glowing light over the old dragon.

—*I ordain as Rainbow Windheart, governor of the Dragonmeet, oldest of the Firefolk, with a hundred centuries under my wings. By the Compact of the Godwars and the vote of the Golden Dragonmeet, I speak for all of us, until the day comes that I am taken back to Mother Flame.*—

Settling a bit, he turned those blind eyes on the blue-green dragon. —*Out of my sight, Jewelclaw. If I see you before a century has passed, I shall not be so kind again as I am right now.*— Heat passed under Daine's tail feathers on its way from Rainbow to the younger dragon. Jewelclaw dodged the bolt with a snarl and jumped into flight, lunging at the girl-goshawk.

Something—not Jewelclaw—clutched her tightly. She felt *squeezed*, as if she had turned to icing in a pastry cook's tube. A strangled cry burst from her lips; she could feel herself dropping as her eyes went dark.

When she opened them again, she lay on the ground, fully dressed, staring at the sky.

—*The only way dragons can live together is to vow to keep their muzzles out of one another's private lives.*— The mind voice was Rainbow's; he sounded close by. —*When we wrote our laws at the Golden Dragonmeet, we made sure of that. When I spoke in my office as governor, they could not argue, under the laws of that same meet.*—

Two ink-blot heads stretched into her vision, one over her left eye, one over her right. Leaf squeaked, "Awake now!"

The next faces Daine saw were those of Grizzle and Scamp. Over their head, within a heartbeat's time, she saw Numair, his dark eyes worried. Behind him, the great blue dragon peered down at her.

"What happened?" she asked, blinking.

Scamp moved out of the way. Into the space she had filled in Daine's vision came the muzzle and blind eyes of Rainbow. His mind voice sounding like wind-tossed leaves, he said, —*Forgive my lack of precision in grabbing you out of harm's way, Godborn. I allowed Jewelclaw to upset me. What you felt was dragon magic, nothing more.*—

"I'm glad it *was* nothing more." Daine felt oddly

peaceful. "Think how upsetting it might be to get squeezed from a shape—like milk from a teat—by something big."

"Is she all right?" Numair asked the blue dragon, worried. "Not—damaged?"

—*She seems well enough now,*— was Diamond-flame's reply.

"You don't know her as I do. She's *never* this philosophical about surprises."

Reaching out, the blind dragon pulled Daine into a sitting position, his grip gentle. "My bones are all wobbly," she confided to him in a whisper. Looking around, she saw that many of the adult dragons had left. "Where'd everybody go?"

—*Where they would have been if Moonwind and her Separatists had not chosen to meddle in business that was not theirs,*— said Diamondflame. —*They have gone home. Ancestor Rainbow ruled that your visit, concerned as it was with returning to my grandchild, was a matter for my clan alone.*—

The blue dragon reared, towering over the girl. Numair and Rainbow steadied her as she got to her knees, then her feet.

—*Who will help me convey these mortals out of the Dragonlands?*—asked Diamondflame.

The young dragons, who had remained, clamored to go. When he looked down his muzzle at them, they silenced instantly. —*Those of you who can fly are too small. The rest of you cannot fly at all—and fly we must. You will remain here, and mind Ancestor Rainbow.*—

Daine's mouth twitched as Scamp grumbled, —*We never do anything interesting.*—

—*I will come with you.*— One of the few adults remaining, a gray-and-gold dragon fifty-six feet in length, came over to them. She was an elegant creature, slender without looking at all fragile. —*I am Wingstar. Your Skysong is my grandchild. The least I can do is bring her humans back to her.*—

—*Climb onto us,*— ordered Diamondflame. —*I believe the Dragonmeet is done.*—

He was right. One by one, the dragons were vanishing from the arena tiers. Only the youngsters and Rainbow stayed.

Leaf went to Daine, Jelly to Numair. Once the humans had settled the darkings into their favored riding spots—around Daine's neck and inside Numair's shirt—Wingstar sank low to the ground. —*I will take you, Weiryn's daughter. You do not appear to have so many bony angles to you.*—

Daine grinned at Numair and climbed onto the female dragon, settling in front of her wings. Numair had to ascend Diamondflame's foreleg to perch on the blue dragon's back.

—*Hold on to my crest,*— ordered Wingstar. —*It won't hurt me if you tug.*—

Under her legs Daine felt powerful muscles flex. "Wait!" she cried, remembering something. The dragons, Numair, and the darkings stared at her. "When we came through last time, we—more me, but both of us for a while—got fair sick. We need to tell you—"

—*Nothing,*— interrupted Diamondflame. —*You were brought here by lesser gods, not by dragons. You will not become ill in the least.*—

Disliking the slur on her parents, Daine muttered, "Pardon *me.*" Leaf giggled under her ear as the flap of immense wings blew her hair into her eyes. She closed them tightly as the dragons leaped up and forward, soaring into the air.

Wind buffeted her. Opening her eyes, she saw that Diamondflame was in the lead, taking them into a cloud bank. Daine shivered; it was cool and clammy, and she couldn't see. Feeling a tickle on her cheek that had to be Leaf's hat, she asked, "Still funfun?"

"More fun," the darking replied.

"You have a happy nature, little one," she grumbled.

Up the dragons climbed, flying a corkscrew pattern through the clouds. Daine sensed Stormwings only a few moments before they came upon them, but as before, she recognized at least one, and very likely three, presences among them.

When the dragons emerged in clear, very cold air, Barzha, Hebakh, Rikash, and their followers awaited them. All of the immortals were armed.

— *You have interesting friends,* — remarked Wingstar.

"If you don't mind, we will go with you to the mortal realms." Barzha's voice sounded odd in the thin air. "We have business to settle."

— *I will not wait if you fall behind,* — Diamondflame warned them.

The Stormwings grinned, steely teeth glinting, as they took up positions to the rear and sides of the dragons. Rikash was the only one to glide between them.

"Is this wise?" Daine asked. "Ozorne's folk outnumber you almost four to one."

"Since when are Stormwings wise?" he called, and laughed.

Diamondflame and Wingstar began their descent,

gliding in a broad spiral that carried them into the clouds once more. Clammy, damp fingers brushed the girl's face and wound in her hair. Gray fog blinded her again. "More fun, more fun," commented Leaf.

They broke through the clouds.

She expected to see Dragonlands or desert. What lay below was a tangled web of barns and gardens, and a sprawling complex of gray stone buildings tucked behind high walls in front and low ones behind. From the high walls, the land sloped down a green, unclut-tered expanse before reaching tree groves around low-lying temples. On the far side of the groves lay a vast city flung on both sides of a broad river.

They were over the capital, and royal palace, of Tortall.

Daine frowned. The voices of the People filled her mind, but they were not tense or wary, as they had been when Port Caynn and the surrounding areas were under attack. Shaping her eyes to those of a raptor, she examined palace and city. Soldiers were everywhere, afoot, on horseback, or patrolling the river, but she saw no fighting, and a great deal of rebuilding. People were hard at work all over the palace grounds, too, piling debris for wagons to carry away. There were patrols on the walls and within the palace grounds, but nowhere did she find evidence of the enemy, except for two large prison stockades that lay east of the palace.

The dragons circled high above the palace; their Stormwing escort did the same. "Why come *here*?" Numair shouted to Diamondflame. "Skysong is at Port Legann!"

—*Why are we here?*— asked Wingstar, mind voice dry. —*You guided us, Diamondflame, and I too thought you would take us to our grandchild. I don't even see an army in this place.*—

—*The god of the duckmoles is here,*— said Diamondflame. —*I want to know why.*—

Wingstar stared at the blue dragon. —*Broad Foot? In this city?*—

—*On the other side of the world from his mortal children,*—Diamondflame replied grimly as Numair and Daine exchanged looks. —*Involving himself in mortal affairs.*—

"How do you know all this?" the mage asked loudly.

—*I am a dragon,*— was the haughty reply. —*My power tells me a great many things that you are blind and deaf to.*—

Silver glittered in front of them, condensing slowly as Broad Foot appeared. Daine reached for him before she remembered where they were. The duckmole was thin, his eyes sunken. "What's happened to you?" she cried. "You look terrible!"

He clapped his bill gently in a duckmole laugh. —*I overestimated my ability to contain Malady. It will not break free of me, but . . . it fights.*— His mind voice—the only way the animal gods could speak in the mortal realms—sounded weak.

—*This is incredible!*— boomed Diamondflame. —*What possible interest have you in the affairs of humans?*—

The duckmole snorted. —*Have you dragons shut yourselves off so completely from affairs in the mortal and divine realms? Can you not feel the battle that is raging? Read the Chaos currents around you!*—

—*Humans and their wars,*— snapped Wingstar, but Daine heard doubt in her voice.

—*If she overturns the mortal and divine realms, how long do you think it will be until she turns on the Dragonlands?*— Broad Foot wanted to know. —*You have made them separate from the Divine Realms, but you share a common border with them, and Uusoae is nothing but appetite. Even when fed to gorging, she hungers still.*—

"Would you dragons mind setting down for a

moment?" asked Numair. "I would like to learn what the situation is here."

—*And I would like to talk to you, duckmole,*—said Diamondflame, gliding down to light on a broad expanse before the palace wall. Daine saw the soldiers' bows follow them down. The catapults on the walls were being turned in order to dump rocks and liquid fire on the dragons, if necessary. She crossed her fingers and prayed that none of the defenders would lose control—she had the feeling that Diamondflame and Wingstar would have little mercy for human error. Looking over, she saw Numair talking into a small, fiery globe on his palm. He'd opened a speech spell to one of the mages below, and was explaining matters, talking with a speed only he could manage.

When the dragons settled on the bare earth, a gate in the wall opened, and two people came riding out. One, mounted on a horse and wearing chain mail, was unmistakably a knight, albeit older than most of the knights on active duty. His long-haired companion wore the brown tunic and trousers of the Queen's Riders and rode a mountain pony. Daine waved. She knew Duke Gareth the Elder and Buri, a commander of the Riders, almost as well as Numair did.

"They're friends," she told Wingstar as the female

extended her forelegs, raising her chest, and the girl, higher in the air. "It's all right."

—*They may well be friends, but do they know that we* are?— The female sank down again. Once she was close enough to the ground, Daine slid off her back and went to their welcoming committee. Numair caught up with her, as Diamondflame, Wingstar, and Broad Foot turned their backs to everyone else and spoke mind to mind.

Tugging an earlobe, Duke Gareth eyed the dragons. "I had thought that I was past being shocked by your companions," the king's uncle said. "Clearly I was mistaken."

"You should have seen where we got them," Numair informed him, shaking hands with Buri. "Where's the queen? For that matter, where's the enemy?"

"Gone, except for our prisoners." Dismounting from her pony, Buri came to give Daine a hug. "They scrambled out of here half a day before a relieving force from the Yamani Islands came in—just pulled up stakes and vanished."

"We still maintain our forces on alert, however," the duke told them. "Just in case the enemy attempts something crafty. The army is camped throughout the Royal Forest, and between here and Port Caynn."

"Thayet took a picked force and some mages and went south on some of the Yamani ships," Buri told them. "They're going to try to break the siege at Port Legann."

Daine gasped. "There's a relief fleet going there from the Copper Isles! They'll be caught betwixt and between!"

"I'd ask how you know, except anybody can tell you've been strange places," the little K'mir remarked, looking at the dragons.

"We'll have to catch up with Her Majesty, then," Numair said. "You're certain everything is well here?"

Duke Gareth smiled. "Enough that you can go to them. We are well situated. You know that Her Majesty would not have left us vulnerable —"

"No more than she'd go if she thought there was still work to do here," added Buri.

Daine looked at the dragons and the duckmole. "Will you take us to the queen?" she asked. "They're at sea, on their way to Port Legann."

—The badger and Gold-streak are with them,— added Broad Foot. He had ended his secret conference with the dragons.

—We will do more than convey you to her,— said Wingstar. —Broad Foot has told us enough that my *mate and I have decided to help you, and our grand-child, fight.—*

"Do you think your fellow dragons might be concerned enough about the danger from Uusoae to fight on our side as well?" Numair asked hopefully.

—If you are prepared to wait a few decades for them to reach the decision,— said Diamondflame, mind voice dry. *—That is one reason why few of us will argue with a personal choice. Long-lived as we are, we still would die of old age before our peers would agree on anything.—*

Numair winced. "Please, forget I asked."

Barzha glided down to join them, her elegant brows knit in a frown. "Why do you gab here like pigeons?" she demanded. "Ozorne is not here. Our people are not here."

—I needed to speak to the duckmole,— Diamondflame said.

"You have spoken, have you not? Then let's find our battle," snapped Barzha. "We didn't come to admire scenery."

Daine and Numair gave Duke Gareth and Buri a hasty farewell and climbed onto the dragons' backs once more. As they flew up, leaving the palace and the capital far below, Wingstar remarked, *—I see no reason* for us to tire ourselves by flying all that way to their queen's ships—not if we can use the spiral spell to transport all of us.—

—Come, Stormwings,— said the blue dragon. — Let us keep our strength for our enemy.— Up they flew until they disappeared into the clouds again.

9

THE BATTLE OF LEGANN

UNDER THE COVER OF DRAGON SPELLS AND THE night, Daine watched as Queen Thayet of Tortall landed her army on a beach a day's march north of Port Legann. All around the girl, men, Riders, knights, mounts, and immortals waded onto the sand as carefully and quietly as they could. The two dragons, as well as centaurs and ogres, towed the ships' longboats. These were packed to the rim with arms and supplies, first to be emptied on the land, then to be sent back for more. In the morning, the relief force would try to cut through a dense forest that lay between this beach and the enemy's main camp. Their task would be easier than it had been for enemies of Tortall: It seemed that Wingstar knew spells that would hide and silence their passage. Ozorne and his commanders thought they were safe from attack on their rear, knowing the forest was nearly impassable, and having mages experienced at the detection of other mages' spells. The dragons had been quick to assure the queen that no mortal or immortal could sense *their* power. Remembering old tales of dragons who walked through cities unnoticed while shrouded in their magic, Thayet had accepted their offer of help.

Daine sighed. She would not be with the army: She was to act as courier between Thayet's force and Port Legann, with Diamondflame himself to take her back and forth. In a pack she carried things that the king and Lord Imrah of Legann should find helpful: bespelled mirrors for use in communicating with the queen and her generals, maps of the plan of attack both for the queen's land army and for the Yamani ships, and descriptions of the extremely varied collection of folk who would be fighting on Tortall's side.

Someone tapped her shoulder; turning, Daine found Queen Thayet. Co-ruler of Tortall, she was dressed in the simple Rider uniform and wore her crow's-wing black hair tightly braided. Only the helmet tucked

under her arm bore any royal insignia, a small gold
crown set over the visor. She also carried a soft leather
bag, which she offered to Daine. Taking it, the girl
realized that it held something heavy that was the size
of her palm.

"If you'd give this to my lord, I would appreciate
it," Queen Thayet told Daine. "And tell him that I said
the *next* time he goes on a long tour of our embattled
cities, he had better take the Dominion Jewel with him.
I don't know how to wield the dratted thing."

"You know he hates to use it." Harailt of Aili, chief
of the mages in Tortall's royal university, came over,
rubbing his hands against the chill. "He thinks it's a
crutch. He doesn't want to be too dependent on it."

"With a relief force coming here from the Copper
Isles, we need all the help we can get," Thayet said
flatly. She kissed the girl's cheek. "Good luck," she
whispered, and went to the longboat that awaited her,
Harailt close behind. Leaning over the rail, Daine
waved to the badger and Gold-streak, who had been
in the boat when they lowered it from the ship. Her
reunion with them had lasted only half a day: They
would stay with the queen and her generals, sending
messages to the commanders through the darkings
who had spied on them until recently.

Daine turned Thayet's leather pouch over in her hands. She'd heard tales that with his jewel King Jonathan could ask the very plants and stones to rise up in defense of the realm. "I'll believe it when I see it," she muttered. Tying the long drawstrings around her neck, she stuffed the pouch inside her shirt, to hang next to the badger's claw. Leaning on the rail, she squinted at the shore. She wanted to get *moving*.

"Fretting about your stork-man?" Rikash inquired, lighting on the rail beside her. He dug steel talons into the wood. "He'll be fine. Mages always are."

"I'd feel better about that if I could be here to look after him."

"Then stay."

"I can't," Daine replied, shaking her head. "I don't want Kitten there without me when the big noise starts. In the Dragonlands, I saw—she's just a baby still. She ought to be in a safe place. Since she isn't, I need to be with her, as much as I can."

"You're breaking my heart," drawled the immortal.

"Got a bit of sand in your crop?" she demanded irritably. "A swallow or two of oil should wash it right out the end that does your thinking for you."

To her surprise he laughed. Around them, she saw gold-skinned Yamanis and Tortallans make the Sign against evil. "I deserved that. Don't mind me." He fell silent again, flexing his talons, digging chips of brightly colored enamel from the rail. All the Yamani ship rails looked tattered after two days of Stormwing company. "Barzha and Hebakh said to wish you happy hunting," he said abruptly. "And if they get to Ozorne first, they'll save you a piece." He grinned, showing all of his pointed steel teeth. "Perhaps it's treasonous of me, but I really think *I* would like to reach Ozorne ahead of them. If I do, they may take all the leftovers from me. How about if I just tell him you said good-bye, before I rip him apart?"

"That's very thoughtful of you," Daine told him solemnly, her eyes dancing with laughter. "I appreciate that."

Rikash looked up at her, green eyes black in the lamplight. "I *think,* if I'm careful, I can at least keep one of his braids for you. I'll try, anyway." He tossed his long blond hair, making the bones that were braided into it click. "Souvenirs are always important." His tone changed to one of mockery. "Gods help us, it's the stork-man, come to make sure I'm not corrupting you. Has your grand conference ended, Longshanks?"

Numair joined them. "It has. There go Barzha and Hebakh now." He pointed to the silvery shapes flapping their way to shore. The rest of the Stone Tree nation was there already, perched on the limbs of trees that edged the forest.

"And I must follow, like a good servant," Rikash commented. "I'll see you both when the dust settles in two days." He took off, gliding over the water. At the last second, he swerved to avoid a collision with the back of Wingstar's neck. The dragon whirled and lunged, jaws snapping. The Stormwing rolled, inches from her muzzle, flipped up his tail, and sped on.

Numair put an arm around Daine's shoulders. "It's time," he said quietly.

"Come with me," she whispered, turning to grab a fistful of his shirt. Jelly squeaked at her. "Well, if you wouldn't hide in his clothes all the time," she snapped.

"Magelet, I can't." Numair caressed her face, eyes intent on hers. "No one else can take on Inar Hadensra, not without risking lives needlessly. He could have been a black robe mage like me, but—he thought the university was too confining. He's in the main camp for certain—I can sense him even at this distance. I *must* be there when Thayet attacks."

"You get into so much trouble without me to look after you," she whispered.

He kissed her forehead. "You belong in Legann.

Make sure that Jonathan understands what Gainel told us. It's not the kind of thing we can trust to a letter or speech spell. He's *got* to see that it's vital to capture or kill Uusoae's pawn, Valmar of the Copper Isles. Diamondflame says he'll get Deniau of the Copper Isles when his fleet reaches Legann." He sighed, staring into the dark with troubled eyes. "And we'll just have to hope she is drawing on those two or Inar Hadensra, or Ozorne, not one of the other immortals that were in our dream, because we have no way to identify them."

Daine threw her arms around the man's neck. They kissed with hunger and desperation, holding each other tight. Jelly shrilled in protest; they ignored the darking.

Slowly, at last, she opened her arms, and Numair let her slide to the deck. "I love you," he whispered. "If you get yourself killed, I will *never* forgive you."

That got a laugh from her, albeit a weak one. Numair offered his handkerchief. "You'll need it," she said, and wiped her eyes on her sleeve.

"Something else." Reaching into his shirt, he pulled Jelly out. "We talked about this," he told the darking firmly. "You'll be much better off with Daine and Leaf."

The darking stretched its neck long until it could

rub its head against his cheek, then retracted until it was a small blob once more. Daine turned. The mage tucked the darking into the compartment of the pack where Leaf already waited.

—If these touching farewells are done with?— Diamondflame hovered effortlessly beside the ship. They hadn't even heard his approach. *—We too must be on our way.—*

Daine and Numair exchanged a last, swift kiss, before the girl climbed onto the rail. Numair steadied her until Diamondflame's magic hands picked her up and deposited her on his back. They began to rise. Daine looked at Numair and blew him a kiss, trying to ignore an inner voice that said she would probably never see him again.

Light sparkled at the corner of her eye: a speaking spell. Phantom lips touched her cheek, and his voice whispered in her ear, "Goddess bless, my darling."

Two days later, in the hour before sunrise, the girl stood on Legann's Northgate watchtower. She knew what lay in the shadows below. Yesterday, as the queen's army advanced, she had mapped battlefields and camps, riding on Diamondflame's back, with his magic to keep them invisible. Copies of her maps went both to the city's defenders and to Thayet, borne by Wingstar. Now the Tortallan rulers knew their opponents' every position. The queen and her forces waited at the forest's edge. It was nearly time to ford the river between them and their enemies, time to begin the day's grim work.

The image of the land before her was etched into her brain. A swath of torn-up ground hundreds of yards wide lay before Legann's outer wall, littered with bodies that had begun to swell, blacken, and stink in the summer heat. With them lay abandoned weapons; shattered spears, arrows, and pikes; stones from Legann's catapults; and wide, scorched gouges where the war mages had battled.

Farther back, out of catapult range, Ozorne's allies had set their defenses. The first of these was a row of logs roped together in X's, their outer ends sharpened to gut any horse that tried to leap over them. Next came lines of trenches, designed to break the legs of horses and men that managed to get through the log fence, and to shelter the enemy's soldiers when arrows were flying. The third barrier was a low, rounded earthen wall. Behind that lay the main enemy camp itself, in a low valley with a river cutting through.

She'd mapped the positions of everything out there.

As the light improved, she saw the shadowy forms of sentries on top of the low earth wall, just as she could see the tall, wooden towers that the enemy used as lookout posts. If the defenders ever let those towers get close enough, they would also give Ozorne's allies a way to reach the top of Legann's curtain wall.

Shivering, the girl drew the blanket that—with the badger's claw—was her only covering even closer. Beside her, Dominion Jewel in one hand, a speech-and-vision-spelled mirror in the other, was King Jonathan. With the mirror, he was in contact with his queen. His generals had such mirrors, too, to pass news to him more quickly than runners could.

"Are you sure you ought to be here?" Onua, Daine's first Tortallan friend, asked the king. She had come to Legann while Numair and Daine were in the Divine Realms, and had reserved the right to stick to the king's side. "It's foolish to risk yourself out in the open. If one lucky Stormwing slashes you, I'm left to tell Thayet why I let you do this."

"I distrust any advice that contains the words *ought* or *should*," he replied coolly. "And I can't wield the Dominion Jewel from inside, Onua. I have to see where I use it."

Daine leaned forward and mouthed, "I told you

so" to Onua. The K'mir smiled, wry. She hadn't really expected Jonathan to take her advice.

Kitten chirped to Daine. The girl awkwardly stooped, clutching her blanket, and used one arm to lift the dragonet into a rectangular notch in the wall. The sky over the hills in the east had gone pink.

In the wide, flat space inside the wall behind the king, light bent as Diamondflame moved. The tower guards couldn't see him, but they *felt* him, and walked, when they had to, pressed against the wall. The dragon's invisibility was less of a problem for his allies than visibility. Not only did it keep him from the notice of the enemy's spies, but at the few times that he *had* appeared, there had been panic in the city.

Hearing the clank of armor, Daine looked around. Lord Imrah, ruler of the fief of Legann, had reached the tower roof. He was no more able to see the dragon than his men, but he knew Diamondflame was there, and at least he did not press against the wall and sidle along. He walked as if he would normally follow the edge of the circular deck, rather than cut straight across it. Daine, with her hands on Kitten, could see that Diamondflame moved his tail out of the nobleman's way.

The girl made room so that Imrah could stand next to the king; the lord nodded his thanks. At first she had not liked this bald, large-bellied man. With his pale eyes and pockmarked face, he looked cruel. The night before, at supper with Jonathan and his leaders, though, she had caught Legann's master feeding Leaf, Jelly, and the Legann darkings under the table. "Well, they look like shadows of their former selves," he'd said then, and winked.

Now he smoothed his salt-and-pepper mustache. "Almost time, isn't it?"

"We'll get the queen's signal at any moment," Jonathan murmured, watching the view to the north. Shadows and light began to mark the landscape, outlining structures and the dead.

"I hope these Yamanis can handle those ships blockading my harbor," Imrah said to no one in particular. "They seem pretty confident they can handle them and that fleet from the Copper Isles."

—*It will not be Yamanis alone,*— Diamondflame said, mind voice crisp. —*Do you but handle your side of this mess. Leave ship warriors to those who can best handle them.*—

"I think your daughter Flamewing believed she could handle ship things, too," Daine said, shivering. "And they handled *her* instead." She smiled briefly at Tkaa, who had come to join them.

247

—She was barely more than a kit,— the invisible dragon said kindly. *—You will see. It is rare for adult dragons to be caught.—*

The sun's rim crested the eastern hill. To the north, beyond the enemy's defenses, light sparked.

Kitten chirped. "Wingstar is in flight," Tkaa said. Like Daine, he rested a paw on Kitten, or neither of them could have seen a thing. Dragons, apparently, could not hide from one another, and those close enough to a dragon to touch it would see what the dragon saw.

Imrah scratched his bald crown. Jonathan drew a deep breath. Daine watched that spark as it rose and grew bigger.

Before Wingstar reached the agreed-upon position, the girl silently called out to her friends among the People. The enemy had gotten careless in the time that she was away. Ozorne must have told his allies that she had gone: They had resumed tethering their mounts with rope and leather, and leaving them unwatched. Now that Ozorne had no darkings to supply him with information—they had all gone over to the badger and Gold-streak—he didn't know that Daine was back.

Steadying the enemy's horses and mules, Daine warned them again of the fright to come. The mounts shifted at her request, stretching their tethers to the limit.

High above the enemy's main camp, placed so that she could also be seen from Legann's walls, the dragon shed the spells that kept her invisible. Stretching out her long neck, she gave a feral shriek that brought sweat to the face of everyone who heard it. Pearl-gray scales blazed silver. Gold scales flared with a brilliance that was the essence of light. Wingstar was a living beacon over the enemy tents.

Even with Daine's warning, the mounts were terrified. They reared and lunged—and each rope and strap, carefully gnawed in the dark by sharp-toothed rodents, snapped. In a thunder of hooves, mules, ponies, and horses fled as soldiers jumped out of the way.

On the wall, Kitten replied to Wingstar with a trill that made Daine's ears hurt. The crenelated granite walls of Legann had been capped with pale gray stones. These now shimmered and glowed, throwing off light, but no heat.

—*She is so much more advanced than our young at home,*— remarked Diamondflame as he rose onto his hindquarters. —*Perhaps more of them should spend time here.*— He launched himself, giant wings pulling him aloft. Daine, Kitten, and Tkaa followed his flight; the other two-leggers were staggering in his back draft, fighting to recover their balance.

"I wish we had a sign that this flaming dragon was part of an *attack* or something," Imrah grumbled. "Those dung heaps might think it's just one of their *own* monsters enjoying the sunrise."

Diamondflame reached the sky over Legann harbor before he shed his cloaking spells. Before him lay the ships of the invading fleet, balked by the harbor's defenders and the chain across its mouth. Daine couldn't begin to imagine how the enemy—or even Legann's friends—felt at the sight of eighty feet of dragon overhead. Diamondflame snarled: Sails burst into flame. Wingstar too snarled. The sharpened logs in front of the trenches and the wooden towers behind the enemy's earth wall began to burn.

"Is that enough sign of an attack for you, my lord?" the king asked.

Imrah of Legann was a deliberate man. He walked over to get a better view of the harbor and its block-aders. The sailors were scrambling to douse their flaming ships as first Diamondflame, then Wingstar, descended on them, howling with fury. Legann's master returned to Jonathan's side. "It'll do," he said, reseating his helmet on his armored hip. With a half bow to the king, he began the climb from the watchtower to the ground.

Onua checked the fit of her arm guards and archer's gloves, and strung her bow.

Daine shifted nervously; she hated waiting for an enemy to come at her. "You stay right there, and don't move," she warned the pale blue dragonet. "If you tumble out, your grandda will cook me—once he and your grandma finish with the enemy's ships, anyway." Kitten chuckled and rubbed her muzzle against the girl's face. Leaf, who was coiled around Daine's neck, squeaked a protest.

Her mind filled with a metallic roar, a shrill hum, and a rattling buzz. Damping her magical hearing as far as she dared, she told her companions, "They're coming."

The K'mir leaned out of the notch in front of her and waved her bow. From the wall below the tower, a familiar voice boomed, "That's the signal, lambkins— string your bows! Wake *up*, Master Wooley! Storm- wings don't wait till you've finished your beauty sleep!" The hectoring voice faded as Sarge, the ex-slave who helped to train the Queen's Riders—and who fought with them—urged Legann's archers to prepare for the assault.

Daine, stretching the cramped muscles of her neck, smiled at the familiar roar that had woken her on so many days in the Rider barracks. She sent a prayer to the Goddess to shield him and his charges: Half of the archers on Legann's walls were as young or younger than she was, teenagers chosen for their precise eye and ability to hit what they shot at.

They needed prayer. Winged legions rose from the second enemy camp to the northeast. Sunlight blazed from Stormwing feathers, and glinted on the silver bones of hurrok wings and claws. With them flew winged apes armed with lances or axes.

At least there were no wyverns. Diamondflame had already told the king that they had sensed the arrival of mature dragons and fled. Though they had been willing to fight on with only a single, very young dragon to oppose them, they dared not try to challenge her grandparents.

"An ugly-looking crew, aren't they?" Marielle, Imrah's lady, joined them, recurved bow in hand, as the immortals came on. A tiny woman, she had lively brown eyes and kept her dark hair cropped short and close. She wore a leather jerkin studded with metal rings over a kilted-up dress; there were archer's gloves on her hands. Unhooking a spyglass from her belt, she surveyed the winged attackers. "You know, these look like they're *running* from something."

"They are," King Jonathan replied. "While Her Majesty's main force attacked in the northwest, her second force hit the camp in the northeast."

"What kind of force?" Marielle wanted to know.

"The badger god," replied Onua.

"Stormwing friends," piped Leaf. Jelly nodded.

Marielle raised her eyebrows. "If you say so, little ones," she said wryly. "Strange friends that we get in wartime."

Another darking stretched to put its eyeless head over Jonathan's shoulder—it was tucked into the king's belt purse. "Centaurs," it squeaked to Marielle. "Forty-four."

"Very true, Inkblot," Jonathan told Ozorne's one-time spy, now his companion and connection to other darkings. "Don't forget Sir Raoul, the Knight Commander of the King's Own. He mustered a hundred-odd ogres, as well as the centaurs. Those who chose to live with our laws are fighting for them."

The noblewoman laughed. "Do you know, sire, I think that if we live to tell our grandchildren about this war, they will accuse us of making it up."

Daine traded places with Tkaa, putting him at the

king's side and herself in front of a stone notch in the wall. Far below, she heard the grind of chains and wood: The portcullises on the north, east, and south gates were being raised, the drawbridges lowered. Imrah led mounted knights and men-at-arms from the north gate, to confront the soldiers who fled the queen's forces. Another company of mixed horsemen, foot soldiers, and archers was leaving by the east gate, Daine knew, and two Rider Groups were trotting their ponies out of the southern gate. If it worked, Ozorne's allies on land would be caught between the queen's relief force and Legann's defenders, just as his seagoing allies, the blockaders, would be pinched between the arriving ships and the harbor's defenders.

Where is Slaughter? Daine wondered. *She'll have plenty of work today.*

The noise level rose, fueled by the howls of winged immortals and the roar of enemy soldiers as they topped the rise between their camp and its outer defenses. Seeing the wooden towers that Wingstar had flamed blazing in front of them, some tried to turn back. Roots—belonging to trees long cut down to clear the battlefield—shot out of bare ground and twined around the ankles of the enemy. More runaways dodged the roots, only to meet Imrah and his knights.

From the valley where the enemy had camped, magic fires erupted and died as Tortallan mages attacked those serving the invaders.

The king was pale and gleaming with perspiration. Marielle and Onua also began to sweat as fear—Stormwing war terror—billowed ahead of the oncoming immortals. No one moved. It affected Daine as it did the others, but all of them had fought under the pressure of that fear before: The choice was fight or die.

"How many Stormwings did you say followed Ozorne?" Jonathan asked, his normally even voice strained.

"Two hundred and forty-eight, Your Majesty—if this is all of them coming at us now." The archers on wall and tower swung their bows up, choosing targets from among the oncoming immortals. Daine's was a winged ape that flew with others of his kind, ahead of the Stormwings. He carried double-bladed axes in feet that were as nimble as hands.

Taking a deep breath, the girl closed her eyes and thought of merlins, fast birds of prey, able to maneuver well in the air. The blanket dropped to the stone deck. Tkaa pulled its folds back, allowing her to take flight.

The air below filled with the snap of bowstrings and the whistle of arrows and bolts. Daine shot straight at the ax-bearing ape, striking him as the hurrok had struck her on the First Bridge, dragging her claws across his brow and scalp. He shrieked and grabbed for her as blood streamed into his eyes. Turning fast, she tore at his wings, ripping holes in them with talons and beak. He fell, dropping both axes as he tried to spin around in midair. When she saw a peaked tower roof loom up underneath, she released her prey. He struck the tower back first, and rolled limply into the city street below.

Swerving fast, she returned to the watchtower roof and the king. A hurrok was her next target; once more she went for eyes first, then wings. Blinded and crippled, the immortal careened into a Stormwing, dragging it down and into the curtain wall as the Stormwing's feathers cut it to pieces. Daine glided back to a place next to the king, watching for a new target.

The archers on the walls shot as rapidly as they could, choosing ape, hurrok, and Stormwing targets with deadly accuracy as they fought Stormwing terror. The king, examining battles on the land and in the air before him, continued to talk calmly into his spelled mirror, relaying what he saw to the queen. In his left hand, the Dominion Jewel glowed, violet light streaming from its many facets.

Jonathan quietly said, "Excuse me," into his mirror, and put it on the stone. Raising the Jewel, he aimed it not at the oncoming Stormwings, but at three hurroks bearing riders to the lower wall and the archers there. The riders were human mages; they lashed the fighters on the curtain wall, burning two of them alive. White threads of fire drifted from the Jewel, falling gracefully onto the hurroks and their burdens.

Kitten cried an alarm: A quartet of Stormwings — two males, two females — had come in low, where no one had seen them, skimming the ground until they reached the base of the curtain wall. Now they sped up its length, ducking the web of fire that was tangling the mages and their mounts, zipping past the archers on the lower levels. Clutching round clay pots in their talons, they were intent on the watchtower and its occupants. Daine recognized the bombs: A spell word from a Stormwing and the pots would explode, showering everyone with liquid fire.

Inkblot jumped from the king's belt purse onto the notch of the wall in front of Jonathan, who did not see his danger. The mages were fighting him and the Jewel with all they had. Jelly, clinging to Kitten's back, leaped to join the king's darking.

Marielle and Tkaa ignored the blots as they leaned

through the crenelated wall. The lady aimed; when her chosen target was only fifty feet away, she loosed. Her arrow took one in the eye; the immortal slammed into the stone with a dying shriek. Jelly and Inkblot dropped to cover the face of the leading Stormwing, blinding him. He thrashed, dropping his bombs in his frantic attempt to scrape the darkings off. They abandoned their victim only when three of the archers on the lower wall had riddled him with arrows.

The two remaining Stormwings came on, deadly rage in their eyes. Tkaa opened his jaws. His throat gave out an ear-piercing song that was part shriek, with a counterpoint tune in it that sounded like an avalanche. The male Stormwing was half caught by the basilisk's song. His left side turned to stone; his right wing and claw thrashed. He dropped as archers scattered from the wall below. Moments later the occupants of the tower heard rock shatter on rock. His companion, the female, had come in to his rear and side; she escaped Tkaa's song. Before the half-stone male began to fall, Daine was arrowing down the side of the watchtower. Abruptly she changed shape to that of a larger, heavier golden eagle, and slammed into the female Stormwing's face. Steel teeth snapped; the girl-eagle got her claws out of the way just in time. Twisting, she slashed the immortal's throat, then jumped away. Cursing, the Stormwing hit the lower wall, silvery blood spraying everywhere, and from there tumbled end over end to the ground.

Daine circled, hunting for the darkings. She was relieved to find them rolling up the watchtower's side, clinging to it as easily as the sunlight did. For the moment the air around the watchtower was clear. Gliding in, Daine carefully picked the two inky creatures up in her claws and carried them back up to the king.

"Good work," Leaf said from its position on Tkaa's shoulder. Jelly went to Kitten; Inkblot flowed out of Daine's talons, pouring itself into Jonathan's belt purse once more. The king grinned, and stroked the purse. Looking for the hurroks and their riders who had run afoul of Jonathan, Daine saw only a heap of white bones on the curtain wall below, and shuddered.

A boom from the north shivered the tower stones. Mushrooming billows of arcane light climbed from behind enemy lines. One cloud was sparkling black, the other a deep ruby shade. Numair had found Inar Hadensra. Daine shifted from foot to foot, ruffling her feathers and praying as she watched tendrils of black fire wind through the red, and red through the black. Numair had tricked the Scanran into protecting their contest from the rest of the battle. Let Inar Hadensra think it was to keep someone from putting a spear through their backs; Daine knew it was to keep the magical battle from hurting anyone else.

Jonathan continued to speak to his queen and generals, passing on the numbers of the enemy and the directions of their movements. His companions defended him from every attack, physical and magical—Kitten and Tkaa easily handled the latter. Now that Numair had engaged the enemy's chief mage, and Thayet's wizards fought most of the rest, few human mages had the attention or strength to strike at those Tortallans who had no Gift, and thus no defense.

Fresh immortals raced onto the battle-torn ground between their camp in the northeast and Legann. Many bore torn nooses of vines and brambles: They had been forced to rip themselves free of clinging plants roused by the Dominion Jewel. On their heels came centaurs, ogres, and knights, all in Tortallan colors, fighting under Tortallan battle flags. When the enemy immortals turned south, to freedom, the ones who escaped the roots that snatched at them from the ground ran into companies of Tortallan soldiers, two Rider Groups, and a small detachment of centaurs who had settled east of Legann.

Behind the Tortallans rose a wall of brambles ten feet high. Anyone who tried to escape the battlefields and camps around the city would run into it. The Dominion Jewel, it seemed, could deliver what King Jonathan had promised.

Metallic shrieks drew the girl's attention. High above the Stormwings, hurroks, and winged apes, Barzha was locked in deadly battle with another Stormwing—a queen. "Jachull," Tkaa remarked, eyes fixed on the crowned immortals. "Queen of the Mortal Fear nation." Daine nodded; so this was the dead-voiced female she'd heard in her dream, the one who had said it wasn't important if some of her own kind died.

Crimson fires edged with gold tangled around the pair like an ill-made knot. For the most part they clawed at each other. The strange queen was adept at quick swipes of her wing feathers; soon Barzha was laddered with shallow cuts and covered in blood. Her enemy bore wounds as well—belly cuts that bled heavily.

Below the queens, Hebakh and Rikash fended off any Stormwings who tried to interfere. Seeing they were outnumbered, Daine called for the People. Sparrows darted into the fray, dashing around Stormwings, pecking and speeding away. Fighting them, or trying to, the immortals smashed into one another, slicing their own allies to pieces. They retreated from Barzha's guards, while the rest of her allies came to help the two males.

A net of scarlet fires wrapped itself around Jachull, its ends lodged under Barzha's skin; Jachull would have to kill the Stone Tree queen to escape. With a snarl, Jachull turned and sped at Barzha, talons forward, set to impale. At the last second Rikash's queen detached the webs of her magic and shot upward, Jachull passing under her by inches.

Barzha fell as Jachull fought to halt and turn; when Jachull stabilized, Barzha was behind her, chopping down with the edges of her right wing. Jachull spun hard to meet an attack she expected from her rear or from above. Instead she jammed her throat and chest into the razor of Barzha's wing. Barzha seized Jachull's face in one talon, dug in her claws, then let her enemy fall. Jachull's allies, who had watched the duel at a distance from Barzha's defenders, wailed.

"Daine?" Jonathan asked quietly. "Would you see how the Yamanis are faring?"

She nodded and took off, changing her shape to that of a gull to fly more easily over the ocean. She kept a wary eye out for winged immortals who might try to kill her. As far as she could tell, they were busy enough, caught between city forces and Thayet's army. Everywhere Daine saw the flash of magic: Stormwing crimson edged with gold; brown and gold from centaurs who were also mages; and varicolored fires that served human wizards. The winged apes laid down a blanket of thick clinging fog, the only magic they possessed, but it did little to hide them. Too many winged creatures and too many other mages took part in the fight; the fog would billow, then shred and blow away.

Soaring over the harbor, she saw that the enemy's ships were in poor condition. Many of the largest vessels had burned to the waterline, seared by dragonfire; nearly all of those left bore scorch marks. Five Yamani ships, half of the fleet that had brought Thayet to Legann, kept all but the smallest vessels from making a getaway. Like dogs herding sheep, they were driving those ships still able to maneuver toward the harbor, where they could surrender to Legann's defenders or be crushed against the breakwater.

Two miles past the blockade Daine found Diamondflame, Wingstar, and the other five Yamani warships. The ten-ship relief force from the Copper Isles, the one she had seen in a Divine Realms vision, was trapped in a circle formed by dragons and Yamanis. Two enemy ships were burning fast. Three more were disabled, their masts broken off. Skins of liquid fire flew through the air, hurled by catapults from vessels on both sides. Any that came too near the dragons swerved, burst, and showered their contents on the enemy's ships. Daine was no admiral, but the outcome of this contest was easy to read.

Circling, she returned to take on her own shape and report to the king. After hearing her description of the sea battle with satisfaction, Jonathan ordered her to rest. A runner gave her meat and cheese between slices of bread, and a cup of heavily sweetened herbal tea. Eating quickly, the girl felt her strength return with every bite and sip.

The sun was almost directly overhead when thick, multicolored smoke rose in an unnaturally straight column from the enemy camp in the northeast. Daine viewed it uneasily: It looked far too much like the Chaos vents in the Divine Realms.

"Sir Raoul, what is that?" Jonathan asked the mirror.

"Booby trap," Daine heard the knight reply. "A squad of men found a box in a tent. One was fool enough to open it before we had a mage check it. The gods-curst thing exploded. It killed everyone in the squad—I don't think it's done making mischief."

The column bent and stretched, colors rippling, until it touched one end to the ground where the eastern road and the road that circled Legann met. Anchored there, it condensed until it was nearly thirty feet in height, and solidified until it formed a monstrous, three-headed serpent. Its scales changed constantly, from pale green to pink to yellow, never holding to one color or pattern. Only the eyes in the three heads remained the same, all blood red, with no pupils that Daine could see.

The smoke-snake turned on the line of Tortallan allies and struck in three directions, each head stretching its long neck for prey, baring overlong, onyx fangs. When the creature straightened again, one head gripped a shrieking man-at-arms in its jaws, the second a green-skinned ogre, the third a female centaur who fought to stab her captor with a javelin that she carried. The serpent devoured them, and searched for its next victims.

The Tortallan centaurs and ogres fled. One knight turned his warhorse to face the serpent. He was a huge man in brightly polished plate armor; his mount was armored as well, her size well-suited to her master's weight. A tight band around Daine's heart squeezed.

Raoul of Goldenlake, the Knight Commander of the King's Own, was not a close friend, but she knew and liked him. She was used to thinking of him as a giant, but the serpent rose at least ten feet over his head before the body split into three necks.

Steel wings and claws flashed in the sun. Rikash—his blond hair with its bone decoration streaming behind him—plummeted, talons first, to slam into the monster's central head. The snake roared, its voice tearing at the ears.

Silvery fire bloomed on the snake's left head: The badger materialized there, burying claws and fangs into the thing's skull as a small, moving shadow dove into one of the creature's nostrils. Daine gasped. That was Gold-streak!

Starlings burst from the trees in a sizable, jeering crowd. Like a swarm of bees they swirled around the serpent's right head, blinding it, digging sharp beaks into its flesh.

Sir Raoul galloped in, massive, double-bladed ax in one hand, hacking at the serpent's body as if he were felling a tree. He struck a vital organ; blood of no particular color gushed forth to splatter his armor, smoking where it struck. His mount screamed when the drops lashed her rump. Hurriedly the knight guided the mare back from the stream of blood. The snake convulsed.

The starlings were not fools. They didn't need a command from Daine to get clear. Pulling back, they left the eye sockets of the head that they had assaulted packed with dead birds. The head that the badger had torn into lolled uselessly on its neck; he had chewed through bone to its brain, without taking harm from the thing's acid blood. Gold-streak looped itself around the badger's forepaw as the god vanished.

The middle head shrilled in rage and pain. It whipped frantically, tossing Rikash into the air. The blond Stormwing slammed into a boulder, and slid to the base of the stone.

The plate and cup slipped from Daine's numb fingers to shatter on the deck.

"*Rikash—no!*" someone cried in a voice that cracked as it rose. "*No! No! NOOOOO!*" It was her voice. If she screamed loud enough, long enough, he would live. She hadn't realized that he meant something to her. She hadn't known he was her friend.

It was the three-headed thing's last defiance. It drooped, then dissolved into a liquid soup with colors that shifted over its surface as it soaked into the ground.

Queen Barzha settled onto the rock that had broken Rikash, shrilling her grief. Hebakh landed beside her, keening, eyes ablaze. They had lost the follower who had brought them hope when Ozorne held them captive. They had lost the only Stormwing who had tried to set them free.

Their voices fell into an odd silence, one of those which came in battles when most fighters stopped briefly to catch a breath. Their eerie wailing sent shivers through everyone who could hear.

The battle resumed, but the tide had turned. Everywhere that Daine looked, she saw the enemy fighting to defend themselves, not to attack. Some humans began to lay down their arms. In the north, black fire flared around crimson still, but the lesser mage fires were dying.

In the northeast, so far away that only an eagle— or a girl who had turned her own eyes into those of a raptor—might see, a long Stormwing took to the air and flapped away. He was trying to escape, leaving the others of his kind who fought on.

Daine had an idea who it was. "No you don't," she muttered, blackly furious. "Not this time, and never again! Sire, I request permission to go after that Stormwing!"

"This is not a good idea," Tkaa said, placing a gentle paw on her shoulder. "You risk capture or death from others of the enemy. He will be pursued, and caught."

She faced the basilisk, eyes ablaze. "That's what I said last time, and *look*!" She swept an arm to include the battlefield before them.

A hand rested on her other shoulder. "Then go," the king said, blue eyes direct. "Go, and the gods look after you."

"If they are not busy themselves," Tkaa pointed out. "Chaos must have plenty of strength to draw upon, with all this."

Daine shed the blanket that she had worn around her human form. Jumping into a wide notch in the stone wall, she leaped out, changing as she did, trading hair for feathers, arms for wings, and legs for talons. As a sparrow hawk, a small, fast bird of prey, she streaked after Ozorne.

10
JUDGMENTS

HER FLIGHT CARRIED HER OVER THE RUINS OF the wooden towers and the enemy's dirt bulwarks. Fighting continued there, but even a quick glance told her that the enemy was losing heart. A growing number of men and immortals sat in clusters everywhere, guarded by wary knights and soldiers in Tortallan uniform.

On she flew. Beneath her lay the enemy's northern camp. The ground was littered with bodies, weapons, and the things men needed to live in hostile country; some wagons and tents were ablaze. Here mages battled, the fires of their Gifts waxing and waning. Some mages had surrendered; others lay dying, the loss of their power turning their bodies into skin-covered skeletons before they were dead.

Beside the river, the fiery black-and-ruby ball that was the interlocked Gifts of Numair and Inar Hadensra pulsed with unchecked fury. Daine glanced at it, then fixed her eyes on her quarry. She couldn't think about Numair, couldn't stop to watch—she was gaining on Ozorne.

Speeding over the river, she saw the queen enter the enemy camp. If she'd had a mouth, she would have grinned. She had been there when Thayet's commanders told the queen that she would not be permitted to ride to battle herself, not when the king was trapped and vulnerable in Legann. They had made Thayet agree that Tortall could not afford to lose both monarchs, but not before she had expressed her feelings in words that Daine usually heard only in the Corus slums.

Rising air bore her above the forest where the relief force had hidden. Her quarry was clearly in view—and much closer. Stormwings could fly, but not gracefully or speedily. Daine shrieked her elation. Ozorne looked back and saw her. He sped faster; Daine matched him.

He searched the land below, trying to spot a place where he might escape her.

It was harder to shape a human mouth and voice box in a bird that it was to give her two-legger self raptor's eyes, or bat's ears. She had no idea why that was true; it just was. After a few moments' struggle she had something that she could talk with.

"Ozorne Muhassin Tasikhe!" she called. "I am fair vexated with you!"

He turned, hanging in midair, smiling contemptuously. There were marks of soot, blood, and sweat on him; the scars of Stormwing battles decorated his chest. The black, glassy stone she had seen in visions of him still hung on a cord around his neck.

"I quiver," he said as she approached. "You have no notion of how terrified I am." For a moment he sounded as he had when she first met him, cool, aloof, and grand, seated on an emperor's throne. In those days he had been someone who placed himself far beyond the kind of life that she knew.

His eyes flickered as he looked over her shoulder. Daine turned. Two Stormwings, and three winged apes, crested the trees between her and Legann. He must have ordered them to wait for just this, so that he could set the trap, and she could fly into it.

The girl-eagle sighed. "Here I was thinking that, just once, it would be nice if you fought a battle *yourself*, without getting others to do your dirty work." She was thinking hard. She would have to be fast now, faster than she'd ever been in her life.

"I am not the one who gets my little animal *friends* killed by the hundreds for defending me," he taunted her.

Any anger that had clouded her mind vanished. "I made my peace with that—and with them—three years ago. Fight, damn you!"

"I won't soil my claws." He sneered. "I was the Emperor Mage of Carthak—"

"Oh, *please*," she retorted, glancing back. The other immortals were coming on fast. "That's finished, and by your own acts did you finish it!"

"How *dare* you judge me!" he snarled. "You're a common-born bastard, a camp follower's brat who spreads her legs for any passing man—just like her mother."

To her own surprise—and quite clearly, to his—Daine laughed. "And you're as ignorant as you are evil," she retorted. "I'm done listening to you!"

Wheeling to face the immortals behind her, she changed, as quickly as thought. A giant strangling-snake, she dropped across two apes who flew close together, wrapping her tail around one throat, and her first three feet of length around the other. To her surprise, two small, blobby forms dropped past. Spreading themselves like kites, they steered until they fell onto the faces of both Stormwings. Leaf and Jelly had stolen a ride on Daine's back.

The Stormwings tried to scream; instead they only pulled darking bodies into their throats. Daine couldn't wait or watch. In one burst of strength, she squeezed, and heard dull snaps as both of her victims' necks broke.

Agony burned her side: The third winged ape wielded a sword. Daine fell away, forcing herself into raven form as she dropped. The cut was long, but shallow; with a grimace she made herself ignore the pain. If she didn't bleed too much, she would be fine. She would *have* to be fine.

Plummeting, she remembered the feel of wind under feathers and the loud calls of raven flockmates. The wind caught her outspread wings and carried her aloft.

There was a crash: The smothered Stormwings dropped into the woods. Leaf and Jelly fell away from their victims, gliding flat until they latched onto the naked limbs of a tall, long-dead tree. Daine swooped to get them as Ozorne screamed a word.

The two darkings flared crimson, and exploded.

Pulling her wings in, stretching her body, she banked, murder in her heart. The last winged ape was forgotten. There was no one bird that she drew on, but many, as Daine shaped angled wings to give her speed, a ripping beak and talons to match for combat, a starling's talent for quick, midair dodges. She stayed as large as she dared: She would need size to fight this battle. Hurtling through the winds, she came at Ozorne.

He lashed her with Stormwing fire. She barrel-rolled, spinning away from his bolts without losing a feather's worth of speed. Behind her, something grunted: The sword-wielding ape fought to catch up. She would have to deal with him: He was quicker than he had a right to be. Twisting herself until the air flowed over and under her just right, she emptied her large bird's bowels squarely into his face.

The ape's furious howl was choked and wet. Daine chanced a look back. He clawed at his throat, his sword falling to the earth. The silly clunch inhaled, she thought coldly, before she fixed her attention on Ozorne once more.

He burned her twice with crimson bolts, or tried to. She bent away from both and picked up her speed. He was sweating; she could smell it, a bitter combination of man oils and metal tang that spread through the air.

On the ground, the forest came to an end; they had reached the coast, far beyond the point where Yamani ships had landed the Tortallan force. Below, the sea battered the feet of high, rocky cliffs. The cliff thermals would help her along; she was beginning to tire, a little.

But if Daine was tiring, so was Ozorne. It cost him to fly. She could see it in his laboring wings and loss of speed. Twice he spun to throw flame at her. Ducking it easily, she gained altitude and circled to his left. He knew she was not directly behind him, an easy target. Forced to keep turning in order to see her, Ozorne lost momentum. Daine closed the gap. Once she was close enough, she changed again, and dropped onto his back, her wildcat's forepaws hooked over his shoulders.

Razor-edged feathers cut into her fur; she clamped her jaws on the back of his neck and bit, hard. Ozorne howled and writhed, falling. Daine bit harder. There was naked flesh on his back, too, where she put her rear claws to use. Red fire raced all over his skin, burning her paws and mouth. She hung on as long as she could, but in the end, she lost control over her shape and dropped off, while Ozorne spun and fell, bleeding heavily.

She strained, trying to regain her wings, but her mind was as exhausted as her body. She couldn't remember how winged creatures felt to her. I can't die! she thought frantically. Not whilst he's alive!

Her back struck a soft, feathered platform that slowed her fall. Gulls had come to her rescue, crowding together so that their outstretched wings overlapped, forming a platform of feather, skin, and bone. They sank to the ground, and drew away from her. She dropped an inch or two, striking thick, springy grass.

"Thank you," she whispered, rolling to her knees. "If I survive this, I will owe you and your kinfolk until the end of time."

She looked up. Ozorne's fall, like her long tumble in the Divine Realms, had been slowed and broken by a tree. He neared the ground, using his magic to cushion his own drop. When he landed, he was scant yards away. For a moment he stood, gasping, sweat-drenched hair in his eyes, bleeding from deep gouges and scrapes.

Daine forced herself to change, dredging up one

last droplet of magic to arm herself. Her skin rippled, grew fur, developed patterns, changed again to human skin. "Like a Chaos thing myself," she mumbled, getting to her knees, and shuddered.

Ozorne shook his hair out of his eyes and grinned, lips peeling mirthlessly from his steel teeth. "What is Chaos to you?" he sneered, panting as he walked toward her.

"If you're for it, then I'm against it," she retorted, keeping her own face down.

"Then you're in trouble," he informed her. "With my help, Uusoae has the strength to defeat the gods at last. She has promised that I will be king of the world."

"And how long will that last? She'll only eat the world, too, when she's done with the gods." Daine thought she had something—her fingers and toenails were cooperating, at least. Driving up from the ground—she had to strike *before* he got those wing blades of his up—she launched herself at him with a scream of raw fury, finger-claws raking at his eyes, knees drawn up to her chest so that the claws on her feet could dig into his gut.

She knocked him back. Intertwined, they rolled down a slope, the girl ripping all the meat from him that her talons could reach, keeping her head down so that he couldn't fasten his metal teeth in her throat. He clawed at her with his own feet, tried to cut her with his wings, but it was hard for him to bend his metal flesh, harder still to grip a head cushioned by thick, long curls in his jaws. He screamed something.

A force lifted her up and knocked her yards away. She landed on her back, the wind knocked from her lungs. Trying to fill them again, Daine felt her claws turn back into toes and fingernails. As surely as she knew her name, she was certain that there were no more shape changes left in her. Perhaps if she had not lost so much blood, or flown so hard and so fast, or had kept her shapes to those of whole animals instead of using parts from many . . .

The sound of metal scraping rock woke her from a weary half-trance. She gasped, and coughed, found the air to roll over, and got on her hands and knees. He was coming for her, panting and exhausted himself, bleeding and triumphant.

"So here you are, without your precious *friends*," he mocked. "There is no one to save you: no human, no animal—no magic. Don't try to deny it," he said when she looked up at him. "Stormwing magic isn't good for much, but we *can* tell when someone is ready to die—when all her weapons are stripped from her."

Daine hung her head. At the edge of her vision the badger's heavy silver claw—the one thing that managed to stay with her through every shape change that she had ever worked—swung on its chain. The end of the claw was sharp; she knew that very well.

She let her curls fall forward, masking her actions. He was still a few yards away. With her right hand, she felt the chain until she found the catch. With her left, she groped for a rock. He would see that; let him.

A flick of a fingernail opened the catch. The chain ran off her neck and through the wire binding of the claw, pooling on the ground like water. Daine straightened, claw tucked into her right hand, a rock visible in her left. She hurled the stone at Ozorne. The weakness in her arm was terrifying; still, her aim at least was good. He threw up a magical shield, but it was barely visible. When the rock struck, the shield's pale red fires rippled and broke; the stone thumped his chest.

"I'm not the only one that's out of magic," she cried hoarsely. Manipulating the claw, she positioned it so that it thrust between the fingers of her fist, pointing out and down. "You couldn't light a candle, could you?"

He smiled, lifting a razor-edged wing as he approached. "I don't need magic to handle you now,

Veralidaine. All I need is this. Why don't you just bare your throat, and make it easy on yourself?"

Come on, she thought, watching through her curtain of hair. And I have to make sure he *never* gets up from this. Just one . . . more . . . step . . .

He took it, bringing him within wing reach—or arm's reach. She threw herself forward, with no grace or coordination of muscle. Grabbing the upper edge of his open wing with one hand, feeling its bite in her palm, Daine slashed forward with the claw.

Ozorne screamed a doomed beast's scream as the badger's talon bit into his neck, and tore. Daine yanked the claw sideways, across his windpipe, through the veins on the opposite side. His blood sprayed, drenching them both; he thrashed like a mad thing. She dug the claw into his belly and dragged it down.

At last he was still.

For a long moment she lay there, too weary to get up—but the mess of blood and flesh made her stomach lurch. She rolled off him, barely feeling the small cuts from his outspread wings, too worn out even to vomit over the mess. When she was able to sit up, she found that the stone he'd taken to wearing was stuck to her bloody chest, with the remains of the cord on which it had hung. Claw must've cut the string, she thought vaguely. Groping, she seized cord and stone and hurled them away from her.

They struck a tree; the stone shattered. Beneath her, the ground lurched, rolled, then sank. Before her appeared an arch and pool of oozing, dripping muck, their shifting colors making her dizzy. In the spot where pond and arch met, a hunched figure straightened. The face changed without letup, no part of it ever still, from unmatched eyes to the overall shape.

Horrible as she looked in Daine's dreams, the physical reality of Uusoae was much, much worse. The girls' hands and feet scrabbled in the dirt as she tried to get away from the Queen of Chaos, but her muscles were as soft as butter. Trembling, Daine covered her eyes. It didn't help. The Chaos queen was in her mind. Her constant shifts of body and face pulled at Daine's belly and ears and heart.

"You *dared* to interfere," the creature muttered, her breath scented richly with flowers and long-dead meat. "For my creature, and my plan—" Hard, sharp, gluey, oozing, pulpy, twining hands seized Daine's wrists.

The girl shrieked at the horror of that touch. Her scream went on, and on—

And ended, as if cut off by shears. They were

nowhere, in a flat, dead space where there was no sound, no light, and no up or down. Mercifully, Daine could no longer feel Uusoae's touch. She only wished that she could no longer see the goddess, but her vision was crystal clear, even without light.

"It is as we said, Father Universe, Mother Flame," boomed a deep voice. Mithros, the Sun Lord, stood nearby. A huge black man with short-cropped hair, he wore gold armor over a kilted white tunic. In one hand he bore a gold spear with a blade that shone white-hot. "In defiance of the ban you laid upon her, she entered the mortal realms and made an alliance with one who influenced mortal lives. She did it to gain the upper hand against us, her brothers and sisters. Are your bans to be set aside lightly by her, or by any of us?"

Uusoae released Daine, and stepped away. The girl huddled in the space where she sat, teeth chattering, her many wounds bleeding and stinging.

Below, light blazed, all the colors of fire, stars, and the moon. "Uusoae, I am disappointed." The voice was somehow female and somehow the essence of light and heat. Daine heard it in her bones. "So soon after the last time, as well."

Overhead, the blackness moved. "It is her nature to strive, to overset, to imagine all as being different."

This voice was male, a distillation of darkness and emptiness. "Still, to follow one's nature is no excuse to openly defy one's parents. Return to the confines of your own realm, Uusoae. There you will be confined in a cage of dead matter and starfire until your mother and I feel better about you."

"How long will that be?" demanded the ruler of Chaos.

A weight settled over Daine's shoulders; folds of black cloth wrapped around her. She looked up into Gainel's shadowy eyes. He smiled and gave her shoulder a gentle pat.

"Until the next star is born, my daughter," Mother Flame told Uusoae firmly. "Rule your subjects from your cage, and think on the consequences of your behavior."

As one, the great powers—parents of gods and Chaos—spoke: "*It is done.*"

Uusoae vanished. So, too, did that infinite blackness, and the ultimate light. Daine knelt on pale marble in the center of a vast courtyard rimmed with graceful columns and dotted with fountains. Half of the sky overhead was dark and blazed with stars; the other half showed daylight, with a sun just past noon.

Mithros sank into a backless golden chair with a

sigh, and gave his spear to a young, brown-skinned boy in a blue tunic. Beside the Sun Lord a black cat slumbered in a silver chair. The Great Goddess tried to shoo it away, but the cat refused to take the hint. At last the Goddess moved the animal. Set on the marble court, the cat sniffed audibly and trotted over to Daine.

She held out a hand for it to smell. It did so, examined her with bright purple eyes, then sat in front of her and began to wash. All around them, gods settled into chairs, or onto fountain rims and benches.

Silver bloomed on either side of the cat: The badger and Broad Foot appeared. The duckmole still looked thin and worn, but there was amusement in his small eyes as he nodded to her.

"I think you'll be glad to know the Sorrows have returned to their kennels, all three of them," he informed her. "The mortal realms are rid of them, for now."

Gold-streak unwrapped itself from around the badger's neck and rolled over to Daine. "Miss you," it said, and trickled up her thighs to nestle in her lap.

Her eyes stung. Tears trickled down her cheeks. "Leaf and Jelly are dead," she told her first darking, the spy that Ozorne had set on her. "They were so brave."

"I know," Gold-streak replied. "They had freedom. They had choosing. They chose you. All darkings know. We never forget."

Sniffing, she wiped her eyes with a finger, and the Dream King's coat began to slide. Gainel, still behind Daine, resettled the garment around her shoulders. There was much less pain from that change than she had felt when he originally put the garment on her. Peeking under the coat's lapel, the girl saw that her injuries were mending themselves.

—*You will have scars,*— Gainel said, —*but those are signs of battles fought bravely.*—

"I don't hardly feel brave," she whispered. "I feel sad, and I feel *tired.*"

"Brother, there are things to deal with." Looking at the speaker, Daine gulped and thrust herself backward, colliding with Gainel's legs. It was a serpent far larger than the one that had killed Rikash: Kidunka, the world snake, the first child born of Universe and Flame. "*Her,* for one." The serpent pointed its large, blunt nose at Daine.

Eyes—gods' eyes—turned to her. Daine wished very, very strongly that she could just sink into the marble floor.

"Leave be!" Sarra came from somewhere in the

crowd to kneel and wrap her arms around her daughter. "You're frightening her!"

"What is there to deal with?" Weiryn demanded, joining his mate and child.

"She must choose," said the Great Mother Goddess, fixing emerald eyes on Daine.

"Choose what?" asked the girl. "I don't understand."

Mithros met her eyes with his. Daine quivered, but refused to look away. He was a god, the greatest of those who ruled two-leggers, but he was no Chaos queen. Her supply of awed terror was used up for today.

At last Mithros shook his head. "You are godborn, Veralidaine Sarrasri. Wherever the Godborn go, whatever they do, trouble—disorder—"

—*Change,*— interrupted Gainel.

Mithros glared at his brother, and went on. "All those things follow. We cannot have that, particularly not on the scale on which *you* seem to create it. We must then limit the area of your influence.

"Either you now return to the mortal realms to live out your life, or you stay here, a lesser goddess. Once you decide, you will never be able to change your mind. You will never again cross between the realms."

Choose? she thought, numb. Choose between

Ma, who never should have died, and Numair? Her father, whom she barely knew, or Queen Thayet, King Jonathan, Onua?

But I could be a *goddess*. I could do magic like Ma does. I could visit Broad Foot's home. And Kit—seeing her won't be a trouble, since she can go where she likes.

What of Cloud, and Zek the marmoset, and Spots and Onua's Tahoi? Was she going to leave the Long Lake wolf pack behind? Confused, Daine buried her head in Sarra's shoulder. What of Alanna the Lioness, and Maura of Dunlath? Could she spend their lives watching them from the Divine Realms, without ever being with them?

Numair. From their very first meeting, he'd given her joy, delight, new things to learn. He was her teacher, her traveling companion, her comrade in arms. He was her love. When he kissed her . . . She could never give him up, not willingly.

She lifted her head as her heart turned to ice. She had promised Ma that she would return. She had given her *word*.

"The immortals, brother." A soft voice, filled with kindness, issued from the hood that shadowed the Black God's face. "For their part in Uusoae's plan, the

Stormwings should be made to return here, and be forbidden the mortal realms for all of time. Perhaps *all* immortals should return. Humans have forgotten how to live with them."

"Too bad," growled the badger. "Once immortals had a place in things. Human mages threw them out— and *you* allowed it. You have a chance to *fix* a wrong here, not repeat it."

The Graveyard Hag thumped her walking stick on the ground to get attention. "The badger's right," Carthak's patron goddess said. "And it's good for humans to have a *few* things to be afraid of. Besides us, of course."

—*For nearly four centuries, I have labored with human dreams.*—Gainel's mind voice was firm.—*The immortals evoke rich dreams without my striving. Mortal spirits were poorer with the immortals gone, human imagination less fertile. I have enjoyed a few years' relief from a thankless task. Will you cripple me twice, brother?*—

Gold-streak put its small head beside Daine's ear and whispered, "Stormwings."

That tiny, high voice broke through her concentration on her choice that was no choice. "What?" she asked dully.

"Stormwings," repeated Gold-streak. "To be prisoned here."

"Good," she mumbled. "They're *evil;* they're—"

Memory silenced her. Cold air touched her cheek as a voice remarked, "That creature would defile what mortal killers left, so that humans couldn't lie about how glorious a soldier's death is." In her mind's eye, a tan-and-silver figure plummeted, claws extended, blond hair and bones streaming. Dark, imperious eyes, and pale, hypnotic ones, accused her.

She did not like raids on nests for eggs and nestlings, but her squirrel, crow, and snake friends did just that. Wolves chose scapegoats to bully, hurt, even reject completely from the pack. The sight of living prey fighting a hyena's devouring jaws or of a killer whale beating a seal pup to death might reduce her to tears, but those predators could not help their natures any more than Uusoae, or the Great Gods, could.

While she thought, the gods spoke, until Mithros cut off discussion with a wave of his hand. "Very well. Those immortals who dwelled in the mortal realms at the spring equinox may remain, if they choose. All others return here. As for the Stormwings—"

Gold-streak stretched itself wire-thin, raising its

head until Mithros could see it. "What of Queen Barzha?" it asked.

Daine rose, gripping the edges of Gainel's coat to keep herself covered. "Gold-streak's right. Barzha's flock for certain—them that followed her into the mortal realms. Even—maybe even some that sided with Uusoae. Stormwings aren't humans. They aren't gods. They are what they were made to be. If you punish them for that, you may as well punish yourselves for what you are." She straightened, looking around at that magnificent assembly. If they wanted to admit her to their number, then they would have to get used to her speaking her mind. "You'll forgive me for saying so, but you don't look like you'd care to punish yourselves."

"Daine!" gasped Sarra, eyes wide with horror.

A weight pressed against her leg. She looked down: It was the badger. —*That's my kit.*— His mind voice spoke to her alone.

"Isn't *order* what makes you happy?" continued the girl. "Well, Stormwings are the nightmare of battle, pure and simple. What's that but a nightmare of disorder? How can you begrudge a mortal home to anyone who might scare two-leggers off war?"

Mithros glared. "The Stormwings may remain," the

Sun Lord barked at last, his voice thunder in her ears.

The marble courtyard shimmered, then stretched, creating an immense bare space at the center. The moment that it ceased to move, Diamondflame, Wingstar, and Kitten popped onto it. Kitten whistled and chirruped, her scales red with anger. Seeing Daine, she trotted over and began to scold.

"I wasn't hardly given a choice," Daine told her, guessing what her charge was upset about. "They just grabbed me when that Uusoae appeared."

—*We* have *come to take Veralidaine home*,— said Diamondflame. —*The humans want to know what happened.*—

"She may not be able to return," said Broad Foot. "She has to choose either the mortal or the divine realms—she may not cross from one to the other."

—*And whose idea was* that?— Wingstar demanded. The duckmole began to explain.

"I ought to stay," Daine told Kitten, tears rolling down her cheeks unnoticed.

The young dragon replied in a stream of chatter and croaks. Tiny lightnings crackled over her scales.

—*She wants to know why*,— Gainel remarked in his soft voice. —*She wants to know why you will not go to your friends in the mortal realms.*—

Kitten reared onto her hindquarters and dug silver talons into the front of the Dream King's jacket. "Kit!" protested Daine, trying to work her friend's claws out of the fabric. "See, I promised Ma I would visit. I gave my word."

"Dear one, no." Sarra had moved away when the dragons arrived. Now she came forward, clothing over one arm. "You don't belong here. You would be so unhappy." She held out the garments. "I believe Gainel would like his coat back eventually."

Numbly Daine reached for the clothes, still trying to understand her mother's words. "But—I gave you my promise. I don't break my promises."

"You're not breaking it. I'm releasing you. There's a good man and true friends waiting for you at home. That man is a fair *strange* man, certainly, but he's a good one." Sarra motioned, and Daine was encircled by a glittering curtain. The girl couldn't see out; no one else could see in. "Hand me Gainel's coat, dear." A hand pierced the wall, and slender fingers beckoned. Daine gave the coat to her mother, who pulled it out of the enclosure.

Where the underthings, lavender dress, bodice, and slippers had come from, Daine could never guess. She put all of them on. "Ma, I'm decent."

The enclosure vanished. Weiryn had one arm around her mother; he clasped a bow and quiver in his free hand. Looking for Kitten, Daine was horrified to find that the young dragon was scolding Mithros quite emphatically.

"Your going back won't be so bad," Sarra told Daine, eyes filling. "We'll come to you on the equinoxes and solstices."

"But I *promised*—"

"We can't restore the years together that were taken from us," Sarra interrupted. "It was misery, but we can't change it. Seeing you here taught me you're adult now. You're needed, and you're valued, and you're loved. Those are wondrous gifts, sweetling. I can't let you throw them away." Tears spilled down her cheeks and her smile quivered, but her blue eyes were steady.

"She is right," Weiryn said gruffly. "The mortals need you, as you do them." He offered the bow and quiver to her. "Since you lost the one you had."

Slowly, feeling numb, Daine accepted the gift. The bow changed subtly, until it fitted her strength and grip exactly, as the last bow Weiryn had given her had done.

"Veralidaine, do you choose?" boomed Mithros. "Diamondflame, take your grandchild in hand!"

—*Skysong, come here,*— ordered her grandsire. Kitten obeyed, still muttering.

"Our daughter is going home," Sarra told the gods, chin high, "to the mortal realms."

Mithros looked at Daine. "Is that so?"

The girl nodded.

"Then I return you—" began the Sun Lord.

—*No,*— said Diamondflame, cutting Mithros off. —*We shall take her back. Sometimes those whom the gods return to other realms—how shall I put it?—they go astray. What a pity it would be if she entered the realms of Chaos, or of death, by mistake. Better not to take chances. Come, Veralidaine.*—

She thought the blue dragon was being unfair. Still, another dragon ride sounded wonderful, and it would give her a brief rest before she plunged back into mopping up Ozorne's army.

Sarra hugged Daine tightly, then kissed her cheeks. "The fall equinox isn't far off," she said. "We'll come to you then."

She stepped back to let Weiryn hug his daughter. "I am glad that you were able to visit us, Veralidaine. Try not to lose that bow."

"I'll try, Da." She knelt to bring herself closer to Broad Foot and the badger. "Thank you," she told them, running a hand over the duckmole's springy fur and scratching the badger's ears. "You helped save Tortall, both of you."

"It was the least we could do for the friend who tricked Uusoae into the open," Broad Foot replied. "G'day, then, Weiryn's daughter. We'll meet again, I know." Silver fire condensed around his form. Inside it, he grew smaller, and smaller, until he was gone.

Daine lifted Gold-streak from the badger's wide back and kissed the blot. "What will become of you darkings now?" she asked.

Gold-streak rubbed its head against her cheek. "Dragons invite us to Dragonlands. Darkings go there for now. We must think of what we will become."

"Good luck to you, then," she said.

"We will always remember you," Gold-streak told her. It trickled over to Wingstar to climb onto the dragon's back.

"Badger," Daine said, tears filling her eyes. "I s'pose you're done with me, now that I'm grown and know my da and all."

He thrust a cold, wet nose into the hollow at the base of her throat. She flinched. Even after he backed away, the sense of coldness remained. Touching the spot, the girl felt a chilly metal curve, its base wrapped in silver wire, attached to a chain. Lifting the claw, she saw that it had been cleaned so thoroughly that there was nothing to remind her of the use she'd made of it. "You left that where it might have been lost," the badger remarked, dark eyes glittering with amusement.

Daine buried her face in his heavy fur, holding him tightly. "Thank you," she whispered, voice cracking. "I'll never take it off again."

"I will check on you often, to be sure you keep your promise. You aren't rid of *me* so easily, my kit." Rearing slightly, he nudged the claw with his nose. "Ozorne always underestimated you. It was a lesson he never seemed to learn."

—*Come,*— ordered Diamondflame. Kitten was already tucked into the circle of his forepaws and talons, safe within the great dragon's hold. —*Gods annoy me.*—

"As dragons annoy us," snapped the Graveyard Hag. She winked at Daine. "Good to see you again, dearie."

"I bet," muttered the girl. Giving the badger a last hug, she climbed onto Diamondflame's back, tucking her skirts so that she could sit astride the dragon's neck. She looked at Sarra once more. "Ma? Can you do something for me?"

Sarra came to the dragon's side. "If I can."

"Can I see you as the Green Lady? Just once?"

Sarra laughed; Weiryn grinned. Light, gold and soft, gathered around Daine's ma. She grew taller. A simple green cotton dress, heavily decorated with embroideries in complex designs, fluttered around her body in a wind that Daine couldn't feel. There was a sheer green veil over Sarra's face and hair; it too fluttered and moved as if windblown. Looking at her, Daine felt comfort and hope.

"You're beautiful, Ma," she said quietly. "I love you."

Sarra raised her veil. "I love you too, sweet."

—*Stand back,*— warned Diamondflame. He opened his great wings, and took flight.

EPILOGUE

When they glided out of the clouds, Port Legann lay below. On the sea, a few ships still burned. Yamani vessels herded those they had captured into the reopened harbor. All around the city the land was tattered, scorched, and frayed. Everywhere lay the dead. Groups roamed the battlefields, gathering the wounded and the dead, giving the death stroke to dying animals, or scavenging weapons and valuables.

On level ground before the north gate, tables had been placed. On one side, Daine saw enemy leaders—nobles of the Copper Isles, Carthaki renegades—well guarded by royal troops. Opposite them were King Jonathan, reunited and handfast with Queen Thayet, Lord Imrah, the Yamani admiral who had commanded the ten ships that had mopped up the enemy fleet, Onua and her big dog Tahoi, and the mage Harailt. Papers were strewn over the wooden tables, and scribes stood by, heating wax for the seals that would be fixed to each document.

Close by his monarchs, Sir Raoul was perched on a camp stool. A healer examined deep cuts in his scalp and left arm as the big knight tried not to flinch. In the distance, Daine saw her Rider friend Evin and Sarge helping to lift the wounded into wagons that would carry them into the city.

Diamondflame landed on a clear space in the battle-field, Wingstar behind him. Freed of her grandfather's hold, Kitten trotted around to his side, whistling and clucking. Daine looked where her dragonet pointed, and saw a tall, thin, reptilian creature race toward them from the north gate, his tail draped like a train over one long arm. Hard on his heels galloped her small, shaggy gray pony. A broken rope that trailed behind Cloud showed how she had managed to get out of the stables, where she'd stayed since Daine first came to Legann.

Tkaa halted and nodded to the dragons as Daine put her bow and quiver on a nearby tree stump. That done, she threw her arms around Cloud's neck. In mind speech she told the mare everything that had happened, while Cloud lipped her sleeve.

I'm glad you came back, the mare said when she was done. I don't have the patience to train a new rider anymore.

Daine laughed, and straightened. "You *never* had patience with any rider, *including* me!"

Tahoi beat Onua in the run to greet them. Rearing on his hind legs, the dog planted his paws on Daine's shoulders and proceeded to wash her face.

"No—no, Tahoi, that's sweet, but really, I'm practically almost clean!" Holding his paws, Daine backed the dog up until he said that he would be good and not wash her. She released him. He lunged, ran his tongue from her chin to her forehead, then sat, tail pounding the dry earth.

"Very funny," muttered Daine, and wiped her face.

Onua gave her a quick, tight hug. "Ozorne?" she asked, examining the girl for any sign of injury.

"Dead," replied Daine, flushing at the memory. "Just as dead as I could make him without dragging him before the Black God myself. Numair?"

"No one knows" was the quiet reply. "The magic-sign of his duel with Hadensra vanished a while back, but no one's had a chance to go that way to check on him. What in the name of the Goddess happened? There was a—a sound, and the next instant, at least half of the immortals disappeared from the battlefield. Just—vanished!"

"It's a long story," Daine told her friend. "Ask Big Blue to tell it to you." She pointed to Diamondflame, then grabbed her skirt with one hand and mounted Cloud. "I'm going after Numair."

—*Big Blue?*— echoed Kitten's grandfather. —*Hm. An interesting nickname.*—

Onua grabbed Cloud's mane, and was almost bitten for her pains. "Daine, there may be enemy soldiers out that way, still. Wait for a cleanup squad—"

Without needing a word from Daine, Cloud walked over to the tree stump. Daine grabbed her father's bow and quiver, and smiled at the K'mir. "It isn't me who has to be wary of them," she said gently. "They'd best be afraid of *me.*" She nudged Cloud, who set off at a trot.

She was glad that her mare knew where she wanted to go. Exhaustion, banished temporarily while she wore Gainel's coat, was gnawing at her. She prayed that her words to Onua weren't vainglory, and that she'd be able to use her bow if necessary. It would be too embarrassing to have survived all this, only to be cut down by a straggler determined to make one last kill before he surrendered or escaped.

Watching where she placed her hooves, Cloud picked her way through bodies and equipment for war. The giant wooden barriers made to deter jumping horses had been pulled aside, opening gaps in their line. Pony and rider passed the wooden towers, now black and crumbling after their encounter with dragonfire, and rode through a break in the low earthen wall.

The ground sloped, leading to the camp beside the river. Here the destruction was complete. Tents and goods had been destroyed, burned, or stolen. The bodies of those who had defended, not run, lay everywhere.

The red-and-black globe of magics had not come from the camp, but from upriver. Daine gripped trembling hands in Cloud's mane and prayed as they turned right, following the water east.

Deep gashes were torn from the earth. The shallow river was half blocked by stones and what looked like a yard-long bank of earth-colored glass. Already the water was carving a new path around the obstruction. Steam drifted in the hollows under the trees.

"Whoever you are, if you're here to kill me, you'll need to do it while I remain prone," a familiar voice said nearby. "Have the decency to be quick about it, so I can get back to my rest."

Daine tumbled off Cloud's back, trying to see where he was. "What I've got in mind isn't near so quick as killing!"

There was a long silence; her heart twisted within her chest. Then she heard a cracked whisper: *"Daine?"* Under the long, drooping branches of a nearby willow, a dark figure lurched to its feet.

She ran to Numair, slamming into him with enough force to drive him back against the willow's trunk. "That *hurt*," he gasped. Before she could apologize, he was kissing her nose, her cheeks, her forehead, her lips. She kissed him back. They came up for air, then kissed again, their hands checking each other's bodies, for serious injury as well as simply for the joy of touch.

They came up for air several more times before they had calmed down enough to let each other go— although Numair kept his grip on Daine's hands. "Will you marry me?"

She grinned up at him. "Maybe someday," she

replied, eyes dancing. "But only if you're very, very good."

"What if I'm very, very bad?" he whispered, the heat in his voice making her shiver agreeably. He gathered her into his arms and eased his mouth over hers, caressing her lips with his, teasing, until all she could do was hang in his grip.

"Still maybe someday," she replied finally, when she could do more than simply gasp. "But you're welcome to try and convince me to make it sooner."

This is as lovely as colts frisking in the sun, Cloud remarked from outside the screen of willow branches, but you're going to have company. Kitten is bringing Tkaa and Onua here.

Daine giggled and told Numair what the pony had said.

"Then by all means, let us totter down to meet them," said the man with a sigh. "I will resume persuading you in regard to matrimony at another time, when we've rested, and eaten, and had baths."

Daine slung his arm around her shoulders. She was tired, but she could feel him trembling as well. From the grayness of his skin, his battle had cost him a great deal. "So that Inar Hadensra was a hard fight?"

Numair dug his free hand into his shirt pocket

and produced a ruby globe: the dead mage's eye. "The hardest. I believe I'll retire and return to juggling for a living." He tossed the ruby into the river. "I could support us with juggling, if you were to marry me."

"We'll see," she said.

"I take it Uusoae was acting through Ozorne?" Numair asked quietly.

Daine nodded. "I'll tell you all of it later. It will take a bit of telling."

There were Stormwings overhead. They descended from behind the cover of the clouds in a spiraling pattern, feathers blazing where they reflected the sun. By the time Tkaa, Kitten, Onua, and Tahoi met Daine and Numair and brought them to the north gate of Port Legann, the Stormwings were at work on the bodies of the fallen. Watching them from a distance, Daine realized that it might be just as well if she told only a few, trusted friends that she had spoken for the Stormwings' right to stay in the mortal realms. Somehow, she had the idea that not everyone would understand.

AFTERWORD

I DON'T THINK MY HUSBAND WILL EVER FORGIVE me for the Skinners. Now mind, this is a man who watches every monster movie there is and reads countless articles, magazines, and books on the subject—particularly the gore effects—but the Skinners flip him out. I don't know if it's that they strip the skin from every living thing they encounter, or that no matter how much they steal to cover themselves, moments after the new skin appears on them, it is gone and they are raw again. Either way, all I have to do is say "Skinners" to him and he jams his fingers into his ears and starts babbling "La, la, la, la" over and over until I go away.

He does understand the necessity. He knows I needed something so bad that Daine's parents would panic and snatch her from the face of the earth. I don't even know where I got the idea—perhaps I was in the grocery store in the fresh chicken aisle. They weren't a nightmare of mine, I know that. I don't have dreams that are so interesting. Most of the time, I don't even remember them.

As for the rest of the book, given Daine's godly connections, I had to fulfill the reader's curiosity regarding her father and the Divine Realms themselves. In this world, the Divine Realms hold the first of everything. That means here you find the first reproductive unit of not only the first male and female wolves, but also the first pack (including babysitters and contenders for the place of first wolf). There is a first flatworm, and multiple first plants of all kinds, because there's no telling whose pollen or seed will take. There's a first copse, a first temperate rain forest, a first kelp forest. And there are the first great creations, such as the first bridges.

Here, the gods great and small play out the important rituals of life: birth, mating, battle, death—and because they are gods, they return after death. The great gods cross freely between the divine realms and the mortal ones, while, as we know, the lesser gods must wait for the weakening of the boundaries on the great holy days, such as Samhain, Harvest, the week of Midwinter, and so on. Without this exception, Daine and Numair would be dead at the Skinners' hands instead of safe in Weiryn's, because their danger fell on a holiday when Weiryn and Sarra had the power to save them.

Connecting Daine with her parents was more ordinary, but still interesting to me. In all this magnificence and strangeness, there was still the matter of meeting the long-absent father and the mother from whom Daine was horribly separated. There was the issue of staying in one's parents' house after living as an adult, a situation I knew something about, and of introducing a potential boyfriend (something neither Daine nor I had done until that time). There was the problem of persuading her parents that the work she and Numair did was vital, and that they had to return to it. Like any parents, Daine's wanted her to be safe and required persuasion.

Daine also discovers that, in a strange twist of the divine, her mother—a flower child of sorts in her mortal days, gentle and somewhat unworldly—has been made a minor goddess so that she may remain with Daine's father Weiryn. In an ironic twist, Sarra now has responsibility for the births and health problems of the women of her former village and surrounding lands, the same women who scorned her and her child for her husband-less, tempting state.

Beyond Weiryn's house, I enjoyed populating the Divine Realms. Since these *are* the Divine Realms, I could show that the gods traveled where they willed, which meant that the male platypus god showed up because he liked Sarra's cooking. (I love platypi, and some of these jokes have always been just for me.) I brought in the God of Dreams, Gainel, a crucial player in the eternal struggle between the Great Gods and the Queen of Chaos. He was born in my mind as a combination of writer Neil Gaiman's Sandman character in the graphic novels of the same name, and of Neil Gaiman himself. (No, we haven't met personally—I had the chance once and was too terrified to take advantage of it.) The Sandman comics and graphic novels show the great stories of the world as always changing and evolving, the gods and great powers falling in love, squabbling, and dying, and the characters often returning to their original roles. I love the Sandman books and wanted to salute them in my own way. It also made sense to me that, of all the Great Gods, the Dream King would be the bridge between Chaos—who has put all of the realms in danger—the mortal realms, and the Divine Realms. Gainel knows better than anyone that the great monsters, the great beauties, and the lesser gods are born of the dreams of Chaos, gods, humans, and the beast people. Because Daine also lives in two worlds, Gainel takes a liking to her and guides her in her dreams, explaining what is going on in the best way he can.

Everyone always wants to know how I came up with the darkings. The story is a bit of a long one. When the movie *Who Framed Roger Rabbit?* came out, my friend Raquel (also known as Thayet, the wolf and bat lover), who was very much interested in movie animation at that time, researched the film before it was released. She explained how, in the sequence where the evil Judge Doom demonstrates the powers of the (car)toon-killing Dip, he plunges a toon into it. The animators at first meant to use a living human or animal toon, but realized it would be too horrible for the younger children watching the movie. They decided to use a shoe, but simply plunging a dead shoe into Dip lacked drama. So they made the shoe animate, with eyes, eyebrows, a cute squeak, and a way of bouncing around like a puppy, craving attention. When the Judge killed Shoe by putting it in the Dip, I wailed out loud in the theater. That taught me the power of the animate inanimate, or bringing inanimate things to life. (The brooms in Disney's *The Sorcerer's Apprentice* were scary, but more robot-like than alive. Shoe was too alive to die so cruelly.)

Not long afterward, the animated movie *Aladdin* was released. Raquel learned that this was the first movie to use computer animation, and it was only used for Carpet and for the sand giant in the desert. Carpet moved and twisted its body with emotion, flirted with its tassels, and was in every way loveable. I let these things—the inanimate made animate, and a machine making an image come alive—settle into my brain, until the point when Ozorne needed barely visible spies to keep watch on Daine. Of course he created his living slaves without knowing the rules of the Divine Realms; his pride leads him to believe he doesn't need to know rules. Of course he used his own blood, thinking that would bind them to him; in the human realms, this would be true. And from his spell he brought forward new beings, darkings, believing that he could order and punish them as if they were his slaves at home, with the added benefit that, because they were made of his blood, he could see through them, hear through them, and make them tell him the truth of what they saw. In the human realms, he could do that with a blood spell. He never bothered to find out the rules of working magic in the Divine Realms.

When I called Raquel to tell her that Ozorne had made living inkblot creatures from his own blood to spy on Daine, she thought they were disgusting. Once she read the final version, she wanted one. I love it when that happens. And in a serves-me-right note, I find the darkings have taken on a life of their own in *my* mind. They always want to pop up in new places. I never know where they'll appear next, and they always seem to have learned something else. So far they have shown up in *Trickster's Queen* and in a short story I wrote for *Tortall and Other Lands*. I have no idea where they will insert themselves next.

So I found plenty of light in all the dark, and there is so much of it in this book: the brushes with the Chaos queen, the blank and furious threat of the Tauros, the perils of the journey to the home of the dragons, the dangers posed by the dragons themselves, and finally, the last battles with Ozorne and his allies.

I said farewell to Rikash, which was awful. He was

clever, and he had the heart to love a little girl in the unforgiving north, writing letters to her even after his travels carried him far away. He outwitted Ozorne and out-diced the Graveyard Hag in the third book, all to free his true Queen and her consort. He was just too cool.

I've had some criticism regarding the love affair between Daine and Numair, but I never felt that he was too old for her. Emotionally, he is young for his age, and looking out for her family as she did, then fending for herself, Daine is older than her physical age. Given all she's been through since coming to Tortall, she was a very good fit with the stork-man, and he with her. Not every man could live comfortably with someone given to changing into animals and racing off to solve the problems of a pack of wolves or a colony of bats. Yet Daine takes it all in stride, as does Numair. They've seen wonders of all kinds, in the Divine Realms and the mortal ones. And I'm sure their adventures are not over, though, for the time being, my writing about them is. You never know where they will find themselves needed!

ABOUT THE AUTHOR

TAMORA PIERCE HAS MORE THAN TWENTY FANTASY novels for teenagers in print worldwide in English, German, Swedish, and Danish, and audio books in Danish and English. *Alanna: The First Adventure* was her first published book and the foundation of the Tortallan quartets: Song of the Lioness, The Immortals, and The Protector of the Small. *Alanna* received an Author's Citation by the New Jersey Institute of Technology's Seventeenth Annual New Jersey Writers Conference and was on the Recommended Fantasy list of the Preconference on Genres of the Young Adult Services Division of the American Library Association, June 1991. Her other publications include short stories, articles, and her two Circle of Magic quartets. She was also an actor and writer for a radio drama and comedy production company in the 1980s and recently resumed her voice actor's motley for Bruce Coville's Full Cast Audio book company. Tammy has been a housemother, a social worker, a secretary, and an agent's assistant. She lives in New York with her Spouse-Creature, technoweenie Tim Liebe, three cats, two parakeets, and wildlife rescued from the park.

Turn the page to go back
to where it all began,
with the adventures of
Alanna of Trebond. . . .

TAMORA PIERCE
SONG OF THE LIONESS

ALANNA
THE FIRST ADVENTURE

"THAT IS MY DECISION. WE NEED NOT DISCUSS IT," said the man at the desk. He was already looking at a book. His two children left the room, closing the door behind them.

"He doesn't want us around," the boy muttered. "He doesn't care what *we* want."

"We *know* that," was the girl's answer. "He doesn't care about anything, except his books and scrolls."

The boy hit the wall. "I don't *want* to be a knight! I want to be a great sorcerer! I want to slay demons and walk with the gods—"

"D'you think I want to be a lady?" his sister asked. "'Walk slowly, Alanna,'" she said primly. "'Sit still, Alanna. Shoulders back, Alanna.' As if that's all I can do with myself!" She paced the floor. "There has to be another way."

The boy watched the girl. Thom and Alanna of Trebond were twins, both with red hair and purple eyes. The only difference between them—as far as most people could tell—was the length of their hair. In face and body shape, dressed alike, they would have looked alike.

"Face it," Thom told Alanna. "Tomorrow *you* leave for the convent, and *I* go to the palace. That's it."

"Why do you get all the fun?" she complained. "I'll have to learn sewing and dancing. You'll study tilting, fencing—"

"D'you think I *like* that stuff?" he yelled. "I *hate* falling down and whacking at things! *You're* the one who likes it, not me!"

She grinned. "*You* should've been Alanna. They always teach the girls magic—" The thought hit her so suddenly that she gasped. "Thom. That's it!"

From the look on her face, Thom knew his sister had just come up with yet another crazy idea. "*What's* it?" he asked suspiciously.

Alanna looked around and checked the hall for servants. "Tomorrow he gives us the letters for the man who trains the pages and the people at the convent. You can imitate his writing, so you can do new letters, saying we're twin boys. "*You* go to the convent. Say in the letter that you're to be a sorcerer. The Daughters of the Goddess are the ones who train young boys in magic, remember? When you're older, they'll send you to the priests. And I'll go to the palace and learn to be a knight!"

"That's crazy," Thom argued. "What about your hair? You can't go swimming naked, either. And you'll turn into a girl—you know, with a chest and everything."

"I'll cut my hair," she replied. "And—well, I'll handle the rest when it happens."

"What about Coram and Maude? They'll be traveling with us, and they can tell us apart. They know we aren't twin boys."

She chewed her thumb, thinking this over. "I'll tell Coram we'll work magic on him if he says anything," she said at last. "He hates magic—that ought to be enough. And maybe we can talk to Maude."

Thom considered it, looking at his hands. "You think we could?" he whispered.

Alanna looked at her twin's hopeful face. Part of her wanted to stop this before it got out of hand, but not a very big part. "If you don't lose your nerve," she told her twin. *And if I don't lose mine,* she thought.

"What about Father?" He was already looking into the distance, seeing the City of the Gods.

Alanna shook her head. "He'll forget us, once we're gone." She eyed Thom. "D'you want to be a sorcerer bad enough?" she demanded. "It means years of studying and work for us both. Will you have the guts for it?"

Thom straightened his tunic. His eyes were cold. "Just show me the way!"

Alanna nodded. "Let's go find Maude."

Maude, the village healer, listened to them and said nothing. When Alanna finished, the woman turned and stared out the door for long minutes. Finally she looked at the twins again.

They didn't know it, but Maude was in difficulty. She had taught them all the magic she possessed. They were both capable of learning much more, but there were no other teachers at Trebond. Thom wanted everything he could get from his magic, but he disliked people. He listened to Maude only because he thought she had something left to teach him; he hated

Coram—the other adult who looked after the twins—because Coram made him feel stupid. The only person in the world Thom loved, beside himself, was Alanna. Maude thought about Alanna and sighed. The girl was very different from her brother. Alanna was afraid of her magic. Thom had to be ordered to hunt, and Alanna had to be tricked and begged into trying spells.

The woman had been looking forward to the day when someone else would have to handle these two. Now it seemed the gods were going to test her through them one last time.

She shook her head. "I cannot make such a decision without help. I must try and See, in the fire."

Thom frowned. "I thought you couldn't. I thought you could only heal."

Maude wiped sweat from her face. She was afraid. "Never mind what I can do and what I cannot do," she snapped. "Alanna, bring wood. Thom, vervain."

They rushed to do as she said, Alanna returning first to add wood to the fire already burning on the hearth. Thom soon followed, carrying leaves from the magic plant vervain.

Maude knelt before the hearth and motioned for the twins to sit on either side of her. She felt sweat running down her back. People who tried to use magic the gods had not given them often died in ugly ways. Maude gave a silent prayer to the Great Mother Goddess, promising good behavior for the rest of her days if only the Goddess would keep her in one piece through this.

She tossed the leaves onto the fire, her lips moving silently with the sacred words. Power from her and from the twins slowly filled the fire. The flames turned green from Maude's sorcery and purple for the twins'. The woman drew a deep breath and grabbed the twins' left hands, thrusting them into the fire. Power shot up their arms. Thom yelped and wriggled with the pain of the magic now filling him up. Alanna bit her lower lip till it bled, fighting the pain her own way. Maude's eyes were wide and blank as she kept their intertwined hands in the flames.

Suddenly Alanna frowned. A picture was forming in the fire. That was impossible—*she* wasn't supposed to See anything. Maude was the one who had cast the spell. Maude was the only one who should See anything.

Ignoring all the laws of magic Alanna had been taught, the picture grew and spread. It was a city made all of black, shiny stone. Alanna leaned forward, squinting to see it better. She had never seen anything like this city. The sun beat down on gleaming walls and towers. Alanna was afraid—more afraid than she had ever been. . . .

Maude let go of the twins. The picture vanished. Alanna was cold now, and very confused. What had that city been? Where was it?

Thom examined his hand. There were no burn marks, or even scars. There was nothing to show that Maude had kept their hands in the flames for long minutes.

Maude rocked back on her heels. She looked old and tired. "I have seen many things I do not understand," she whispered finally. "Many things—"

"Did you see the city?" Alanna wanted to know.

Maude looked at her sharply. "I saw no city."

Thom leaned forward. "*You* saw something?" His voice was eager. "But Maude cast the spell—"

"No!" Alanna snapped. "I didn't see anything! Anything!"

Thom decided to wait and ask her later, when she didn't look so scared. He turned to Maude. "Well?" he demanded.

The healing woman sighed. "Very well. Tomorrow Thom and I go to the City of the Gods."

* * *

At dawn the next day, Lord Alan gave each of his children a sealed letter and his blessing before instructing Coram and Maude. Coram still did not know the change in plan. Alanna did not intend to enlighten him until they were far from Trebond.

Once Lord Alan let them go, Maude took the twins to Alanna's room while Coram got the horses ready. The letters were quickly opened and read.

Lord Alan entrusted his son to the care of Duke Gareth of Naxen and his daughter to the First Daughter of the convent. Sums of money would be sent quarterly to pay for his children's upkeep until such time as their teachers saw fit to return them to their home. He was busy with his studies and trusted the judgment of the Duke and the First Daughter in all matters. He was in their debt, Lord Alan of Trebond.

Many such letters went to the convent and to the palace every year. All girls from noble families studied in convents until they were fifteen or sixteen, at which time they went to Court to find husbands. Usually the oldest son of a noble family learned the skills and duties of a knight at the king's palace. Younger sons could follow their brothers to the palace, or they could go first to the convent, then to the priests' cloisters, where they studied religion or sorcery.

Thom was expert at forging his father's hand-writing. He wrote two new letters, one for "Alan," one for himself. Alanna read them carefully, relieved to see that there was no way to tell the difference between Thom's work and the real thing. The boy sat back with a grin, knowing it might be years before the confusion was resolved.

While Thom climbed into a riding skirt, Maude took Alanna into the dressing room. The girl changed into shirt, breeches and boots. Then Maude cut her hair.

"I've something to say to you," Maude said as the first lock fell to the floor.

"What?" Alanna asked nervously.

"You've a gift for healing." The shears worked on. "It's greater than mine, greater than any I have ever known. And you've other magic, power you'll learn to use. But the healing—that's the important thing. I had a dream last night. A warning, it was, as plain as if the gods shouted in my ear."

Alanna, picturing this, stifled a giggle.

"It don't do to laugh at the gods," Maude told her sternly. "Though you'll find that out yourself, soon enough."

"What is that supposed to mean?"

"Never mind. Listen. Have you thought of the lives you'll take when you go off performing those great deeds?"

Alanna bit her lip. "No," she admitted.

"I didn't think so. You see only the glory. But there's lives taken and families without fathers and sorrow. Think before you fight. Think on who you're fighting, if only because one day you must meet your match. And if you want to pay for those lives you do take, use your healing magic. Use it all you can, or you won't cleanse your soul of death for centuries. It's harder to heal than it is to kill. The Mother knows why, but you've a gift for both." Quickly she brushed Alanna's cropped hair. "Keep your hood up for a bit, but you look enough like Thom to fool anyone but Coram."

Alanna stared at herself in the mirror. Her twin stared back, violet eyes wide in his pale face. Grinning, she wrapped herself in her cloak. With a last peek at the boy in the mirror, she followed Maude out to the courtyard. Coram and Thom, already mounted up, waited for them. Thom rearranged his skirts and gave his sister a wink.

Maude stopped Alanna as she went to mount the

pony, Chubby. "Heal, child," the woman advised. "Heal all you can, or you'll pay for it. The gods mean for their gifts to be used."

Alanna swung herself into the saddle and patted Chubby with a comforting hand. The pony, sensing that the good twin was on his back, stopped fidgeting. When Thom was riding him, Chubby managed to dump him.

The twins and the two servants waved farewell to the assembled castle servants, who had come to see them off. Slowly they rode through the castle gate, Alanna doing her best to imitate Thom's pout—or the pout Thom would be wearing if he were riding to the palace right now. Thom was looking down at his pony's ears, keeping his face hidden. Everyone knew how the twins felt at being sent away.

The road leading from the castle plunged into heavily overgrown and rocky country. For the next day or so they would be riding through the unfriendly forests of the Grimhold Mountains, the great natural border between Tortall and Scanra. It was familiar land to the twins. While it might seem dark and unfriendly to people from the South, to Alanna and Thom it would always be home.

At midmorning they came to the meeting of

Trebond Way and the Great Road. Patrolled by the king's men, the Great Road led north to the distant City of the Gods. That was the way Thom and Maude would take. Alanna and Coram were bound south, to the capital city of Corus, and the royal palace.

The two servants went apart to say goodbye and give the twins some privacy. Like Thom and Alanna, it would be years before Coram and Maude saw each other again. Though Maude would return to Trebond, Coram was to remain with Alanna, acting as her manservant during her years at the palace.

Alanna looked at her brother and gave a little smile. "Here we are," she said.

"I wish I could say 'have fun,'" Thom said frankly, "but I can't see how anyone can have fun learning to be a knight. Good luck, though. If we're caught, we'll both be skinned."

"No one's going to catch us, brother." She reached across the distance between them, and they gripped hands warmly. "Good luck, Thom. Watch your back."

"There are a lot of tests ahead for you," Thom said earnestly. "Watch *your* back."

"I'll pass the tests," Alanna said. She knew they were brave words, almost foolhardy, but Thom looked as if he needed to hear them. They turned their ponies then and rejoined the adults.

"Let's go," Alanna growled to Coram.

Maude and Thom took the left fork of the Great Road and Alanna and Coram bore right. Alanna halted suddenly, turning around to watch her brother ride off. She blinked the burning feeling from her eyes, but she couldn't ease the tight feeling in her throat. Something told her Thom would be very different when she saw him again. With a sigh she turned Chubby back toward the capital city.

Coram made a face and urged his big gelding forward. He would have preferred doing anything to escorting a finicky boy to the palace. Once he had been the hardiest soldier in the king's armies. Now he was going to be a joke. People would see that Thom was no warrior, and they would blame Coram—the man who was to have taught him the basics of the warrior's craft. He rode for hours without a word, thinking his own gloomy thoughts, too depressed to notice that Thom, who usually complained after an hour's ride, was silent as well.

Coram had been trained as a blacksmith, but he had once been one of the best of the king's foot soldiers, until he had returned home to Trebond Castle and become sergeant-at-arms there. Now he wanted to be with the king's soldiers again, but not if they were going to laugh at him because he had a weakling for a master. Why couldn't Alanna have been the boy? *She* was a fighter. Coram had taught her at first because to teach one twin was to teach the other, poor motherless things. Then he began to enjoy teaching her. She learned quickly and well—better than her brother. With all his heart Coram Smythesson wished now, as he had in the past, that Alanna were the boy.

He was about to get his wish, in a left-handed way. The sun was glinting from directly overhead—time for the noon meal. Coram grunted orders to the cloaked child, and they both dismounted in a clearing beside the road. Pulling bread and cheese from a saddlebag, he broke off a share and handed it over. He also took the wineskin down from his saddle horn.

"We'll make the wayhouse by dark, if not before," he rumbled. "Till then, we make do with this."

Alanna removed her heavy cloak. "This is fine with me."

Coram choked, spraying a mouthful of liquid all over the road. Alanna had to clap him on the back before he caught his breath again.

"Brandy?" he whispered, looking at the wineskin. He returned to his immediate problem. "By the Black

God!" he roared, turning spotty purple. "We're goin' back this instant, and I'm tannin' yer hide for ye when we get home! Where's that devils'-spawn brother of yours?"

"Coram, calm down," she said. "Have a drink."

"I don't want a drink," he snarled. "I want t' beat the two of ye till yer skins won't hold water!" He took a deep gulp from the wineskin.

"Thom's on his way to the City of the Gods with Maude," Alanna explained. "She thinks we're doing the right thing."

Coram swore under his breath. "That witch *would* agree with you two sorcerers. And what does yer father say?"

"Why should he ever know?" Alanna asked. "Coram, you know Thom doesn't want to be a knight. I do."

"I don't care if the two of ye want t' be dancing bears!" Coram told her, taking another swallow from the skin. "Ye're a girl."

"Who's to know?" She bent forward, her small face intent. "From now on I'm Alan of Trebond, the younger twin. I'll be a knight—Thom'll be a sorcerer. It'll happen. Maude saw it for us in the fire."

Coram made the Sign against evil with his right

hand. Magic made him nervous. Maude made him nervous. He drank again to settle his nerves. "Lass, it's a noble thought, a warrior's thought, but it'll never work. If ye're not caught when ye bathe, ye'll be turning into a woman—"

"I can hide all that—with your help. If I can't, I'll disappear."

"Yer father will have my hide!"

She made a face. "Father doesn't care about anything but his scrolls." She drew a breath. "Coram, I'm being nice. Thom wouldn't be this nice. D'you want to see things that aren't there for the next ten years? I can work that, you know. Remember when Cook was going to tell Father who ate the cherry tarts? Or the time Godmother tried to get Father to marry her?"

Coram turned pale. The afternoon the tarts were discovered missing, Cook started to see large, hungry lions following him around the kitchens. Lord Alan never heard about the missing tarts. When the twins' godmother came to Trebond to snare Lord Alan as her next husband, she had fled after only three days, claiming the castle was haunted.

"Ye wouldn't," Coram whispered. He had always suspected that the twins had been behind Cook's hallucinations and Lady Catherine's ghosts, but he had kept those thoughts to himself. Cook gave himself airs, and Lady Catherine was cruel to her servants.

Seeing she had struck a nerve, Alanna changed tactics. "Thom can't shoot for beans, and I can. Thom wouldn't be a credit to you. I will, I think. You said yourself a grown man can't skin a rabbit faster'n me." She fed her last piece of bread to Chubby and looked at Coram with huge, pleading eyes. "Let's ride on. If you feel the same in the morning, we can turn back." She crossed her fingers as she lied. She had no intention of returning to Trebond. "Just don't rush. Father won't know till it's too late."

Coram swigged again from the skin, getting up shakily. He mounted, watching the girl. They rode silently while Coram thought, and drank.

The threat about making him see things didn't worry him much. Instead he thought of Thom's performance in archery—it was enough to make a soldier cry. Alanna was much quicker than her brother. She rarely tired, even hiking over rough country. She had a feel for the fighting arts, and that was something that never could be learned. She was also as stubborn as a mule.

Because he was absorbed in his thoughts, Coram never saw the wood snake glide across the road.

Alanna—and Coram's horse—spotted the slithery creature in the same second. The big gelding reared, almost throwing his master. Chubby stopped dead in the road, surprised by these antics. Coram yelled and fought to hold on as his mount bucked frantically, terrified by the snake. Alanna never stopped to think. She threw herself from Chubby's saddle and grabbed for Coram's reins with both hands. Dodging the gelding's flying hooves frantically, she used all her strength and weight to pull the horse down before Coram fell and broke his neck.

The gelding, more surprised than anything else by the new weight on his reins, dropped to all fours. He trembled as Alanna stroked his nose, whispering comforting words. She dug in a pocket and produced an apple for the horse, continuing to pet him until his shaking stopped.

When Alanna looked up, Coram was watching her oddly. She had no way of knowing that he was imagining what Thom would have done in similar circumstances: Her twin would have left Coram to fend for himself. Coram knew the kind of courage it took to calm a large, bucking horse. It was the kind of courage a knight needed in plenty. Even so, Alanna was a girl. . . .